STAR WARS®

HEIR
TO THE
JEDI

BY KEVIN HEARNE

Star Wars: Heir to the Jedi

THE IRON DRUID CHRONICLES
Hounded
Hexed
Hammered
Tricked
Trapped
Hunted
Shattered

THE IRON DRUID CHRONICLES NOVELLAS
Two Ravens and One Crow
Grimoire of the Lamb

STAR WARS®

HEIR
TO THE
JEDI

KEVIN HEARNE

DEL REY • NEW YORK

Star Wars: Heir to the Jedi is a work of fiction. Names, places, and incidents either are products of the author's imagination or are used fictitiously. Any resemblance to actual events, locales, or persons, living or dead, is entirely coincidental.

2015 Del Rey Mass Market Edition

Published in the United States by Del Rey, an imprint of Random House, a division of Penguin Random House LLC, New York.

DEL REY and the HOUSE colophon are registered trademarks of Penguin Random House LLC.

Originally published in hardcover in the United States by Del Rey, an imprint of Random House, a division of Penguin Random House LLC, in 2015.

This book contains excerpts from *Star Wars: Aftermath* by Chuck Wendig and *Star Wars: Battlefront: Twilight Company* by Alexander Freed. These excerpts have been set for this edition only and may not reflect the final content of the forthcoming editions.

ISBN 978-0-345-54486-5
eBook ISBN 978-0-345-54487-2

Printed in the United States of America

randomhousebooks.com

9 8 7 6 5 4 3 2 1

Del Rey mass market edition: December 2015

THE DEL REY

STAR WARS®

TIMELINE

I THE PHANTOM MENACE

II ATTACK OF THE CLONES

THE CLONE WARS (TV SERIES)
DARK DISCIPLE

III REVENGE OF THE SITH
LORDS OF THE SITH
TARKIN
A NEW DAWN
REBELS (TV SERIES)

IV A NEW HOPE

HEIR TO THE JEDI
BATTLEFRONT: TWILIGHT COMPANY

V THE EMPIRE STRIKES BACK

VI RETURN OF THE JEDI

AFTERMATH

VII THE FORCE AWAKENS

ACKNOWLEDGMENTS

When *The Empire Strikes Back* first came out in 1980 and I saw Luke summon his lightsaber to his hand in the wampa cave, I remember thinking, "Whoa! Awesome!" And then, after I'd seen it maybe ten more times, I wondered, "Where'd he learn how to do *that*?" My nine-year-old self never suspected that one day I'd get the chance to provide the answer, and I'm grateful to Del Rey and Lucasfilm for making it happen.

Many thanks are due to Alan O'Bryan for discussing with me the potential hyperspace applications of eigenvalues and eigenvectors. It was one of the most nerdtastic conversations ever.

ACKNOWLEDGMENTS

A long time ago in a galaxy far, far away. . . .

... A long time ago in a galaxy far, far away ...

The destruction of the Death Star brought new hope to the beleaguered Rebel Alliance. But the relentless pursuit by Darth Vader and the Imperial fleet is taking its toll on Alliance resources. Now the rebels hide in an Outer Rim orbit from which they can search for a more permanent base and for new allies to supply much-needed weapons and matériel.

Luke Skywalker, hero of the Battle of Yavin, has cast his lot with the rebels, lending his formidable piloting skills to whatever missions his leaders assign him. But he is haunted by his all-too-brief lessons with Obi-Wan Kenobi and the growing certainty that mastery of the Force will be his path to victory over the Empire.

Adrift without Old Ben's mentorship, determined to serve the Rebellion any way he can, Luke searches for ways to improve his skills in the Force. . . .

CHAPTER 1

THERE'S NO ONE AROUND to answer all my questions now that Ben's gone. It's a stark fact that reasserts itself each time I wonder what I'm supposed to do now. That brown robe he wore might as well have been made of pure mystery; he clothed himself in it and then left nothing else behind on the Death Star. I know Han likes to scoff at the idea of the Force, but when a man's body simply disappears at the touch of a lightsaber, that's more than "simple tricks and nonsense."

And I know the Force is real. I've felt it.

I still feel it, actually, but I think it's like knowing there's something hidden in the sand while you're skimming above it. You see ripples on the surface, hints that something is moving down there—maybe something small, maybe something huge—living a completely different life out of your sight. And going after it to see what's underneath the surface might be safe and rewarding, or it might be the last thing you ever do. I need someone to tell me when to dive into those ripples and when to back off.

I thought I heard Ben's voice a couple of times during the Battle of Yavin, but I'm wondering now if that really happened. Maybe I only thought it did; maybe that was my subconscious speaking to me—a kind of wishful thinking. He's been silent since, and I don't feel I can talk to anyone else about the Force. My confidants at this point consist of one blue-and-white astromech droid.

Han and Chewie are off somewhere trying to earn enough credits to pay off Jabba the Hutt. They lost all their reward money from the Battle of Yavin and they're back to being broke and desperate—the galaxy should beware.

Leia is cloistered with the leaders of the Alliance in the fleet, which is currently hiding in the Sujimis sector around an ice planet no one has paid any attention to since the Clone Wars. Not that she would want to hear about my worries any more than I would like to speak them. She has much more important things to do than to waste time putting a bandage on my insecurities. Threepio is with her, no doubt feeling unappreciated for his predictions of imminent doom in over six million forms of communication. That leaves Artoo and me free to run an errand for Admiral Ackbar.

I've been dispatched to Rodia in an effort to open a secret supply line to the Alliance. I'm not supposed to call it smuggling—Ackbar has serious issues with the very concept, but the truth is the Alliance can't operate without it. Since the Empire is trying to shut down our lines of supply in the Outer Rim by going after smugglers' dens, and the established black markets in the Core are a bit too risky for us to employ, we have to look for other sources to exploit. Rodia is under Imperial control, but Leia suggested that the Chekkoo clan on the Betu continent might be open to working with us. She said they despise the ruling

Chattza clan and are highly skilled at manufacturing weapons, armor, and other hardware we could use to fight the Empire. Leia was betting they'd defy the Empire to spite the Chattza clan, and we stood to benefit. Mon Mothma was unsure of the idea, but Ackbar surprised everyone and weighed in with Leia, and that decided it.

I don't know what it is about Ackbar that tends to quash arguments. He has a kind of moist charisma, I guess, that no one wants to challenge. I know I don't want to dispute him, anyway.

Once it was agreed, I volunteered for the mission, and they loaned me a beautiful personal yacht to fly in. My X-wing would set off all kinds of alarms if I dared to enter Rodian space in it, but a small transport with minimal weapons would be no big deal. Both Artoo and I whistled when we first saw it in the docking bay of the *Promise,* one of the Alliance's frigates. It was less of a yacht and more of a showpiece.

Painted a metallic red and trimmed in silver, the cockpit and living quarters of the ship sat forward and the wings swept back in an unbroken arc, like a half-moon thinking about going crescent. The rear end looked a bit like someone had taken a bite out of a cookie, and it was packed with big sublight engines, jammers, sensor arrays, and shield generators. The power was all invisible from the front or the sides— it spoke of luxury and decadence—but the back told anyone pursuing that they wouldn't be keeping up for very long. It was built for speed and quite possibly spying while doing its best to look like a rich person's pleasure craft.

"Nice, isn't she?" a voice said, causing me to tear my eyes away. "That's the *Desert Jewel.* You fly her safely, now." The speaker was a tall woman with dark skin and a cascade of tightly curled ringlets framing a narrow face. She gave me a friendly smile and I smiled back.

"Is she yours?" I asked.

"Yep! Well, I guess I should say she's my father's. But both his ship and his daughter are at the disposal of the Alliance now. Just got here last week." She extended a hand. "Nakari Kelen. Glad to meet you."

"Kelen?" I said, taking her hand and shaking it. She had a strong grip, and I tilted my head to the side as I connected her name and the ship's to a memory. "Any relation to the Kelen Biolabs on Pasher?"

Her eyes widened. "Yes! Fayet Kelen is my father. Are you from Pasher?"

"No, I'm from Tatooine."

"Ah, another desert planet. So you understand all about my fascination with ships and how they can take me far away from home."

"Yeah, I understand that very well. I'm Luke Skywalker."

"Oh, I know who you are," she said, finally letting her hand slip from mine. "They told me you'd be taking my ship out for some kind of spooky mission, but no one told me you hailed from Tatooine."

"Ha. It's not really spooky. Kind of a boring business trip, in fact, but this looks like it will prevent any Imperials from thinking I'm with the Alliance."

"I should hope so. My baby's classy and elegant and ill disposed to rebellion."

"Hey, speaking of ill disposed, mind if I ask you something?"

Nakari nodded once, inviting me to proceed.

"I've always wondered why your dad chose Pasher for his biolabs. You'd think a jungle planet would be better suited simply because there's more actual biology there."

She shrugged. "He started small and local. The poison

and glands of sandstone scorpions and spine spiders turned out to have medical applications." She chucked her chin at the *Desert Jewel*. "Very profitable applications."

"I'll say."

"What did you do on Tatooine?"

"Moisture farming. Spectacularly dull. Some weeks were so boring that I actually looked forward to going into Tosche Station to pick up some . . . power converters. Huh!"

"What?"

"I just remembered I never did pick up my last shipment. Wonder if they're still there."

"We all have unfinished business, don't we?" That was an unexpected turn to the conversation, and I wondered what she meant by it. I wondered why she was there at all, frankly. The comfortably wealthy rarely stir themselves to get involved in rebellions. But I had to admit she wasn't dressed like the privileged child of a biotech magnate. She wore desert camo fatigues tucked into thick-soled brown boots, a blaster strapped to her left hip, and what looked like a compact slug rifle strapped to her back, held in place by a leather band crossing diagonally across her torso.

I flicked a finger at the rifle. "You hunt sandstone scorpions with that?"

"Yep. Can't use a blaster on them. Their armor deflects heat too well."

"I'd heard that."

"And since so many people are wearing blaster armor these days, a throwback weapon that punches through it is surprisingly effective if you know how to shoot one."

"Hunt anything else?"

"Of course. I've been to Tatooine, actually, and bagged a krayt dragon there. Its pearls paid for the upgrades on the *Jewel*. She's still Dad's ship, but I've modified her quite a bit, and I hope to have the credits soon to buy her from him outright. Come on, I'll show you."

Both of us were grinning and I was excited, happy to have found someone with a similar background way out here in an icy part of the galaxy. I couldn't speak for Nakari, but meeting someone with shared experience filled up a measure of its emptiness for me, especially since she clearly understood why ships are important: They take you away from the deserts, even if it's just for a little while, allowing you to think that maybe you won't shrivel and waste away there, emotionally and physically. Not that the rest of the galaxy is any more friendly than the dunes. My old friend Biggs, for example, loved to fly as much as I did, and he escaped Tatooine only to die in the Battle of Yavin. I miss him and wonder sometimes if he would have done anything differently if he'd known he'd never set foot on a planet again once he climbed into that X-wing. I console myself with the guess that he would have gone anyway, that the cause was worth dying for and the risk acceptable, but I suppose I'll never know for sure. The Empire didn't fall and the rebellion continues, and all I can do is hope the next mission will prove to be the one that topples the Emperor somehow and validates my friend's sacrifice.

A walk-up loading ramp into the *Desert Jewel* put us in the narrow corridor behind the cockpit. Unfortunately the ramp was also the floor and with it down we couldn't move forward—a clear shortcoming in design—so we had to close it and leave poor Artoo on the hangar deck before we could enter the cockpit.

Nakari pointed to hatches on either side of the corridor. "Galley and head on the left, bunks and maintenance access on the right," she said. "Your droid can plug in there. There's a lot of emergency supplies, too, survival gear that comes in handy when I'm scouting planets for Dad. Breathing masks and an inflatable raft and suchlike. The bunks are kind of basic, sorry to say. I spent all my credits on speed and spoofs."

"A wise investment," I assured her. "Can't enjoy any kind of bunk, much less a luxurious one, if you can't survive a panicked flight from a Star Destroyer."

She sawed a finger back and forth between our heads. "Yes! Yes. We are thinking alike here. This is good, because I want to see my ship again."

"I'd—" I stopped cold because I almost said *I'd like to see you again* as an unconscious reply, but fortunately realized in time that she might misinterpret that as an incredibly inept pass at her. I finished with, "—think that would be good for both of us," and hoped she didn't notice the awkward pause.

"Indeed." She waved me forward. "After you."

"Thanks." Five steps brought me into the cockpit, where I slid into the seat on the left side. Nakari rested a hand on the back of my seat and used the other to point at the banks of instruments. "She's got top-of-the-line jammers and sensors from Sullust, a holo-display here, which is kind of low-end because I'd rather have these high-end deflector shields, and twin sublight engines on either side that will shoot you through space faster than an X-wing. Oh, and she's got a point-eight hyperdrive for the long hauls."

"Wow. Any weapons?"

"One laser cannon hidden underneath where I'm standing. You activate it right there, and a targeting display pops up."

I winced. "Just one cannon?"

"She's built to run and keep you alive until you jump out of trouble. Best not to get into any trouble."

"Got it."

"Good." She clapped me on the shoulder. "Be safe, Luke."

I turned in my seat, surprised that the tour was over so quickly. "Hey, thanks. What will you be doing in the meantime?"

She opened the boarding ramp and then jerked a thumb at the rifle stock behind her shoulder. "I'm training some of the soldiers in sharpshooting. Heading dirtside to shoot frozentargets on Orto Plutonia. I'll be plenty busy." Her eyes flicked down to the hangar deck, where something made her smile. "I think your droid is ready to come aboard."

"Is he in your way?"

"A bit."

She began to descend, and I called after her as she disappeared from view. "Sorry! He'll move."

Artoo rolled up a few moments later, and I found the button that would secure the ramp behind him. He chirped and sounded impatient with me, but as usual I couldn't understand him. "You can jack in to the right," I said, and he scooted in there while continuing his electronic scolding.

We had to navigate several different hyperspace lanes to get to Rodia from the Sujimis sector and I was getting used to the way the *Jewel* handled, so our trip probably took more time than strictly necessary. Fortunately, we weren't in a hurry and I enjoyed every minute of it. The *Jewel* was sheer pleasure to fly; the cockpit was quiet, unlike the high-pitched electronic whine of my X-wing.

Artoo successfully installed a program into the *Jewel*'s computer that would translate his digital beeps into readable language. His words streamed on the holodisplay that Nakari had pointed out to me, and I kept the ship's intercom on so that he could hear my words.

"Artoo, take us to Llanic, will you? We need to stop there to see if we can find someone to smuggle for us if the deal in Rodia works out."

Situated at the intersection of the Llanic Spice Route and the Triellus Trade Route, Llanic bustled with smugglers and other ne'er-do-wells in a way that might have moved Ben Kenobi to call it a "wretched hive of scum and villainy," even if it was not quite as wretched as Mos Eisley. Plenty of illicit credits flew through there, and because of that the Empire kept a watch on it. Leia had given me a briefing, warning me that Moff Abran Balfour patrolled the spice route often, and he represented the nearest Imperial presence to the current location of the Alliance fleet. I was not supposed to give him the idea that perhaps the fleet was somewhere in his sector.

I was expecting a lively screen full of contacts when I entered the system, but perhaps not quite so lively as it proved to be. One of Moff Balfour's Star Destroyers showed up immediately, though it was too far away to pull me in with a tractor beam or engage in any meaningful way. Flying much closer to me were two TIE fighters, pursuing a ship that didn't appear able to put up much resistance. They were firing on it, and its shields were holding for the time being, but I doubted that would continue for much longer, especially since it was slower than the TIEs. I imagined there would be unidentified rattling noises on the ship, not indicating anything dire, just a general statement of decrepitude and imminent destruction. Didn't seem like a fair fight to me, but I wasn't going to make it my problem until I realized the ship was of Kupohan manufacture. The Kupohans had helped the Alliance in the past, and might do so again.

Not that there were necessarily Kupohans inside, or even Kupohans that were friendly to the Alliance. I had innumerable reasons to mind my own business and leave the ship to its fate, but I decided to dive in anyway on two guiding principles: If they annoyed the Empire this much, they were at least marginally on my side; and since I could help them, I should— and no one was around to argue with me about that last principle.

"Artoo, plot us a course out of the system right away," I said, and accelerated to intercept speed. "We're going to have to get out of here in a hurry after this. And hold on to something." The artificial gravity generator would keep him glued to the floor, but it wouldn't prevent torsion from the extreme maneuvers ahead. Normally he's wedged snugly into my X-wing and there would be no worry about such things.

I engaged the ship's baby laser cannon and waited until I got a system go-ahead, then dived on the lateral axis toward the TIE fighters. I flipped on the deflector shields and locked on the targeting computer. One look at the ships and I knew the TIE pilots were hanging on to the orientation of the Star Destroyer from which they had deployed; they had a sense of which way was "up" and they were sticking to it, which is a limiting and even dangerous perception to hold on to in space. Up and down don't really have a meaningful use until you're in atmosphere. I deliberately rolled as I dived, adjusted my nose so that the leading TIE fighter was in my sights, and fired.

The *Desert Jewel*'s bolts turned out to be blue and shot in bursts of three. The first burst missed entirely, but the second tagged the TIE fighter and destroyed it. The second TIE rolled away to the left in an evasive maneuver and I pulled up, planning to flip a loop and dive again; the Kupohan ship was still moving, free of Imperial pursuit for a few moments.

I expected the TIE to bank around and try to acquire a firing solution on me, and for a couple of seconds it looked like it was going to, but then it veered away to reestablish an attack vector on the Kupohan ship. That struck me as very strange behavior—to ignore a mortal threat and give someone a free shot at your unshielded ship while you pursued a fleeing target. I almost didn't believe it and checked to make sure there wasn't another ship on my scanners that I'd missed somehow, something waiting in ambush, but there was only me, the remaining TIE, and the Kupohan in the immediate vicinity. It looked like the Star Destroyer had just launched an entire squadron of additional TIEs, but it would take them a while to catch up.

"They must want to erase that ship in the worst way," I said, thinking aloud. The TIE pilot had probably been given an order from the Star Destroyer that amounted to "Kill the Kupohans, or don't come back." From my perspective, that was all the more reason to help out.

Without the danger of being fired upon, I lined up another run and pulled the trigger on the TIE fighter, even as it was doing its best to blast the Kupohan ship to pieces. The Kupohan's shields held under the onslaught, but the TIE fighter came apart at the first touch of my lasers.

"There," I said, and checked the position of the Star Destroyer again. It wasn't in range yet, but it was moving full-speed to catch up, and the squadron of TIEs was still a couple of standard minutes out. "Maybe I can get some answers. Artoo, prepare the next jump and see if you can raise the Kupohan ship."

The droid's reply appeared on my holodisplay: JUMP READY NOW. INITIATING CONTACT.

"Good. I hope that they can still—" I cut off as the Kupohan ship jumped to hyperspace without so much as a thank-you. "Well, I guess they *can* still jump. We should do the same. Take us to hyperspace as soon as you're ready, Artoo."

The tension drained from my shoulders as I disengaged the laser cannon, but my mouth twisted in regret as the stars blurred and streamed past the cockpit window during the jump. I couldn't help but feeling somewhat disappointed. I wondered who was on that ship and why they mattered so much to the Empire— and whether compromising my mission and putting this ship on Imperial wanted lists was worth it. It was worth it to the crew of the Kupohan ship, no doubt— they still had their lives. But I wasn't sure if I'd done the Alliance any favors with that particular episode, and now, with the opportunity to evaluate it coolly, I saw how rash the decision had been. Now I had to skip Llanic entirely and go straight to Rodia, hopefully ahead of any Imperial alert to be on the lookout for me.

Perhaps I'd do well enough there that Leia and Admiral Ackbar would forgive me for tweaking the Empire's nose when we were supposed to be hiding.

CHAPTER $\Delta 2 = a_2 - a_1$

THE *DESERT JEWEL* ENTERED the atmosphere of Rodia without earning a scrambled visit from a squadron of TIE fighters. Following a route painted by Artoo, I dropped down on the coast of Betu, a continent away from the Chattza clan, the Grand Protector, and the bulk of Imperial activity. The Chekkoo clan lived there, and while they weren't in open rebellion, lacking the resources to follow their hearts, simple geography gave them the opportunity to exercise some passive resistance and keep a few secrets.

Set upon a high rocky cliffside with ocean waves pounding the base, the Chekkoo Enclave sported a single gray tower thrust out of a series of stone walls draped around it like skirts, each one bristling with weapons emplacements. A thriving city nestled in between the walls, but the spaceport waited outside them and we touched down there. Beyond that, the jungle awaited, humid and humming with the drone of insects and the occasional screech of something wanting to eat or something else dismayed at being eaten.

I wasn't prepared for the smell; a diplomatic person

would say it was *pungent*. I couldn't muster any words, diplomatic or otherwise; it was all I could do not to gag openly as the ramp opened and the odor of bad cheese and fungal feet wafted in, hot and cloying and fat in my nostrils, much too big for the space, like a Hutt squeezed into an armchair.

A single Rodian waited for me at the bottom of the ramp and pretended not to notice my expression of disgust. She was dressed in a long blue tunic edged in gold and matching pants tucked into buckled brown boots. She had a spray of golden spines sticking up between her antennae and falling in a line down the back of her head.

"Welcome, Luke Skywalker," she said. "I am Laneet Chekkoo. I'll be your guide while you visit Rodia."

"Pleasure to meet you," I managed. "Are you only a guide, or will I be negotiating with you, as well?"

"Only a guide. I am primarily concerned with keeping your presence here unobserved by other clans. If you will follow me, we will depart for Toopil."

"Toopil? Aren't we going to the enclave?"

Laneet twitched her head once to the left, which I believe signaled negative among Rodians. "Too many Imperial spies there and even more from other clans. At the enclave we are meek and subservient to the Grand Protector and display very little in the way of our true wealth and power. Toopil is a different place entirely. You will see. This way, please."

I followed Laneet out of the relatively quiet spaceport and into a teeming open-air market with labyrinthine passages and a shifting crowd of shoppers unconscious of personal space. A whole new spectrum of smells hammered my nose. Some of it was supposed to be appetizing, I think, since I spied food vendors, but it wasn't making me hungry at all. Artoo's dome swiveled about as he trailed behind, taking it all in, but he kept silent.

We made several turns before ducking into an electronics vendor boasting of aftermarket jamming systems and other fine accessories for the discriminating bounty hunter. The vendor's stall turned out not to be a stall at all but its own maze of a structure with multiple levels and merchandise grouped in small rooms, each with its own resident merchant and with multiple exits to other showrooms. When we rounded a corner into a room displaying racks of neural disruptors and occupied only by a giant Ithorian, Laneet signaled with her right hand and the Ithorian lumbered forward to block the narrow passage behind us with its bulk. No one would be able to squeeze past it until it reemerged, and we took the opportunity this afforded to slip into a hallway concealed behind a wall panel filled with weapons that might have been designed to melt internal organs. Once the panel closed behind Artoo, Laneet paused in the dimly lit passage and looked back at us.

"We just want to make sure we are not followed. Our transport awaits ahead, but please move silently. We are still moving through the market, and the walls are thin. We don't want to give away the presence of this passage to anyone."

I nodded and trailed after our guide in near darkness, the only illumination coming from wan glow panels spaced in intervals that were farther apart than was comfortable for human eyesight. Sounds of the bazaar trickled through the walls on either side, merchants haggling with customers or bawling out specials to passersby in the hope of attracting a full purse. Eventually we reached the end of the passage, where two armed guards and a gauntlet of automatic guns in the walls trained their weapons on us. Laneet identified herself and introduced us, and after some unseen processing behind all the weaponry, we were allowed to pass and descend a ramp to a small docking platform where a personnel speeder waited at the entrance to a subterranean tunnel. We piled in and Laneet fired up the repulsors, rocketing down the tunnel for maybe ten minutes.

"We can talk now," she said. "Please forgive the unpleasant security measures. We welcome all business, you understand, especially that which will prove inconvenient to the Chattza clan or the Empire. But we must be careful. It is for our protection as much as yours that we go to such lengths."

"Well, it's impressive. I've never even heard of Toopil," I said.

"It doesn't exist officially," Laneet replied. "It's simply a cantina, a few meeting rooms, and some sleeping arrangements underneath Utheel Outfitters. Utheel makes everything from stealth armor to big-game grenade launchers, and they test their products in the surrounding jungle. They invite prospective customers out for hunts, and thus they have dormitories on site for the purpose. But underneath those are secret dormitories accessible only through a few well-guarded entry points like the one we used. Energy usage is thereby concealed. We also have a private docking bay and smugglers' den with an entrance camouflaged from the air. Most light freighters would fit in there. We do plenty of business in that bay, all of it hidden from the Empire and other clans, and the money is laundered through Utheel Outfitters."

I thought Han would be impressed with their setup; I sure was. "And the Empire truly has no clue you're doing this?"

Laneet snorted in derision, which sounded like a phlegmy sneeze through the Rodian snout. "I'm sure they have their suspicions. We suspect every other clan of similar practices."

We arrived at a dock that appeared at first to be unguarded, but I sensed somehow that wasn't the case. After all the security I saw getting this far, I couldn't imagine they'd leave this wide open. Laneet caught my expression and interpreted it correctly. "There are guards. They're in stealth armor."

"Oh, really? I've never seen stealth armor."

Laneet made a noise similar to a chortle but closer to a digestive problem. "Hence the name."

It reminded me of Ben's assertion that your eyes can deceive you. The Force would help me pierce through such illusions if I could learn how. "Do you manufacture the stealth armor yourself?"

"Yes, Utheel is quite diversified. It doesn't have shipyards or produce heavy artillery, but almost anything smaller can be found here, save perhaps blasters. Other manufacturers are more efficient at producing such basic weapons. We produce a broad range of higher-quality items in smaller batches. You will see more inside. Come."

We stepped out of the speeder and onto an empty concrete dock with a single door waiting at the back of a concavity lined with automatic blaster turrets and presumably the aforementioned guards in stealth armor. With so much firepower concentrated here, I wondered if even a Jedi could make it to the door unscathed. No one would penetrate it without fully committing to heavy assault. Laneet paused at the door, spoke some words at a console, had her hands and eyes scanned, and then the door chimed as it opened. I followed after. Once through the door, we found ourselves in a small magnetically sealed room. Laneet pointed first at the floor, where there was some discoloration, and then at the ceiling, where there were matching stains. "If anyone were to get this far without receiving a go-ahead from the door outside, the weighted ceiling drops down quite fast. Squashed at least one Chattza spy."

The inner door chimed before opening, and a narrow hall provided more opportunities for defense before finally leading us to a rather luxurious meeting room sporting tables surrounded by thickly upholstered chairs. The room was carpeted and chandeliered and attended by liveried servants rather than droids; even the tablecloths looked posh. I got the impression the Rodians had gone to some effort to make it smell pleasant to humans, but the competing scents of Rodians and florals made the air difficult to breathe.

Several Rodians waited to be introduced, all employees from different divisions of Utheel Outfitters, ready to discuss what business they could with the representative of the Rebel Alliance, and I admit I found that thought enjoyable. Leaving aside the odor, this sort of work was much more entertaining than moisture farming.

Long tables lined the perimeter of the room, laid out with weapons instead of a buffet. After a drink and a brief chat during which I complimented the Chekkoo security arrangements I'd seen thus far, they gave me a tour of the weapons, some of them prototypes, and several of these were presented as gifts. I got a proximity stun mine, a handheld EMP detonator, and a needle gun I never intended to use. Thinking of Nakari's slug gun, however, and her assertion that it would work in situations where blasters might not, I asked if they might have anything with that kind of punch behind it, something with high-velocity armor-piercing rounds. One of the weapons engineers said he could secure something for me to look at the next day.

"If it wouldn't be too much trouble, I'd like to see the smuggling bay that Laneet mentioned earlier before we make any deals. Your equipment is fine, but it will be useless if we can't get it offplanet safely."

They agreed that would be best, and as it was getting on toward planetary nightfall and the end of their shift, they said Laneet would take me to the bay and they'd continue with me the next day.

Artoo and I followed Laneet into a busy cargo bay located underneath Utheel Outfitters but on the opposite side of the dock from where we had entered. There we took another speeder a few klicks down a much wider tunnel until we reached a giant lift suitable for loading large pallets or even vehicles. Laneet drove the speeder directly into the lift and we took it up to a large cavern carved out of the rock. Laneet pressed a single button to activate a sliding door, which opened up a slice of cliffside in a narrow canyon. The other side loomed above, already cast in shadow under clouds painted pink from the setting sun, and Laneet led us to the edge and pointed up. "We are low enough that the lip of the other side provides a shadow from satellite surveillance. You would enter and exit the canyon from that direction," she said, gesturing to the left. "Follow it to the end and you will emerge at a waterfall that is something of a tourist destination just ten klicks from the spaceport near the enclave. Its beauty is reason enough for ships to visit, and no one thinks anything of the occasional traffic coming in and out."

"Huh. Not much here," I said, looking around at the empty cavern.

"It's for loading and unloading cargo only. We keep it powered off during downtime to prevent it being scanned," Laneet said, "and we patrol the perimeter during operations to make sure no one can do a fly-by and see it. Should you need rest and relaxation or refueling, all those facilities await at the spaceport. This was designed for discretion."

I gave a nod of appreciation. "Yeah. I think this will work for us. All right, we can go back and start thinking about doing some business."

"Excellent. I will inform Soonta. May I tell her you will join her for breakfast in the morning?"

"Sure." Laneet referred to Taneetch Soonta, one of the Rodians I'd met earlier. I believe she'd introduced herself as a sales executive for Utheel Outfitters.

As we walked back to the lift and Laneet closed the cavern wall with another push of the button, she said, "I'll take you to your room now in Toopil. Do you have all you require?"

"Almost. Just need a powerfeed for my droid and maybe some dinner."

"Of course. And your droid can download our inventory and pricing for you to peruse at your leisure."

My room in the secret complex of Toopil proved to be my favorite place so far on Rodia, for it had been scrubbed of smells as much as possible rather than doused with a surplus of perfumes. Artoo displayed the weapons and armor inventory after he downloaded it, and I frowned at the prices. I didn't precisely know the state of Alliance funding, but I wasn't sure we'd be able to afford any large orders. War was expensive—and not just in lives lost. I'd make a point of testing out the weapons tomorrow to make sure they deserved such a steep price.

I left Artoo in the room when it was time to meet with Soonta for breakfast. Laneet knocked softly on my door and led me upstairs to a special chamber of the Utheel Outfitters complex. It was a solarium that also functioned as a café, though there weren't any families dining there. It appeared reserved for an exclusive clientele. Richly dressed Rodians and an assortment of other species held quiet conversations barely audible against the notes of a Bith symphony floating above them via hidden speakers. Sunlight filtered through a huge stained-glass window that reached from floor to ceiling, bathing all the diners in colored light. White porcelain cups and saucers rested in front of us on a small round bistro table, each cup tinted a different hue thanks to the windows. I was wearing white also, but Soonta had dressed herself in an ensemble of dark greens highlighted with glints of silver thread. Diners at other tables kept their voices low, their conversations amounting to no more than a soft hum over the Bith music, and I wondered if maybe that incredible window was responsible for creating the strange atmosphere of reverence. The other visitors sitting with Rodians were no doubt as interested in Chekkoo weapons as the Alliance was, and it struck me as weird for everyone to be negotiating the purchase of deadly weapons in such a serene setting. This kind of commerce normally involved a certain seediness that the Rodians were deliberately refusing to provide.

After our server departed with our orders and Soonta inquired politely about my sleep, I expected her to ask if I'd had the opportunity to review their catalog and suggest a discounted selection or something of that nature. She surprised me.

"Forgive me if I'm intruding, friend Skywalker," she said, "but I noticed something unusual as you sat down—a flash only, obviously not meant to be seen, but so interesting that I cannot help but ask, at risk of giving offense. Are you perhaps carrying a lightsaber?"

I froze. My lightsaber was indeed concealed beneath my outer tunic, but clearly I had not taken enough care in dressing this morning to make sure it stayed hidden. I didn't like to leave it lying around to be discovered when I was away and so kept it on my person at all times. Though it wasn't a strictly prohibited weapon, its association with the Jedi would tend to make one guilty by association in the eyes of the Empire. The Chekkoo's willingness to conduct some business on the side with the Rebellion might not extend to consorting with a sympathizer of the Jedi. We were stepping lightly on quicksand here.

"That's an interesting question," I replied carefully. "Let us suppose purely for argument's sake that I am. Would you be offended or scandalized, or perhaps feel bound to report me to Imperial authorities?"

"Far from it, far from it," she assured me. "I would have to confess that my views on the Jedi do not align with the official Imperial view."

"Is that so? What are your views, then?"

"I can hardly give them words. I suppose I harbor doubts about the Empire's version of recent events. The victors' view of history rarely matches that of the vanquished, after all."

"So you don't believe that the Jedi betrayed the Emperor?"

"I believe they had a serious disagreement with him, no doubt, and I find it easy to believe that he personally felt betrayed. His public behavior and rhetoric paint him to be the sort of man who views any disagreement as a betrayal. But I don't feel the Jedi were in the habit of betraying others. I believe they were more likely to keep oaths than break them. Of course, I have no proof of any of this. It is a feeling, nothing more."

"That's an extraordinary feeling, if you don't mind me saying. How did you come to hold it?" I asked.

"A member of our clan was a Jedi Knight. He was my uncle, in fact, and though his devotion to the Order usually kept him far from Rodia, I saw him a few times when I was young. Of course, he was here on Jedi business—and of course the Jedi do not maintain their family ties—but I was told who he was and even had occasion to meet him once or twice. He seemed to me the very personification of honor."

I could relate to that feeling, because Ben Kenobi had affected me the same way. He was in my life for only a short time, yet he earned my trust and respect immediately, even though from a logical standpoint I had little reason to trust a stranger. Now, meeting someone else who had personally known a Jedi Knight, I found it hard to hide my excitement, but instead of shouting *No way! Tell me everything!* I carefully schooled my expression into a polite smile and said, "That's fascinating, Soonta. If you don't mind me asking, what was he like, apart from honorable?"

"His name was Huulik. He was a good pilot—or at least fairly proud of his skills. But he used to talk about another Jedi who could fly like no other, and his name also happened to be Skywalker. That's why that fleeting glimpse of a lightsaber piqued my interest. I don't suppose you had any relatives among the Jedi?"

My heart pumped faster. "Yes. My father was a Jedi who fought in the Clone Wars."

Soonta blinked and tilted her head. "A *son* of a Jedi Knight? I thought the Jedi weren't allowed such relationships."

That wrung an ironic half grin out of me. "Guess I'm not allowed, then."

"It certainly explains the coincidence. It must have been your father of whom my uncle spoke. Apparently this Skywalker saved his life at the Battle of Sedratis. They were swarmed by droid fighters, and my uncle's shields were depleted when Skywalker flew in between him and the next blast that would have killed him. Skywalker destroyed the immediate threat and gave Huulik's shields a chance to recharge. They were eventually victorious that day, and I'm given to understand that they fought together on several occasions."

That was the first specific exploit of my father's career as a Jedi I'd ever heard. It was gratifying to hear of him saving the life of a friend.

"Thank you for sharing that."

"Did your father survive the Clone Wars?" Soonta asked.

"No," I said, shaking my head. "He was betrayed by Darth Vader."

"I am sorry to hear. But how do you know that, specifically?"

"I was told so by another Jedi, Obi-Wan Kenobi."

"Kenobi! I know that name! He came to Rodia during the Clone Wars to help return a kidnapped child from another clan. Am I to understand he's still alive?"

For a moment I felt my throat close up, but then I was able to say, "Not anymore. He died at the Battle of Yavin."

"Ah! So a Jedi was involved in the destruction of the Death Star. The Alliance's victory there makes much more sense now. The Jedi have a way of turning daunting tasks into routine ones."

I decided not to mention that I'd been the one who'd delivered the fatal shot to the exhaust port.

Besides, Obi-Wan *had* helped me. "So what happened to your uncle?" I asked.

"Like your father, he was betrayed. He was shot by clone troopers who were supposed to be on his side. He made it into his ship, recorded a brief message about what happened to him with his astromech, and gave it orders to bring him back here. He could not think of anyplace safer in the entire galaxy, which I thought was sad. This has never been a safe planet. But he was already dead when his ship landed, his wounds too severe to survive the journey."

"That's terrible. I'm sorry," I said. "Did his astromech survive the trip?"

"Only in the physical sense. The clan wiped its memory to prevent it falling into the wrong hands and putting us at risk. We scuttled his ship and built my uncle a small tomb out in the jungle, not knowing what else to do."

"Oh. I don't suppose it would be . . . well, look, Soonta, that *was* a lightsaber you saw on my belt, one left for me by my father, and I'd like to be a Jedi myself someday if I can. If it's not rude of me to ask, do you think I could go pay my respects to your uncle?"

The antennae on top of Soonta's head—they looked like suction cups on short stalks—drew back in what I thought must be surprise. Or maybe it was shock and a certain sense of outrage. I'm not well schooled in Rodian body language, and my shoulders tensed, bracing for an angry retort. Instead, Soonta sounded pleased.

"That would be most thoughtful of you. I should pay my own, in any case." Soonta took a sip from her caf cup and then said, "You're a prospective customer. We can borrow a couple of speeders by way of a test drive and visit now, if you'd like. The tomb isn't far from here."

"That sounds great," I said. "I'm actually not hungry. We can go now if you're willing."

"So be it."

Leaving the quiet solarium and crossing the length of Utheel Outfitters was at once refreshing and uncomfortable. It was nice to walk in open surroundings instead of in subterranean tunnels or the close confines of a ship, but manufacturing facilities are not renowned for their peace and quiet. Welding and the whir of machinery assailed our ears and the vibrations of shearing metal shook our bones to the point that I began to miss the silence of space.

Taneetch Soonta spoke to the warehouse supervisor and secured two brightly colored demo speeder bikes for a day trip. We shot north into the tangle of the jungle, slicing through the wet air as if we were waterskiing. I followed Soonta's lead, weaving through trees just below the canopy and above the undergrowth. The humidity was truly ridiculous, and I felt the close pressure of it even with the wind of the ride. Sweat trickled down my neck and back, my clothes stuck to my skin, and I resigned myself to marinating. The dry heat on Tatooine felt like being in an oven sometimes, but this was more like bathing in a stew pot. After we flew over the canyon I recognized as the one that led to the smuggling bay, we descended for a klick until the trees stopped growing so close and poor drainage maintained a swamp of dark water frosted with green algae. It wasn't an endless expanse of water, however. Small islands of spongy loam peeked out of the swamp, providing places for trees and bushes to take root, and Soonta led me to one that boasted some solid rock on it. Only a little bit was available on the edge—the island was so choked with trees and thick undergrowth, there was truly nowhere else to land. I didn't see the mausoleum until we set down on a moss-covered stone shelf a mere half a meter above the swamp. It was a small stone structure hidden under the canopy of a thinekk tree and further camouflaged by creeping vines. Before the whir of our speeder repulsors faded, Soonta urged me to dismount quickly. The stress in her voice jarred against the languid croaking of frogs and the bored conversation of alien birds.

"We should move away from the water's edge," Soonta said. "Just in case there may be ghests nearby."

"Ghests?"

"Yes," she said, putting her hand on the small of my back and gently ushering me away from the speeders and into a thicket of bushes that dared me to pass through without getting stabbed and scratched by thorns. "They're large creatures that like to move quietly in the water before erupting to pluck food off the shorelines, especially herbivores and birds, and we just flew down from the sky to land at the shore—"

Soonta's sentence was cut off as an enormous scaled figure splashed out of the swamp and pounced on my speeder bike, wrapping it up with clawed hands and biting down into the front steering vanes with a mouthful of sharp teeth. We scrambled back as the ghest roared, frustrated to find it had ambushed something that was not meat, and it slammed the speeder into the rock shelf with its powerful arms, destroying the vanes in the process and effectively totaling the vehicle. The ghest turned its pale round eyes on us and hissed as it slipped back into the water, disappearing completely, leaving us with thudding hearts in our chests and a single working speeder.

"Your point is well taken," I said. "Will it try again?"

"When we try to leave, yes. There is no doubt,"

Soonta said. "It prefers ambush. It knows the speeders are not food now but that we are. It will be watching." I noticed that there was no way for us to watch the ghest in return. The swamp water revealed nothing of what moved underneath the surface.

"Can we shoot it?" I asked.

"Yes. But it is notoriously difficult to get off a lethal shot before a ghest bites you in half. They are not hunted so often as they used to be, but when they are, they are hunted in teams, and those teams often return with a dead ghest and at least one dead Rodian."

"Hmm. It won't come after us on the land?"

"It's technically possible but highly doubtful. Ghests are much slower on land and perceive that as a weakness. They prefer the quick strike."

We stood in silence for a couple of minutes, looking for any signs of movement in the dark waters. The surface remained still and gave no hint that something stalked us from below. During that time it occurred to me that this had been horrible planning on Soonta's part.

"Why did we land so close to shore?"

"There was no place else to land. You saw that for yourself as we came in."

"So you risk an attack like that every time you visit your uncle's final resting place?"

"Hardly ever. Someone in the family clears a path and landing area each time we visit. But the jungle is robust, new growth shoots up, and it's been too long since anyone visited. I might have been the last one to visit, and that was almost a standard year ago."

"So how are we getting back?"

"We'll have to double up on my speeder."

I gestured at the still waters where the ghest waited. "But that thing would never let us get off the ground. You can't call for someone to come get us?"

"I know from experience that my comm won't reach anyone from this place."

"What about an emergency beacon?"

The Rodian gave that single twitch of her head to the left that meant no. "These demonstration models are stripped down, built for speed rather than safety. Our clients always want a demonstration of speed but never ask for a demonstration of emergency services."

I sighed in frustration. "Well, let's do what we came to do, and worry about getting out of here afterward," I said.

"Agreed," Soonta said, and we turned to the mausoleum. Soonta produced a handheld sonic cutter to clear a path through the undergrowth, which allowed us to reach it in a few minutes while saving our clothes and skin from tears and perhaps puncture wounds.

The mausoleum didn't have a marker on it or any engraving explaining who was entombed there. Soonta knelt in the soft dirt before the gray stone door and I joined her, bowing my head. She said a few things in her native language that I didn't understand, but they sounded solemn and respectful and I hoped my silence would be taken in the same spirit. But I could not help wondering what might lie inside the tomb. I know that Soonta said her uncle's body had been found inside his ship once it landed, but was it truly still there now? I don't think I'll ever forget the sight of Obi-Wan's empty robe. That method of dying still didn't seem plausible to me—and I had seen it with my own eyes. I wondered if perhaps this Huulik had eventually faded to nothingness in the same way.

When Soonta had finished her oblations I asked, "Forgive me if it's rude to ask, but . . . might we see him?"

The Rodian tilted her head ever so slightly in my

direction and regarded me with her giant black eyes. "Did you speak the truth earlier? Do you wish to become a Jedi yourself one day, or was that merely an idle fantasy?"

"Yes, I truly wish it. More than anything."

"Then we should enter."

I helped her open the door, and the smell inside was every bit as damp and moldy as the outside. Assorted slugs and a snake wriggled away from the sudden glare of sunlight. A sarcophagus squatted in the middle of the room, almost covered in a carpet of lichen.

"There's something in there for you," Soonta said, pointing with a green finger.

"I . . . there is? What?"

"Help me move the lid."

I didn't argue since it was what I wanted anyway, but her eagerness puzzled me. I supposed I didn't know much about Rodian cultural taboos regarding the dead and decided to go with it. We hefted a corner of the slab together and shoved it aside until the top half of Huulik's remains lay revealed. There wasn't much left, but clearly he hadn't passed on to some other state of existence like Obi-Wan. Apart from the bones there were still fragments of the robe left, a few curling clumps of hardy threads that had survived this long against the elements and denizens of the swamp. Soonta leaned over and thrust her hand into the sarcophagus, obstructing my view. She emerged holding a thick black cylinder.

"This is Huulik's lightsaber, I believe. We buried it with him since we didn't know what else to do with it."

"Does it still work?"

"I don't know." She handed it to me. "Try it and see. It's yours."

I blinked. "You're giving this to me? Wouldn't someone else in your family object?"

Soonta shrugged her antennae. "At this point I suspect I am the only member of my family who still comes to visit him. And it is not doing any good sealed away like that. I think it's an inheritance better suited to you than me. Perhaps you can learn something from it and one day become a Jedi like your father and my uncle. It would be good to have the Jedi return, I think."

It was a stupefying gift and I had difficulty mustering a response. "Thank you," I managed after a time, though the words were inadequate. "I'm honored."

Huulik's lightsaber was designed for a Rodian hand and wasn't quite comfortable in my fist. It had a matte-black finish to it and an odd slick feeling—I didn't know if that was its original state or if some kind of biological ooze coated it. Pointing it carefully away from both of us, I thumbed it on, expecting the power cell to be long depleted by now. But it ripped into life and thrummed with energy, a brilliant amethyst blade.

"Now something like that," Soonta said, "might allow you to survive a direct attack from a ghest."

It took a moment for me to process her meaning, but when I did I stared at her. "You mean walk out there as bait, holding a lightsaber in front of me?"

"You have two now, correct? Your odds of ensuring the ghest has to eat a lightsaber before it eats you are pretty good."

I grinned. Soonta had a strange sense of humor, but she also had a point. I'd be better off protecting myself from a quick attack with two lightsabers than with a single blaster that I'd have to aim and fire in a fraction of a second before I got chomped. I thumbed off the Rodian lightsaber and asked, "I don't suppose

Huulik brought anything else home with him, like a handy step-by-step manual on how to train yourself to become a Jedi?"

"No, nothing like that, unfortunately. I would have attempted it myself had that been the case, even though I can't feel the Force."

"Well, I'm very grateful for this much." I turned the lightsaber hilt over in my hands, thinking. "You said he was shot by his own clone troopers?"

"That was what his recording said. We, of course, had no way to confirm it. Asking the local garrison of troopers if someone may have shot a Rodian Jedi Knight offplanet would attract the wrong sort of attention. But it's stunning in its implications, isn't it? Looked at in that light, it might have been the Jedi who were betrayed, not the Emperor."

Not for the first time, I wished I'd had more time with Ben. Not only could he have taught me about the Force, but he could have filled in many giant gaps in my knowledge regarding the history of the Clone Wars. The Empire's version of events was undoubtedly self-serving, but there was no alternative version of events available. My aunt and uncle would never talk to me about it no matter how much I begged them. I felt handicapped by my ignorance.

"You've given me a lot to think about. That is, if I can get us out of here." Even if Soonta were to leave me here to go get help, she'd need to get on her speeder bike safely—and there was no guarantee she could do that. If the ghest was still waiting in the swamp, it could easily pounce before she could take off. We needed to remove the threat before either of us tried to mount the speeder bike. I withdrew my own lightsaber from my belt, walked forward to the edge of the island, one weapon in each hand, and turned them both on. I crouched to minimize myself as a target as I advanced, holding the lightsabers parallel to the ground and angled to protect each side of me so that I was at the base of a triangle. The ghest would have to be extremely fast and agile to take me out without getting cut. The problem was it had looked like it might actually be that fast and agile.

The dark water gave no sign of the ghest's whereabouts, only a promise that it hid a food chain within its depths and I was not at the top of it. Just stepping near the water made me feel like something's lunch.

Insects and birds and amphibians continued to drone and chirp and croak, heedless of my problems, but their noise existed on another level than auditory. When I stretched out with my feelings and tried to locate the ghest through the Force, all I got was an overwhelming sense of the life surrounding me—nothing so specific as a single bird or fish or predator. I knew that many of the creatures were hungry and wanted to eat other creatures, but there was no sense that a certain one wished to eat me.

There I stood, shifting my weight a bit and moving slightly to look alive, lightsabers humming, for five full minutes.

"Maybe it's moved on," I finally said. "How about you try taking the remaining speeder back—I'll guard you as you get on—and come back to pick me up?"

Soonta said, "I suppose—" and then the ghest erupted from the swamp on my left, a flash of movement faster than I could track. By reflex I whipped the blade in my left hand toward it while simultaneously falling backward and swinging a fraction later with my right hand as well. Both swings connected, but the ghest connected, too. Its head got above and through my awkward defenses and it sank its teeth into the soft tissue between my left shoulder and my neck. It didn't bite through or try to move up to my throat, however; by the time we hit the ground, its head and shoulders weren't connected to the rest of the body. The swing I'd taken with my lightsaber had shorn through entirely, leaving me alive but with a dead ghest's teeth buried in my flesh.

Soonta rushed over to help. "Are you all right?" she asked.

"I'll live. I think."

"Most people don't survive being attacked, so that was well done."

The soggy head affixed to my body didn't make me feel like a winner. "Ugh. It wasn't really a skill thing. More like panicked reflexes and really good weapons. You were right, there's no way I would have gotten off a blaster shot in time." I thumbed off the light-sabers and shook a little bit from adrenaline and the thought of how close I'd come to death. A couple of centimeters more and the ghest would have had my throat, and I would have bled out regardless.

The ghest's jaw hadn't locked up, so prying it loose was more painful than difficult. "We need to get you to the infirmary," Soonta said, tossing the head into the swamp before helping me to my feet. The ghest's long serpentine body trailed off into the water, a greenish log that ended in blood on the rock. "The sooner the better. Limping into town doubled up on the speeder will be a bit faster than going back for another one and returning."

She took holos of the damaged speeder and the ghest's body with her datapad before we left. "I need to explain what happened if I don't want to have my pay docked."

We crowded onto the remaining speeder; I wrapped my right arm around Soonta's waist and did my best to deal with her personal pungency. I knew that later I'd look back on the experience and count it as a good one on the whole, because there was no telling what I could learn from Huulik's lightsaber, but at the time, feeling weak and light-headed from blood loss, foul smells, and excessive humidity, I thought that was the worst speeder ride ever.

$$\frac{\sum_{i=1}^{n}}{n-1} \text{(CHAPTER 3)}$$

ONCE I WAS PATCHED UP and back in my room in Toopil, I was too wired to sleep and could think of no better use of my time than to take a closer look at Soonta's gift.

Doing my best to relax and leave myself open to the Force, I activated Huulik's lightsaber and marveled again at how the hilt didn't feel quite right; even though I'd wiped it down with a damp cloth and removed all hints of debris, it still seemed to want to escape my grip with a slippery, viscous surface tension that was absent from my own lightsaber. Was it a function of Rodian versus human manufacture? Or was my lightsaber better suited to me because it had been constructed by my father?

The blade was not pure light, of course: It was energy from the same sort of power cell that fueled blasters, given form by passing through a kyber crystal as superheated plasma that arced at the top and returned to the hilt. It didn't give off heat until it touched something solid; the rest of the time its power was contained by a force field. I knew that much but very little else. I wanted to see how it worked—how it was constructed. I had never dared take apart my lightsaber for fear that I wouldn't be able to put it back together again, but Soonta had given me Huulik's lightsaber to learn something if I could, so I was going to risk it.

I deactivated it and inspected the hilt closely. There were no screws or switches or any of the usual markers of assembly. Except for the button to turn it on and the dial that adjusted its strength, it appeared to be a solid artifact, as if it had been shaped that way in nature. Perhaps the barrel was a solid piece, albeit hollow, that had been slipped over the rest of the assembly. And perhaps the key to opening it wasn't visible with the eyes.

My room had a basic desk and chair, and I seated myself at it and placed the lightsaber on the desk, emitter pointed away from me for safety. As before, I kept myself open to the Force, but now I tried to focus on the lightsaber and feel the Force inherent in it. Closing my eyes, I explored the top of the hilt right below the emitter with my fingers, searching for any tactile clues. The surface retained that same strange slick feeling, but I detected nothing unusual at the top, or around the button or dial, or even on the rest of the hilt. When I ran my finger fully around the base, however, clockwise and then counterclockwise, eyes still closed and trying to feel the Force, a *snick* announced the appearance of a fissure lengthwise down the hilt; after another soft *click*, the casing popped free, revealing yet another metal sheath, one that looked more like mine and had visible screws. Artoo unscrewed them for me and I was able to lift off one half of the sheath and reveal the innards.

The power cell at the base was insulated and held no interest for me. Above that was a platform for the primary focusing crystal that gave the lightsaber its color. Two additional crystals floated above it, balanced so precariously on mounting ridges that they could easily be disturbed—and they had been. They lay askew, and I feared I must have done that in the process of disassembling it. The lightsaber wouldn't work properly now, even if I put it back together; without proper focusing there was no telling what would happen if I tried to turn it on. It might explode. And aligning those crystals by hand would be impossible— I sensed that it had to be done with the Force, and only through the Force would I know whether it was aligned properly or not. They were wafer-thin slices of crystal, too, a beautiful clear amethyst, and might scratch or cloud with handling. Moving them precisely with the Force would ensure that they remained pristine.

The lightsaber's construction confirmed for me what I had already suspected: Far from being merely a feeling of interconnectedness that could guide your actions or a method of tricking the weak-willed, the Force could be used to manipulate solid objects. However, the skill required to construct a lightsaber—or even put this one back together—was a parsec or five beyond my current abilities.

I had Artoo take holo stills of the lightsaber as I deconstructed the rest of it for future study, and then I thought I should work on those Force abilities if I ever wanted to reassemble it or make my own.

Obi-Wan had never addressed telekinesis with me. It was likely that I wasn't strong enough to begin training in such an advanced field of study. That didn't mean I shouldn't try. I could begin with something small and harmless. At the far corner of the desk, there were a few sad vegetables lounging on a plate left over from lunch. I imagined that the cranker root, especially, looked unhappy where it was and wouldn't mind moving a tiny bit. The humblest of Rodian vegetables, it sat, steamed and soggy, in a puddle of oil on a ceramic plate. Its outlook would be vastly improved if it escaped the valley of the plate, say, and moved to the crest along the edge, where it could enjoy the fabulous vista of the desk and the tumbled remains of Huulik's lightsaber.

Before I began, I gave myself permission to fail. It was to be my first try, after all, and there was no use in getting upset or even angry at myself if I didn't succeed right away. Obi-Wan said the man who killed my father, Darth Vader, had been seduced by the dark side of the Force. I assumed he was referring to darker emotions like fear, anger, and guilt, but his word choice puzzled me—I would never think of dark emotions as being seductive, with an agenda to consciously corrupt someone. To me they were emotions triggered by events that were felt intensely and then faded away, not natural states of being. But Obi-Wan probably knew what he was talking about and I didn't think I could risk ignoring the warning of Vader's example. That meant I needed to be extremely cautious since I didn't have anyone around to train me. The cranker root looked thoroughly nonthreatening. I hadn't read the histories of those "seduced" by the dark side, but I doubted that any of them had been corrupted by a vegetable of questionable nutritional value. This had to be safe.

I pulled the plate nearer to me so that it filled my vision on the desk. The cranker root lay inert, jaundiced and phlegmatic in the yellow light of the room's filtered glow panel. Its weight was negligible. It should be a simple matter to use the Force to move it off the plate, especially since conditions were optimal.

The first step—the only step I really knew—was to clear my mind and reach out to the Force. So simple to say but not so easy in practice. Sometimes it just kind of happened for me, but whenever I actually told myself to clear my mind, the words sort of hung around in my consciousness, an image of white letters on a green screen: CLEAR YOUR MIND. That didn't help. Thinking THAT MEANS YOU didn't help, either. Sending in more thoughts to clear out the old ones from my brain cycled through the same problem again. How did the Jedi do this reliably and on cue?

Meditating and getting to a quiet place when alone was somehow much different from feeling the Force in combat or while piloting or practicing against drones. When I opened myself to the Force in those situations, it was more of an instinctive process, and I felt guided and warned in an almost effortless way, perhaps owing to a combat-ready state of action and reaction where there is no time for thought, and a profound sense of personal danger.

The cranker root represented the opposite of danger. Maybe that was my problem—I needed pressure to push my abilities, to switch me into a nonthinking instinctive mode. But even if that were true, I couldn't settle for such a standard. I had to be able to do this on my own, by conscious effort—or would it be an unconscious effort if I managed to clear my mind?

CLEAR YOUR MIND, I told myself again. The words remained stubbornly uncleared and began to blink insistently for my attention. That wasn't working.

I sighed, and that gave me the idea of focusing on my breathing. Each breath quieted the roiling of my thoughts a bit more. The three blinking words that annoyed and mocked me gradually faded as my lungs filled and emptied and the rhythm of it took over. The Force swirled through and around me, eddies of energy that I could sense and feel but had yet to push or control. Stretching out through the Force, eyes closed,

I located the plate, a cold ceramic disk. I found the cranker root, dead now, but a thing sensed as fundamentally distinct from the plate. That was a beginning. But now what? If I merely imagined the cranker moving, would it happen? What if I—

Laneet Chekkoo burst in. "Forgive me, friend Skywalker, but there is dire trouble. The Empire has issued a planetwide alert for a ship matching yours, and if you do not leave right away you may be discovered here."

"What? Can't we just hide it in the smugglers' bay?"

"The chance of being seen by spies is too great. We're trying to prevent the ones we know about from investigating the spaceport, but we can't hold them forever and there are probably others we don't know about. If you're seen here, we want you to be seen leaving. We can smuggle goods to the Alliance, but we can't openly defy the Grand Protector or the Empire now."

"All right, I understand. Just a moment." I collected the pieces of Huulik's lightsaber and placed them in a small bag. "Come on, Artoo," I said. "We have to run and hide again."

$$s_k^2 = \frac{1}{n} \sum_{j}^{n} \left(\textbf{CHAPTER} - \overline{4} \right)$$

WE TOOK A LONGER ROUTE back to the fleet, a circuitous path that involved forging a new hyperspace lane between Kirdo and Orto Plutonia—but only after scanning the ship for tracers and spyware. Without immediate pressure and with the luxury of time, Artoo minimized the inherent risk of traveling along unknown hyperspace lanes in conjunction with the nav computer of the *Desert Jewel*.

Admiral Ackbar and Princess Leia surprised me by taking a shuttle over from the command ship *Redemption* to the *Promise* where the *Desert Jewel* was being kept. They wanted to see me right away, and they arrived in the captain's quarters with C-3PO whirring behind them. The protocol droid looked like he had recently enjoyed an oil bath and a shine, and he was almost jubilant to see R2-D2.

"It was a somewhat successful trip," I said. "Artoo has the full catalog of Rodian weapons—"

"Excellent," Ackbar wheezed, waving that away as unimportant. I noticed the Mon Calamari often cut off or disregarded any talk that didn't immediately advance his current goal. "But we're more interested in what happened to you in the Llanic system."

How had they heard about that? "I never could make that stop on Llanic," I said. "There was this ship in trouble and I couldn't stand to see it destroyed by TIE fighters, so I helped it escape. I know it was stupid and compromised the mission and maybe the safety of the fleet, and I apologize for that."

"We'll send someone else to Llanic, Luke," Leia said. Her long dark hair was braided in a queue that fell down her back, and she wore a practical, casual outfit of pants, tunic, and boots. "And don't worry— helping that ship the way you did was vital. It carried information that could change things for us."

"It did?"

"There was a Kupohan spy on that ship who delivered some vital intelligence. Apparently, there's a Givin woman newly arrived on Denon who can, if reports are accurate, slice almost anything. She's a cryptographic genius who makes intuitive leaps that droids can't and customizes her own hardware. The Empire is keeping her in a sort of luxurious imprisonment there, trying to convince her to apply her skills to slice through our codes and those of other groups they're monitoring. She's been given freedom to move on the planet, but she's guarded around the clock. Through a Kupohan contact on Denon she smuggled out a message entirely in mathematics that took Threepio most of a day to figure out. She says she'll work for us against the Empire if we can get her family to Omereth and then take her there to join them."

"Where's Omereth?"

"Out past Hutt Space," Ackbar answered. "It's a water-based planet with a few archipelagos. I've seen holos. Looks delightful, but it has little to offer most species in the galaxy besides fish, so it's practically uninhabited."

"No sentient water species there?"

"Only those daredevils that like to visit from other planets, I'm told. The problem is that many of the native fish are quite large and hungry. Makes for dangerous swimming. Not the kind of ocean I'd like to swim in."

"Luke, we can have Major Derlin and his crew take care of relocating the family," Leia said, "but we'd like you to snatch the cryptologist from Denon and fly her to Omereth."

"Why me?"

"You're one of the best pilots we have, and it's going to take some skillful flying to get her out of there. Once the Empire realizes she's been taken, they'll be anxious to reacquire her. We know this because the pursuit of the Kupohans was relentless. If not for your interference, they wouldn't have made it."

"Are you sure about that? There were only two TIEs on its tail and I took them out easily. I mean, one of them swung around to attack and then deliberately broke off and gave me a free shot. What if this is a setup?"

"I don't think it is," Ackbar said. "The Kupohan ship's shields were almost exhausted and the TIEs would have destroyed it in the next couple of minutes. They couldn't have known you'd show up at that time. They were genuinely doing their best to eliminate the Kupohans and seal their security breach."

"We still don't have the *Millennium Falcon* available," Leia continued, "so I think, when you consider that you need a very fast ship with room at least for a passenger and a droid, the *Desert Jewel* might be our best option."

"She's a wanted ship now," I reminded her, but Leia shrugged it off.

"The *Millennium Falcon* is wanted everywhere. We just change the transponder codes and it's fine."

"But the *Jewel* is virtually unarmed," I pointed out. "That's a serious drawback if we're going to face significant Imperial interference. We need to be able to defend ourselves. That ship's not ready for this kind of mission without upgrades."

Leia exchanged an uncertain glance with Admiral Ackbar. "Upgrading weapons on such a custom ship might be difficult," Ackbar said, consonants slipping and vowels bubbling as his voice, accustomed to water, struggled in the dry air of the ship.

"Why?"

"The Alliance is low on money. We're having trouble maintaining the fleet we have, much less upgrading it. However, there's some time before you need to go. The Kupohans need a couple of weeks to establish the Givin's routine and search for weaknesses in her security so that they can give you the best chance of success. If you can find the resources to upgrade the ship by then, by all means, do so."

Something didn't add up. "You just had me go on a trip to see the Rodians about purchasing weapons and now you're saying you can't pay for weapons?"

"We'll have money eventually, Luke," Leia assured me, "but we're not sure when. Expecting a rebellion to have reliable cash flow is like—" She paused to grasp for an apt comparison, then finished: "—expecting Han Solo to behave rationally." She turned her head to the droids. "Threepio, you enjoy calculating these sorts of things. What's more likely, reliable cash flow for the Alliance or Han behaving rationally?"

"While both have very little chance of occurring, Princess, reliable cash flow is far more likely."

She frowned. "That's what I thought."

It occurred to me that Leia might be feeling some resentment at Han being away trying to help himself instead of helping the Alliance. I wouldn't say a thing about that to him, of course: He would interpret it to mean that she missed him. Speaking of missing people . . .

"Is Nakari Kelen back from that training mission on the surface?" I asked.

"Yes," Ackbar replied. "Why?"

"Well, she might be able to solve the funding problem. Unless I'm mistaken, her dad is practically made of funding."

"We know about that, but according to her, the use of his ship is all he's willing to consider right now."

"He might change his mind if Nakari's directly involved. Can I have her go along on this? I could use someone to watch my back anyway, and she must be competent with that slug gun if you're having her train the rest of the troops."

"You're right, she's more than competent. I don't have any objections," Ackbar said.

"Great." I felt a surge of something like victory and then wondered why. The obvious answer was that I had become smitten after a single brief meeting with her, but I hoped that wasn't it. I didn't truly know her, after all. All I knew was that I had seen enough to want to learn more, and if I wished she would turn out to be as truly likable as she seemed at first, who could blame me for that? Hoping neither my voice nor expression betrayed any of my feelings, I said, "Threepio, would you mind asking Nakari Kelen to join us? She ought to be on the ship somewhere."

"Certainly, Master Luke."

I'm not sure that my voice remained neutral there.

Leia's eyes narrowed and she pursed her lips together as if to ask a question, but I forestalled that by diving into a description of the Chekkoo smuggling bay and their shadow business operations underneath Utheel Outfitters. When the rebellion refilled its coffers again, they'd find an excellent supplier on Rodia.

Nakari had a wide grin for me when she joined us. She wasn't decked out for the field this time; she wore flats instead of boots and had no weapons. "Thanks for bringing my ship back in good shape," she said.

"No problem," I replied. We briefed her quickly on what we wanted to do. "Do you think your father might upgrade your ship to take part in a mission like that?" I asked.

She shook her head. "He doesn't spend money on anything unless it will benefit his business somehow. The only reason I was allowed to fly the *Desert Jewel* in the first place was for scouting missions to new planets and to go hunt rare beasties with some kind of biological oddity his labs could exploit. I upgraded most of the ship, but he helped me get the hyperdrive. A faster ship meant a faster turnaround time and a potential edge on his competitors."

"Oh." That was disappointing but understandable. I couldn't think of how arming the ship to fight off the Empire would help his biolabs.

"We might be able to earn his gratitude, however," she mused. "You said we have a couple of weeks, right?"

"Yes. There's some give to the schedule because we're waiting on more intelligence."

"Well, he lost contact with a collection crew recently and desperately wants a salvage run."

"What's a collection crew?"

"Basically they're hunters and gatherers. Four or

five people who go to various planets to collect specimens for the labs." She deepened her voice and tucked her chin against her neck, presumably imitating her father. " 'Go, my minions, and fetch me three hundred Yathik acid slugs!' " Her voice and posture returned to normal. "That kind of thing."

I was amused by her impression and cracked a smile, but I didn't laugh because Admiral Ackbar blinked his giant eyes and seemed impatient. "Okay, got it."

"So one of Dad's scouts made a discovery recently on this moon orbiting a planet in the Deep Core, and when Dad got the news, he sent a full crew out—his best one. Hasn't heard from them in a couple of weeks, and he wants to know if his collection crew is still there, and, if so, whether anything can be salvaged—especially if there are any living or dead crew and critters on the ship. He'll pay handsomely for any news of it."

"Why doesn't he simply send someone else to go check it out?"

"It's a new discovery, as I said, and he'd prefer to keep it quiet. Industrial espionage is huge in his business. Crews can make a lot of cash on the side tipping off his competitors. He knows firsthand because he pays bribes to the crews of his competitors, as well. He was hoping I could go by myself because he doesn't really trust anyone else, but I told him I was serving the Alliance now and I am. And the other thing is, the hyperspace lanes to this system aren't well established yet, and being in the Deep Core with all those mass shadows makes it even more risky. So he needs someone who's not only loyal but also willing to take a leap. The nav computers on the *Jewel* are pretty good, but I don't know if they're *that* good."

"Add an astromech droid and you'd probably be fine," I said, thinking of R2-D2.

"Yeah, well, my guess is that Dad will convince someone to go out there soon because time is a factor. I mean, he's going to say he's worried about the crew because they might still be alive and need help, but I can be honest: He's really worried his competitors will find out about the moon and exploit it before he can. The point is, Luke, if we wanted to do this, it should be a quick trip. We can go there, find out what happened, and bring back some kind of news—any kind of news—for my father; he would be grateful, and then we could get the *Desert Jewel* upgraded in time for this mission on Denon."

Ackbar jumped into the discussion. "What are the names of this planet and moon, if I may ask?"

"The planet is called Sha Qarot and it orbits a red sun. The moon is a strange purple place called Fex."

"Does the Empire know about Sha Qarot and Fex?"

"Maybe. I'm not sure who discovered it, how long ago, or who they sold the information to besides my father. My father's under the impression that its existence is not widely known."

"Are there any sentient species?"

"Not that I know of. I don't think anyone has set foot on the planet yet; it has a poisonous atmosphere and heavy volcanic activity. We just have holos and scans from orbit. But Fex is very interesting, even though we haven't found sentient life yet."

"If searching for this lost collection crew will earn you the credits to upgrade your ship, I think you should do it," Ackbar said. "But it might also serve another purpose—a more important one as far as I'm concerned. It's possible that the moon might make an ideal base for the Alliance, so I want you to scout it with that in mind. Keep an eye out for the Imperial fleet and put down beacons for future reference if you find any satisfactory sites—but don't lose track of time. Extracting that cryptologist from Denon is your main priority."

CHAPTER 5

NAKARI ASKED ME when I wanted to leave and nodded when I said as soon as possible. There is very little excitement on a Nebulon-B frigate like the *Patience*, breathing recycled air and drinking recycled water, and the chance to check out a funky purple moon sounded like a good time to me. I still remember my years of deadly boredom on Tatooine, when every sunset signaled another lost opportunity to experience something besides sand dunes and moisture vaporators, so a chance to evacuate a sterile environment galvanized me to action like nothing else. Almost becoming snack food for a ghest was vastly preferable to twiddling my thumbs on the hangar deck.

Nakari evidently felt the same and said immediate departure was fine with her.

"Let me get cleaned up and packed, maybe grab a bite, and I'll meet you at the ship in a couple of hours?"

"You sure that's enough time?" Nakari asked.

"It's more than I need. That's taking it easy."

She smirked and tucked a curled string of hair behind her ear. "All right. See you then."

I bade farewell to Leia and Admiral Ackbar and brushed past the droids on my way out. My exit triggered the abrupt departure of R2-D2 just as C-3PO was complaining at length about a microsecond lag in his lateral relays. "Wait! Where are you going?" he called. Artoo's response didn't please him. "But you just got here and I'm not finished catching up yet!" The door closed on any further complaints and Artoo chirped a question at me.

"We'll be flying out on the *Desert Jewel* again soon. I hope you liked her. We're going to be depending on you two to get us in and out of the Deep Core safely." I didn't understand his reply, but since the digital beeps sounded generally positive I didn't worry.

"Luke? Wait up," Leia called from behind. Surprised, I stopped and turned, telling Artoo to go ahead to my quarters. Once she saw that I was waiting, Leia didn't hurry, and when she reached me, she didn't speak right away. Instead she glared at me and paced back and forth, hands on hips. I checked the hallway behind me to make sure she wasn't angry with someone else, but no, it was just the two of us, which meant she was mad at me.

"What?" I asked. "What did I do?"

"It's what you're *doing*."

"What am I doing?"

"You're taking a poorly mapped hyperspace route to a planet where people have gone missing because she's pretty."

"No, that's not it—" The flash in Leia's eyes made me stop and backtrack. "Well, yeah, she *is* pretty, but that's not why I'm going. I'm going because the ship needs weapons if we're going to pull off this mission on Denon, and you heard Admiral Ackbar— this moon might turn out to be a great hiding spot for us."

"We can send someone else to check out the moon, and we can find a safer way to get the credits you need to upgrade the ship. You don't have to take this risk."

"How is it any riskier than anything else I've done? I mean, the Battle of Yavin was pretty risky."

"You were surrounded by people you could trust then."

I blinked. "Oh, I see. You think she's working for the Empire."

Leia shook her head and huffed in irritation. "No, not exactly. It's just that she's an unknown quantity and I don't trust her yet."

That was disappointing; I'd need a better reason than that to rethink the mission. On the one hand I wanted to do whatever I could to make Leia happy, but on the other we now had Admiral Ackbar's orders. We really did need a better place to hide than this orbit. I knew the leadership had some ideas about where to build a new base, but they hadn't settled on anything yet.

"Come on," I said, "I can't scrub the whole trip based on unknowns. How can you ever trust someone if you don't give them a chance?"

"That's a very noble attitude, Luke, but not a very safe one."

"If safety is always the number one priority then we would never talk to anyone."

"This isn't about dealing with high-minded blanket statements. When you get betrayed, it's never by someone who looks like Vader. Betrayal always comes wrapped up in a friendly cloak. It's one of the first things I learned in the Senate."

"All right, fair enough. I agree that a certain amount of suspicion of anyone new is warranted, but I don't want to be paranoid, either. You sound like you have a specific reason to be wary of her. What are you not telling me? What should I be looking for?"

Leia crossed her arms and looked away, annoyed. "I don't know. Something under her cloak."

I snorted, she sniggered in response, and then we were both laughing.

Leia covered her mouth. "I'm sorry. I didn't mean it that way."

"I know. Still funny, though."

"Usually I'm more careful with how I phrase things." The smile on her face scurried away, chased off by darker thoughts. "It just shows you I'm worried." She gestured down the hall to where she had left Admiral Ackbar. "I know we can't scrap this now that it's a scouting mission for the Alliance," she said before letting her hand fall down, "but please don't think it's routine. And don't be so trusting."

"I won't."

"Okay." She threw her arms around my neck for a quick hug. "Be very careful, Luke. Come back safe."

"Thanks. I will," I said, though I wasn't so anxious to leave anymore. It felt good to see Leia shed her all-business demeanor for a few moments and speak to me on a personal level—especially without Han around. But I could hardly prolong the moment when I had a mission waiting.

An awkward silence stretched between us. Eventually, Leia spoke. "Well. I'd better get back," she said, giving me a tight grin. "See you soon."

"Right! Yes. Soon." I resumed walking to my quarters, and Leia returned the way she had come, leaving me to wonder why my brain had seized up so badly. It must have been the infinite number of things to say and how most of them would have been the wrong thing. I'd just have to hope I did better next time.

In an hour I was showered, dressed, packed, and

loaded up on soup and crackers. Having nothing better to do, I headed down to the hangar early, thinking I'd go through some of the weapons in the Rodian catalog to see what might work for the *Desert Jewel*, only to find Nakari already there.

"Turns out I'm pretty anxious to leave, as well," she said. "Can't wait to do anything besides sit here and hope the Empire doesn't find me. There's something about skulking that doesn't suit me. It's not engaging, but it isn't restful, either."

Copying her gesture from when we first met, I waved a hand back and forth between us and said, "Same here!"

We let Artoo board first and followed him up.

"We have to stop on Pasher on the way to get all the details from my dad," Nakari said. "I think we have to pick up some custom armor, too. The creatures the collection crew were after are supposed to be dangerous."

"What are they?"

"Not sure. My dad's information protocol means he never gives specifics like that in messages in case they're intercepted. We'll find out soon enough. Plus, I want to impress upon him that we're doing this as a special favor and expect a special favor in return."

She invited me to pilot, content to be a passenger. "I'm already familiar with the ship and what it can do. You might need some additional time to get acquainted."

It was true I wasn't as comfortable yet in the *Desert Jewel* as I was in my X-wing, but I complimented her on what I'd experienced so far. The *Desert Jewel* deserved every admiring glance she received.

Pasher was located in the Inner Rim at a sort of interstellar dead end. Entering the system and viewing it from orbit reminded me of Tatooine, though

Pasher didn't have any moons, and since it lacked the intersecting hyperspace lanes of Tatooine, it wasn't a popular haven for smugglers. Kelen Biolabs was the largest industry on the planet and Fayet Kelen had many demands on his time, but he carved out some for his daughter when we arrived at the sprawling complex of his industrial kingdom. I probably did not make the best impression on him, but it was Nakari's fault. Her earlier impersonation of him turned out to be uncannily accurate, so much so that I could not suppress a goofy half smile in his presence, which he may have found annoying. It was difficult to tell. He was portly, had decided to shave his head rather than try to hang on to a halo of hair, and was gifted with an abundance of jowls. He used his deep voice to boom imperious orders at his employees—whom he actually called minions—and then softened them at the end by adding on "there's a love" or "just because you're brilliant." When we first walked into his office, he turned to an assistant standing nearby and barked, "Minion! Fetch us caf!" And then immediately modulated his tone, saying, "But only because you are kind and deserve a long paid holiday soon." I guess his employees were all in on the joke, or at least compensated well enough that they overlooked his idiosyncrasies. He noticed my expression, however, and shouted at Nakari, "Daughter! Who is this and why is he laughing at me?"

"This is Luke Skywalker, Daddy. He's with the Alliance and he'll be going with me to Fex."

"Pleasure to meet you, sir," I said, nodding at him.

"Hmph! Skywalker. Where have I heard that name?"

"He's the one who destroyed the Death Star, Daddy."

"Ah! The pilot!" He lowered his voice and said to

his daughter, "So you've decided to go to Fex after all? Good idea bringing him along."

"Yes, we'll go, but we expect to be compensated for the trip."

"Compensated! For what?"

"For finding the collection crew and bringing back whatever we can."

"Ah! Very well! The more you bring back, the looser my purse strings. But you must be prepared. *Minion!*" he bellowed. A different assistant, a lean, tall, older man, walked through a door set in the wall to our left and asked Fayet Kelen how he might serve. "Fetch two suits of the new Fexian armor prototypes immediately for my daughter and her pilot! And a case of stun sticks! Have them delivered to her ship as soon as possible! And," he added, more quietly, "please give my regards to your family. I hope your son is doing well at the university."

The man bowed and departed without a word, accepting both the order and the good wishes. It was just as well that he didn't try to speak, for Fayet had already turned his attention back to us and pointed at R2-D2, who had followed us in. "Can I transfer coordinates and other data to your droid?" he asked.

"Of course," I said.

"Does this droid interact with anyone besides you?"

"He occasionally interacts with other members of the Alliance," I said. "But mostly he's my personal astromech."

"It's good to have a minion, isn't it?"

Artoo bleeped something and the tone did not fail to communicate his annoyance with such a demeaning label. Fayet Kelen paused, considering the droid, then looked at me. "You should make sure to lavish him with compliments for his service."

"Oh, I do. He's the finest droid in the galaxy."

Fayet nodded, satisfied, ignoring Artoo's blat of disgust. "Are you returning to the Alliance after leaving here, or traveling straight to Fex?"

"Straight to Fex," Nakari answered.

"Good. After the mission is complete I want all of the data I'm about to give you erased from the droid's memory, agreed?"

"Sure," I said. I could simply have Artoo make his own observations and record them for the Alliance's benefit should we want to use the moon as a base. We'd erase everything he gave us but would have our own data to use afterward.

"Excellent." He picked up a datapad from his desk and stabbed at it rapidly with a thick finger. "*Droid!* I am uploading the encrypted mission files to our system for your access. They will be accessible for fifteen minutes and you may connect to any socket on your way out. Filename *Fexian,* download using the password *Violet,* and decrypt the files using the key *Skywalker.* Acknowledge!"

Artoo chirped an affirmative as Kelen's first assistant returned with almost comically tiny cups of caf, barely half a swallow, resting on porcelain saucers on a round tray. We all paused to drink and return the cups to the saucers, thanking the assistant for bringing them before she withdrew.

"And now, my daughter," Fayet said, stepping forward and placing his massive hands on either side of Nakari's face, "go and return to me safely. You are my pride and my world, and my love for you is as vast as the dune sea outside our city walls. You know this, do you not?"

"Yes, Daddy."

He nodded, satisfied. "Good." He dropped his hands but then waggled a finger at her. "Now, this moon is an extremely dangerous place. Do not step outside your ship without your armor. Review the files I have given you carefully on the way."

"I will." She lunged forward and pecked him on the cheek. "I know you're busy and you have to go." She embraced him briefly and stepped back. "Thanks for seeing us."

"Always." His eyes flicked to me, then he thundered, "And you! Pilot!"

"Yes?"

"Exercise prudence on your journey. You will not show off. Let your skills commend themselves by your judicious use of them."

"Understood, sir."

"And stop grinning at me!"

I did my best to master my expression and said, "Yes, sir."

"Come on, Luke, he's late for a meeting," Nakari said, tugging at my sleeve and leading me to the door. Her father was already shouting for another minion before we could make our exit.

Artoo paused in Fayet Kelen's reception area, where a dataport in the wall allowed him to download the pertinent files for the mission. The tall, lean gentleman who had a son at university was waiting for us at the ship with three black cargo cases. "Two armor units and some stun sticks, as ordered," he said. "I'd practice somersaulting in the armor if I were you."

"Why?" Nakari asked.

"I'm assuming Mr. Kelen shared our survey files with you. Watch the holo of what you're hunting and you'll see what I mean." With that cryptic comment, he wished us a safe journey and departed, but not before I noticed his brief shudder.

"Well, my curiosity is piqued," I said.

"Mine, too. Why would we need somersaults and stun sticks? Why can't we just set our blasters to stun?"

"My guess is that we're not going to have a chance to deal with whatever they are from a distance. That would explain the armor and hand-to-hand weapons."

Nakari frowned. "Yeah, I figured, but I don't understand why we can't ensure that we have plenty of distance before we engage."

"Should make for interesting in-flight entertainment."

Artoo decrypted the *Fexian* file and used the coordinates therein to plot a route as we left the atmosphere of Pasher. I asked him to plot a safe trip into a well-known Core system before trying to navigate the Deep Core. When making a dangerous jump like that it was always best to pause, confirm your position among the stars, and recalculate using the latest possible data.

"I liked your dad," I said as we waited for the first jump.

Nakari searched my face to see if I was being serious or merely polite. "He's a bit eccentric."

"Yeah, but it seems like it's in a good way."

"Not everyone views his yelling as a good thing."

"He tempers it with tenderness, though. Unless that's an act?"

"No, he's genuinely sweet. If anything, the yelling is an act."

"Why does he do it?"

"I don't know for sure, but I have a collection of theories."

"Have you tested any of these theories?"

"I can't test them because he won't be honest or even answer me if I ask him. I did ask him, you know. 'Why do you yell at your minions, Daddy? And why do you call them minions? Isn't that kind of disrespectful?'"

"What did he say?"

She imitated his voice again and grimaced. "'Think

about it, daughter!' And so I did and still do. I cultivate my theories and let them grow for a while—if you'll allow me a farming metaphor—and see which ones flourish in the light of day and which ones wither."

"Which of them flourishes the most right now?"

"Oh, no, you won't get answers that easily. Think about it, pilot!"

I smiled. "Okay, fair enough."

"The best answer, however, is that there are many different viable alternatives. More than one solution to a problem. What's *your* dad like?"

I gave a tiny shrug. "I don't know. I've never met him. He was a Jedi Knight in the Clone Wars and a good pilot, and that's all I know."

"Your dad was a Jedi? How did that happen?"

"The way it usually happens, I would imagine."

"But he was a good pilot, eh? Like father, like son?"

Shrugging, I said, "I guess so."

"I'm sorry if I stepped on an exposed nerve there."

"Oh!" I realized that my expression must have given her the wrong impression. "No, don't worry, it's not you or the question itself. It's just the uncertainty that bothers me. I'd like to think that he was a good guy, but since I'll never meet him all I can do is set him on a pedestal and layer on the wishful thinking. He might have had all the charm of a bantha."

Nakari nodded and changed the subject abruptly, which suggested to me that she didn't want to exchange tales about our mothers next. "Let's take a look at those files if they're ready."

"All right." I flipped on the ship's comm and asked Artoo if he had everything decrypted and spooled up for viewing.

JUMPING NOW. HOLO NEXT, his reply read. The stars blurred and streaked past the cockpit as we jumped into hyperspace, and then a blue holoimage of Fayet

Kelen sprang up in front of us. Nakari hadn't been kidding about her holoprojector being low-end.

"Behold, my minions!" he boomed. He'd obviously recorded this before he knew Nakari and I would be taking on the assignment. "You are traveling to Fex, which might be the richest new discovery for biotech in decades. The red sun of the system has given rise to an unusual purple landscape ranging from pale lavenders to deep violets. High silica and mineral content in the soils have resulted in some fascinating crystal structures that another division may exploit, but we are concerned with how those conditions have manifested themselves in the wildlife. Many of the herbivores, for example, have extraordinary crystalline spikes or horns growing around their heads, or, like a tortoise, have the ability to withdraw their heads into a highly armored body cavity." A series of stills began to flash in the holo in place of Fayet, though he kept narrating. The creatures all had heavy, nightmarish heads of spines and other protuberances and long bodies with tails to balance out the weight. "This tendency for natural armor often goes midway down the back but does not apply to limbs or the lower torso. Bellies are unprotected. We even found this head-and-shoulder armor on display among the predators, which we thought highly curious. What environmental threat on Fex posed such a danger to heads that herbivores and carnivores alike evolved these extreme defenses? We hypothesized that there must exist some sort of arboreal or even aerial apex predator that attacked the head of anything it came across, and thus our first collection crew was sent out with armor suits, as well—but not nearly as strong as that which you currently have. That first crew, unfortunately, discovered why such headgear is necessary. Three were scouting and collecting development leads on the moon while their ship, the *Harvester,* orbited above. I will now play back a vid of their deaths, which they themselves recorded from their helmets."

"Um," I said, "are we going to see a decapitation?"

"I don't know," Nakari whispered.

The holo shifted to helmet footage of a Bith in full armor walking through the Fexian forest. He wore a giant helmet to cover his fleshy, bulbous head, and when he turned briefly to check on his partners, his black eyes could be seen through his faceplate. He was leading the person with the cam and talking about what he was seeing, his alien speech overdubbed with a monotone translation in Basic that conveyed none of the excitement—and later panic—that he obviously felt. Our view switched to his feed, presumably, since the Bith disappeared and we saw nothing but the forest ahead and the quality of the sound changed from a comm crackle to a muffled internal echo like one often hears in the confines of a helmet.

"The crystalline flowers we've seen are valuable just as they are for the jewelry trade, before we put them under a microscope for medical use," he said. "And—" An impact to his head shook the cam. "Auggh! Chobb's knob! What was that?"

The holo switched back to the original view, where we could see the Bith ducking and shaking his head and slapping at the top of it. Odd how he never actually made contact with his helmet, and his hands came away pricked with blood.

"*Gaahh!* Something's on my head! Get it off!"

"What? Where?" The owner of the first helmet cam spoke. "I don't see anything!"

"Right on top! I think it's trying to get through! Hurry! *Aghk!*"

The Bith suddenly ceased moving—or rather, I should say he ceased struggling, for his arms fell limp at his sides and he collapsed face-first to the ground, dead of completely mysterious causes. There was nothing visible attached to his head.

"What in five bloody—" the first speaker began, and then his helmet rocked as well. "Aw, no! No! What is it? Hafner, stun me, quick! Stun my head, and Priban's, too!" The view swung around to reveal a third member of the party, a green-skinned Duros with wide, terrified red eyes behind his visor.

"What? I don't understand." The view switched to the cam of the Duros named Hafner, as he watched the original speaker, a human male, gesturing madly at him. Beyond the human, we could see Priban's still body on the forest floor.

"Stun me now or I'm just as dead as Priban! Do it!"

Hafner's cam shook; I guessed he was fumbling for his blaster.

"Hurry! It's drilling through! *Uhk!*"

The human's limbs went slack, his eyes rolled up in his head, and he fell forward just as the Bith had. Hafner finally got it together, much too late, and shot a stun blast at the unnamed human and at the Bith. Tiny squeals resulted, and the predators lay revealed: small six-legged creatures with spindly limbs that ended in clawed fingers designed to clutch and hold on to prey. Their heads were long snouts with a bulbous skull at the top ringed by eight eyes evenly spaced around it. Their bodies had sharp rigid spines in four rows of four each, presented radially so that anything trying to slap away the creatures would get poked. In each case, the creatures had their snout inserted into a hole in the helmet. Hafner leaned in closer to the human to get a better look.

"Are you seeing this through the feed, *Harvester*? What is it? I couldn't see it before. It didn't appear until it was stunned. That implies conscious control of a very powerful natural camouflage system. It bored right through the helmet! I think you should come pick us up now. We aren't prepared for this kind of thing."

Reaching out with the tip of his blaster, Hafner thrust it underneath the creature's neck and lifted, pulling the flexible snout out of the cavity only to discover that there was another, thinner snout, like a translucent hose, inside of that one, and as it came free, blood and chunks of brain slipped out and plopped wetly onto the helmet.

"I knew it! These things eat brains! That's why all the animals on this moon are so armored." Hafner looked up and saw branches overhanging high above. "They must drop down from the trees. If they stay up there, a creature close to the ground probably wouldn't smell them in time. And you can't see them unless they're unconscious. Or dead, I suppose. But how did they . . ." The cam view returned to the creature. "That feeding tube couldn't have drilled through the helmets, and the outer snout looks like regular skin over cartilage. I'm going to take a closer look while it's still stunned and then get out of here. I hope you guys are on your way, *Harvester*."

A garbled reply came in. "On our way."

For the record, scientists scare me a little bit. I think a normal reaction for most people, upon witnessing two colleagues' brains get eaten by invisible aliens, would not be a calm request for pickup but rather a screaming demand for an air strike to turn the entire surface of the planet to glass. This Hafner should be running away and soiling his armor, not taking a closer look at the brain-slurping alien.

He set his blaster down on the forest floor and Nakari exploded, shouting at the holo, "No! What are you thinking? Don't put down your weapon, that thing could wake up at any time!"

"We already know this isn't going to end well," I said. "Your father said as much."

Being careful to avoid the spines, Hafner picked up the limp alien form with his gloved hands. "Not heavy. Thin bones but very strong ones," he said. "And look at the skin. Colors radiate wherever I touch it." We couldn't see that in the holo, or at least not clearly. There were hints of color, but the low quality of the projector fed everything through a strong blue filter and subtlety was lost, though we could see variations in the tone next to the points where his fingers applied pressure. "Must be a highly advanced chromatophore system in their skin." Cradling the creature by its lower extremities in his left hand, he grabbed hold of the snout with his right. The clear feeding tube retracted by reflex on contact. Hafner continued his commentary. "Hmm. The snout looks completely flexible, but that's not entirely the case. There's a bone inside it along one edge—wait. It moved to the bottom now. How strange."

"It's not strange, it's waking up!" Nakari said. "Run, idiot!"

Hafner's fingers probed at the bone, and it moved again. "Look at this. The bone inside that runs along the snout actually rotates in a full circle. Must be an extraordinary socket and musculature system at the base of the skull, and that feeding tube must retract far up inside for it to be allowed such free movement."

His fingers clutched around the end of the snout. "Down here there is a ring of bone, near the orifice. Yes, it is a ring indeed. I wonder if . . ."

He squeezed and pulled down against the skin of the snout—and unveiled a horror. It was a rotary blade of teeth, pointed down and insulated by its angle from cutting the inside of the creature's snout. But they could cut through a helmet—and then a skull—just fine. The teeth were discolored but otherwise undamaged.

"This is incredible," Hafner mumbled. "They use these teeth and a rotary motion to drill through the skulls of their prey, damaging the brain, and then when their victims fall down, they insert their feeding tubes and . . . well. Feed. What must they be made of, to penetrate through these helmets like they did? Some sort of crystalline coating to the teeth, perhaps, as hard as diamond?"

The picture was rocked as a weight fell down upon Hafner's head. "Oh! I have one on me! *Harvester,* come quickly! I'm stunning myself and the beast!" We saw him pick up the blaster on the ground, heard the stun blast, and then the cam view slipped down and sideways as Hafner hit the forest floor. The picture was replaced by Fayet Kelen.

"Unfortunately, the *Harvester* did not arrive in time to save Hafner. Before it could arrive, the beasts had all woken, finished their meals, and departed. The *Harvester* crew did not land, but rather extracted the bodies with cables and claws. They stunned the bodies to make sure none of the beasts was hitching a ride into the ship, and then left the system to report back to me.

"The brains had been completely removed from the victims. The Bith, Priban, had also been poisoned. Those spines contain a toxin. They were otherwise untouched, but their deaths have revealed the most stunning biotech find in a good long while. A poisonous, adaptive creature with a natural drill mechanism capable of penetrating most armors and perhaps fooling weapons scanners? The potential from this single species alone is worth millions of credits, never mind all the other species on Fex.

"For now we are calling these creatures Fexian skullborers. I sent another crew, the one you are going to find, with upgraded armor and infrared goggles to spy the creatures when they are in camouflage. The armor you have is even better than theirs but cannot accommodate the goggles. Do not leave your ship without the armor on. Stun anything you bring into the ship to make sure no skullborers are hiding on it in camouflage. If you can bring back any skullborers, dead or alive, my bounty will be great. At minimum I need confirmation that the crew is dead or alive and a report on the condition of their ship, the *Harvester*. That ship was fitted with a remote-activated beacon. If it has not been obliterated, it should broadcast a signal in response to the codes I am including in this file. I'm also including other stills and reports for your review. Good luck and safe hunting."

The holo winked out and Nakari looked at me. "Hey, Luke."

"Yes?"

"I know that it's really early and we haven't even made it into the system yet, but I'm going to gently suggest that the Alliance does not try to establish a base on that moon."

"Yeah, I think that's a good call."

"Now we know what the stun sticks are for. They make perfect sense."

"Did the second collection crew have them, I wonder?"

"Maybe that's in the rest of the information he included."

"Maybe. We should review all that." I called out, "Artoo, can you give us everything else Nakari's father included in that file?"

INCOMING, came the reply. We got a toxicity report that indicated the Bith would have fallen stone dead of heart failure if the skullborer hadn't penetrated his brain first—so slapping at them was not an option. There were some speculative reports on the skullborer's skeleton and the composition of the drilling teeth. The helmets worn by the first crew were about an eight on the hardness scale, so the teeth were at minimum a nine and possibly a ten, considering the speed at which they had bored through the material. Our helmets were now nine point five on the hardness scale, including the visor, while the rest of the armor was standard, albeit insulated from stun blasts. Since stunning had proven to be effective, recommended tactics suggested immediate application of the stun stick if attacked.

"I'm taking two of those things with me," Nakari said. "And if one lands on me, you bash my head with your stunners, too, you hear?"

"Same here," I said, nodding. "We'll see what we can salvage from the ship and get out. No walking around underneath the trees."

"Definitely not." We fell silent and Nakari bowed her head, obscuring her face behind a curtain of dark curls. It was probably a good time to make a clever quip of some kind, but my mind remained blank, still in shock at what I'd seen. Perhaps that's all Nakari felt, as well, and in that case there was nothing I could do to fix it. I wondered, though, about her father. What sort of person would send his child to face such dangers when he could risk someone else? Was he that confident in the new armor? Or was he that confident in Nakari? Judging by her next words, she was thinking much along the same lines.

"Can't believe he'd send me out to do this," she said.

"Well, didn't you tell me you've hunted a krayt dragon before? He must figure you're up to it."

"Maybe," she said, and then laughed with equal measures of amusement and rue. "Or maybe he's more confident in the armor and figures anyone can do it now. You hope it's one and not the other. Sometimes I think the galaxy might be entirely populated by people with daddy issues."

"Of one kind or another, probably so," I agreed.

CHAPTER 6

IT WOULD BE HOURS BEFORE we made it all the way into the Core, where we could take time to make final calculations prior to making the last jump to Fex. We had time to kill, and Nakari whipped out a couple of frozen nerf steaks from the galley's freezer.

"Fancy," I noted.

"Enjoy it now. We'll be choking down protein sludge after this." She put me in charge of "all things nerf," and pointed to a collection of vegetables she had stashed away, which she would be preparing. It was only enough for one meal. Everything else, as she said, would be protein and nutrient rations of one kind or another.

"Why do you bring so little real food?" I asked her.

"Jobs like this one usually don't give you enough time to prepare it or enjoy it. We'll be working nonstop and on alert at all times once we hit atmosphere. Food's just fuel then."

"Okay, but why not save something for when the job's through?"

"That feels like celebrating prematurely. And my

desire for real food just pushes me to get home as fast as possible."

It turned out neither of us was particularly skilled in the culinary arts. "You sure can thaw a nerf steak" was about all Nakari could muster as a tribute after taking the first bite of my cooking. She was right: I had thoroughly thawed that nerf, then kept going until I had burned it into a dry, tough piece of leather.

I speared a root on my fork and regarded it doubtfully as it sagged on either end. It should have kept its shape. "Wow. These vegetables are really steamed," I said.

We eyed each other for a couple of seconds to see if either would take offense, then broke into laughter and said, "Sorry," at the same time.

After our meal, the armor begged to be tried on. The body was a strong but fairly lightweight insulated mesh, padded and reinforced on the torso and spine, designed to stop kinetic rounds and claws, I supposed. The helmets, by contrast, were almost absurdly heavy and cumbersome. We first had to put on a thick rubber insulation mask that the instructions claimed would shield us from the inevitable use of stun sticks to our own heads. It swept down across our collarbones and across the breadth of our shoulders. Then the helmet was fitted on top of that, so heavy that maintaining balance would be a problem. Any sudden movement forward or backward would tug your body in that direction, as I demonstrated by trying to look down. Nakari threw her head back to laugh at me and fell backward, pawing unsuccessfully at the walls to keep herself upright. We both toggled our comms and laughed at each other.

"Remember that guy on Pasher as we got on board?" I said. "He advised that we practice somersaults in these!"

"No way that's going to happen!" Nakari said. "He must have been messing with us."

"Yeah, because I'm not sure I can get up now."

"What? Whoa. That could be a problem."

It was a problem, though not an insurmountable one. We managed to regain our feet, but not quickly and not without considerable strain. If we went down on Fex, we would not spring back up again. Running for more than a few steps might be impossible.

"Did they even test these before giving them to us?" I wondered aloud, steadying myself against the walls of the passageway.

"We should try out the stun sticks," Nakari suggested.

"Agreed. If we can't take a hit now, think of what kind of mess we'll be in on the surface of Fex. We'll wind up like that first crew and maybe the second, too."

"Who goes first?"

"Go ahead and try it on me," I said. "It's only fair. I ruined the nerf steaks."

"Very well, they shall be avenged." She staggered over to the case of stun sticks and pulled out two, flipping them both on. The air around them rippled for a moment with an energy field and then settled. Lurching toward me and grinning through her visor, Nakari reached out with her right hand and thwacked me on the pate, which I could feel but hardly hear inside the helmet.

Her voice crackled through the comm. "Anything?"

"I'm not unconscious, so that's good," I said.

"Copy that. Double strike incoming." Both sticks pounded on the top of my helmet, but I felt only the indications of a soft impact. She wasn't striking hard and shouldn't have to.

"No effect," I said, encouraged. "Try the sides and the visor, too."

Experimentation continued and we discovered that the visors were not as well shielded. The stun stick didn't knock me out, but I did feel a shock, jerk away involuntarily, and then topple backward from the weight of the helmet.

"Okay, good to know," I said.

"Good to know they work, that's for sure," Nakari said as she helped me up. "I'm going to have a ton of notes on these suits for my father, but I think they should keep us alive long enough to stun anything that lands on us."

We had enough empty hours ahead that some rack time was not only feasible but advisable, so we took advantage and asked Artoo to wake us when he was ready to jump into the Deep Core. He did so, and after we guzzled some black, bitter instant caf that succeeded in clearing our heads while savaging our taste buds, I annoyed him by asking to triple-check his coordinates with the *Desert Jewel*'s nav computer. It took him less than ten seconds, but he sounded affronted.

"Sorry, Artoo, but I've never jumped into the Deep Core before. It's crowded in there and things move fast and this isn't a well-established route yet, so I think an abundance of caution is warranted." That seemed to mollify him, and I let him take us in for the jump. It was only fifteen minutes until the white lines of the stars collapsed into pinpoints again and we were in the Sha Qarot system, a red sun and a black planet crisscrossed with a web of crazed orange faults. Fex appeared from orbit to be a serene contrast to the angry planet, a cool soft plum scoop of ice cream. The whole system was beautiful from orbit, and since we were in the Deep Core the sky was thick with stars.

I reminded Artoo to take holos for the benefit of the Alliance, even though we wouldn't use Fex as a base. Maybe the orbit itself would be useful. I wanted to remember it regardless; we were among the first ever to see Sha Qarot and Fex in person.

Nakari sent the signal to activate the *Harvester*'s beacon, and we set a course for it as soon as our sensors picked it up. While the *Jewel* took us in on autopilot, we climbed into our bulky armor but decided to leave the helmets until it was time to open the air lock.

We followed the beacon signal down to a plain of lavender grasses on the edge of a forest, a canopy of leaves like purple cotton perched on toothpicks. The *Harvester* rested there, seemingly undamaged from the outside.

"So far, so good," Nakari said, landing the *Desert Jewel* on the far side, putting the *Harvester* between us and the forest. "Nothing can drop down on us going from ship to ship."

Scans revealed life-forms inside, but not enough to make up the entire crew of the *Harvester*. Attempts to raise them via comm failed, so we had no choice but to investigate in person. Swathed in our armor and practically teetering from the weight on our necks and shoulders, we set armored boots on the surface of Fex and trudged toward the ship, stun sticks in each hand and blasters on hips. Artoo burbled something that might have been an admonition to be careful as the ramp closed behind us. The *Harvester* was a Corellian XS-800 light freighter with entry allowed from the ground via a ventral air lock situated behind the cockpit and in front of the living quarters, and also via two loading elevators to the cargo areas nestled on either side of the ship.

"Cargo areas first, agreed?"

"Yeah."

We approached the portside cargo bay and Nakari sent remote codes to call down the freight elevator. It descended flawlessly and without any bodies on it, which was encouraging. The platform had a rudimentary console connected to the rest of the ship, and Nakari punched in codes to light up the interior. Hydraulics whined as we rose together, though we didn't see much at first beyond the glow panels and cargo hooks in the ceiling. Might there be a Fexian skullborer perching up there even now, invisible to our eyes?

"Stun sticks ready?" she asked.

"Ready."

The clanking of our boots on the deck sounded muffled and far away, like someone else was walking elsewhere in the ship.

A pallet of crates shrouded in tarpaulin hunched in one forward corner as the elevator stopped, but farther aft along the right wall a line of specimen crates with thick, clear glass was stacked three high, like one might see in a pet merchant's stall. I doubted these held any promise of a nurturing relationship.

"Check the crates first, leave nothing behind us," Nakari said.

The crates underneath the tarp turned out to be bulk food supplies—mostly protein sludge mixtures.

"It's our diet for the near future," I said, "nothing more."

"Okay, let's head aft." There was an airtight hatch back there leading to a machine shop, bathrooms, and the galley, and from there to the other cargo bay on the opposite side; or we could go forward through the common area and living quarters to see what waited for us on the bridge. As we drew closer, most of the specimen crates were empty and inactive, save for ten closest to the hatch. We clumped our way forward to get a better look and saw that five of them in the middle row contained Fexian skullborers lying on their sides—unconscious for sure, since we could see them, but more likely dead.

"You know, this makes me wonder," Nakari said. "How do you keep a Fexian skullborer alive in captivity? Does anybody sell brain chow on the market?"

"I'm sure butchers would be able to supply nerf brains or something like that," I said.

"Ugh."

"The skullborers might find them delicious."

"Uh-oh, Luke. Look at this."

"What?"

Nakari pointed at the top five containers closest to the aft exit of the cargo bay. The thick polymer glass in these—much like our visors—had been cut through in narrow arcs with uneven edges. The units were still functioning in that the glow panels in the lids, calibrated to mimic the UV light and radiation from Sha Qarot's star, remained on and warm. But the containers, clearly occupied at one time, no longer held any residents.

"I bet the glass is all over the floor, but I don't want to look down or I might join it," Nakari said. I thought the debris might be more like chunks than shards; the glass was quite thick and might in fact be a clear polycarbonate.

"That means we have five skullborers loose in the ship?"

"Maybe. If we're lucky, they just snuck out past us real quiet and invisible when we lowered the freight elevator."

"Not sure if we're that lucky."

"Nope. But I wonder why only the top five escaped and not these five below them."

"Maybe one figured out it could bore through the glass and the others saw what it did and copied it."

"Okay, that's plausible. The ones below wouldn't have seen anything except maybe the glass falling."

"Or the ones in the bottom cages might have already been dead."

"True. I actually hope that was the case. Because whether the five on top followed a leader or acted independently, that implies a level of intelligence I'd rather not face. Let's press on. We need to find the crew—there were six of them. Maybe they'll respond to a shipwide announcement." She stepped forward to the aft hatch leading to the rest of the freighter, which we noticed was partially open. It had tried to close automatically and failed, prevented from doing so by the booted right foot of . . . someone.

"Oh, no," Nakari said.

"That means they got into the rest of the ship."

"That it does. But maybe someone's locked away somewhere." Using the console pad on the wall by the hatch, she toggled the comm. "*Harvester,* this is a rescue crew sent by Kelen Biolabs. We are in the port cargo bay. If anyone is alive, please respond." She lifted her finger away, and we waited for a reply. Nothing. She repeated the message and we waited again in vain. "All right, we press on," she said to me, pushing the button to open the hatch and then bracing herself against the hatch edge so that she could look down without being pulled off balance. I did the same on the other side of the hatch.

A Cerean lay facedown in a standard Kelen Biolabs uniform—bareheaded, in other words—with two holes in the back of his conical skull, one for each of his two brains.

"They weren't wearing armor," I said. "They thought

they were safe on the ship with the skullborers locked away."

"Wonder how long he's been here," Nakari said.

"Same as the others," I replied.

"How do you mean?"

"This ship never took off, but it's still functional. The skullborers either killed everyone or isolated them from the bridge. Otherwise you can bet it wouldn't still be sitting here like this."

Nakari's lips pressed together into a thin line through her visor. "Okay. We go from room to room together, clearing each and locking it behind us."

"Can they bore through the hatches?"

"That would be excellent intel to have right now. We'll see. Let's check all the way aft first. Maybe someone made it into an escape pod."

I stepped past her into the next chamber, an all-purpose area that had some scientific equipment set up. It had a bathroom and a galley; both were unoccupied. The armor that the crew should have been wearing was piled in a corner next to the bathroom, and the infrared goggles that would have allowed the crew to see the creatures—and wouldn't fit our helmets—were stowed in a box underneath a table. In the center of the back wall was a pair of doors that led to the engineering area and the escape pods.

A rudimentary machine shop was incorporated in the engineering area, and it had been thrashed by someone desperate for any kind of weapon—and that someone was dead, facedown like the Cerean, but with a wrench within centimeters of his right hand. Nakari gasped when she saw the body.

"I know him. Knew him."

"Was he the pilot?"

"No, a scientist. I was on a collection crew with him once."

"I don't see any blood on the wrench," I said. "Though I don't know what skullborer blood looks like. Impossible to tell if he scored a hit with it or not."

"If he wasn't already holding it and the skullborer landed on his unprotected head, he probably wouldn't have had time enough, considering how fast they drilled through armor."

I winced. "Good point."

Moving in tandem, we checked both escape pods and the remainder of the engineering compartment. No more crew. And no dead skullborer bodies.

"Nakari."

"What?"

"It's likely there's one in here, right? The door was closed."

"Not necessarily. It could have escaped when someone else entered or left. And we can't assume they're too dim to figure out the doors. The crew might not have coded them locked and simply allowed them to function with the press of a button. The creatures were smart enough to bore out of their cages in an organized fashion."

"At least one row of them was."

"Yeah. Well, nothing's jumped on us and you have to think anything trapped in here would be hungry, so let's call this clear and move forward," Nakari said. "But we'll do the starboard cargo bay before we head up into the living quarters and the bridge."

"Okay." We exited the engineering compartment and Nakari strode to the starboard cargo bay doors, which she tried to open with a single touch. A red light stopped her and a chirp demanded the full code. She carefully punched it in with one hand while bracing two stun sticks in the other. The doors slid aside and I stepped in, arms out for balance as much as readiness.

The bay contained more pallets of equipment and a couple of speeder bikes coated in lavender dust, but no bodies of any kind and no brainsucking predators that we could see. Considering their natural camouflaging abilities, I wondered if we had truly cleared the rooms so far, or merely caught them napping. If a skullborer remained quiet, how would we know it was there?

"You know," I said, "after we clear the ship this way, I want to go through it again with just one stun stick and a portable scanner to make sure we didn't miss any that might be hiding."

"Good call," Nakari said. "Ready to go forward?"

"Yeah. How many cabins?"

"Eight of them, four on each side of the hallway leading to the bridge. But first there should be a common lounge area." Her fingers hovered over the datapad next to the door. "All set?"

Raising my arms, I said, "Go," and she pressed the door release. It wasn't locked like the cargo bay doors, so it slid aside quickly and gave me my first view of the carnage.

There were three bodies. One of them, a jowly, thick-lipped Sullustan male, was still seated in a lounge chair with a datapad in his lap, the large orbs of his eyes open and filmed over in death; he'd been killed before he could get up. A human female slumped, lifeless, near the hatch leading to the cabins, and nearby a horned Zabrak male lay facedown blocking the door leading to the medical bay, the back of his head an open bloody mess, albeit a dry mess at this point.

"They have to be in here," I said, moving forward to allow Nakari to follow me inside. "Some of them, anyway." The helmet wouldn't allow a decent range of motion, but I saw some scratches and smears of blood high up on the bulkheads. The skullborers couldn't camouflage their tracks.

The door hissed shut behind us and I paused, expecting an attack at any second, but the time ticked by and none came.

"Let's secure the medical bay before we go forward," Nakari said.

Zabrak have some horns on their heads but they are short and stubby and obviously no deterrent to a skullborer, since they don't grow on the vulnerable pate. The Zabrak's body was half out of the bay—like the Cerean we had seen earlier, he'd been trying to exit, perhaps seeking help, when the skullborer brought him down. Peering past his body into the bay, I could see an examination table and the metal arms of various scanners and surgical tools; such bays were customized for multispecies crews like this one and packed full of instruments and medicines that a human would never need. I thought that the tangle of apparatus suspended over the examination table would be attractive to creatures that liked to lounge in branches waiting for prey to walk by.

"That door should open up fully without a code," Nakari said, "since it never closed."

"Got it." I thumped the console with my elbow and the door slid wide, allowing me to step past the body of the Zabrak. Three steps in I felt something land on my head. "They're in here!" I shouted as I whipped the stun sticks at my head from either side. The one on my left hit nothing but helmet, but the right one made contact with something with a bit more give to it, like flesh. No squeal or anything, but the extra weight slid off and plopped onto my shoulder, which startled me. I moved my head too fast to get a look at it as it fell, and the unwieldy helmet pulled me off balance; I managed to stagger backward and get my hands down to control the fall, but the fall was inevitable. And as soon as I hit the ground, two more weights landed on me in quick succession, *thunk-thunk,* right on my visor, though I saw nothing. A white circle of abraded polymer appeared directly above my left eye and I could hear the material scream as it was torn to shreds by the invisible creature drilling directly toward my head. Its teeth would have no trouble plowing through my eye and then to my brain directly behind. I pounded at the area with each of my stun sticks, but the drilling continued as a body became visible, and I lost a couple of precious seconds realizing what had happened—one skullborer had landed on top of the other, draping over it protectively, and while I had stunned that one to unconsciousness, the first one was still invisible and hungry for my gray matter. I couldn't get to it with the stun sticks, and meanwhile the drilling continued with palpable progress. Dropping the stun sticks, I grabbed for my blaster and didn't bother to check its setting. I leveled the barrel on a plane even with the outside of my visor and pulled the trigger, letting rip a bolt of red plasma that momentarily blinded me but halted the shriek of drilling. It also left a scorch mark across my visor.

"Luke! Are you okay?" Nakari asked.

"Yeah. Three down, right?"

"I'll say. No problem seeing them after you blasted them. There's nasty purple goo all over the bay now."

"What about the first one I stunned?"

Nakari dropped a stun stick and drew her blaster. She fired at the unconscious form out of my line of sight. "He won't wake up, either. I don't have any interest in bringing these things back alive. They've killed my friends."

"Friends?"

She gestured with her blaster. "I knew this Zabrak,

too. He knew how to . . . cook." Her eyes flashed at me behind her visor. "Sorry. Didn't mean to imply criticism of your nerf steaks."

I hadn't even thought of that until she said it. Last thing on my mind. I'd been thinking that I knew all about what she was feeling right then. In the shock of seeing someone you know dead, one of the first things you think of is how you will remember them. Things like "he could cook" or "she could sing" or "he was my best friend and I'll miss him forever." The crush of grief rolls in behind that, but sometimes you can shove that in a closet for a while until you have time to deal with it; I knew I still had plenty to deal with. I imagined Nakari was walling up her feelings like that now. "Not a problem," I said. "Sorry about your friend. Give me a hand up?"

"Sure." She holstered her blaster and strode forward, right hand extended, while her left still held a stun stick. She had to balance herself carefully to lean down, but before I could take her hand, she reared back from me, her left hand bashing the top of her right with the stunner. A skullborer appeared and slid off her hand as she simultaneously dropped the stun stick and screamed. She yanked out her blaster and shot at the back of her left hand, killing another of the creatures—and taking some of her own blood with it.

"Ahh!" Dropping her blaster, she clutched her injured hand to her chest. "Why did they attack my hands?"

I rolled over and levered myself up to a standing position. "They're smart, just like you thought. Problem solvers. They saw us kill the other three using things in our hands. So they attack the hands to disable you, and then they can get to what they really want."

"Oh. Oh, you're right! These things are at least

semi-sentient. We shouldn't be messing around with them. Except this last one who's only stunned. Would you mind?"

I considered simply dropping it outside the ship, but it wouldn't do to have it lingering around where it could attack us again when we had to return to the *Jewel*. I shot it, and that made five dead skullborers to match up with five empty cages. "At least you're already in the medical bay," I said. "Let's see if we can patch you up."

The skullborer had chewed through her glove like tissue and had sawn through the web of tendons in the back of her hand, though it didn't break any of the bones; Nakari had blasted it to jelly before it could drill so far. It was impossible for her to make a fist now. I slapped a bacta patch on it, gave her something for the pain, and let the automated medical system continue from there. She'd need a true surgeon to repair the damage, but the system could keep her stable and free of infection.

"I'm going to check the rest of the ship, just in case," I told her. "We should still have one crew member left, right?"

Nakari nodded, biting her lower lip. The pain medication probably hadn't kicked in yet and her adrenaline was wearing off.

"I'll be back as soon as I can," I told her. "I want to see if I can get the ship fired up, too."

"I don't know how you can see anything," she said, breathing quickly. "Between that chewed-up spot in the visor and the burn, it's a wonder you're not blind."

"I'll be careful. I'm taking two sticks with me just in case."

Nakari requested that I give her one of hers, and only when she felt sufficiently armed did she lie back on the table to let the medical program run. She quizzed me on the codes for the doors before I exited.

Though my theories would probably be laughable to anyone with a better knowledge of biology, I wondered if the skullborers might get smarter depending on what they ate. Would the prions and neurons of their meals accrete somehow and improve their thinking? If such a thing were possible, maybe eating the double brain of a Cerean would explain how their tactics adapted and improved—because they *had* been pursuing a tactical strategy by going after Nakari's hands. And come to think of it, when they attacked my face, the way that one of them landed on top of the other was clever, too—I couldn't get to the one on the bottom using the stun sticks, and they hadn't seen the blasters get used yet, so they wouldn't have been able to account for that. But that possibility raised other questions. The one that landed on the other's back would have necessarily been punctured by the first one's spines, so if that had been planned, it had been a planned sacrifice. Could they even see each other while camouflaged? Maybe that one–two business had been a complete accident. The two that attacked Nakari had obviously coordinated their attack, though, which made me wonder how they communicated. We had heard no vocalizations from them until we caused them pain.

The simplest explanation—and far more likely than the idea that they could get smarter by eating brains—was that the skullborers were at least semi-sentient, maybe even sentient to begin with. But between them killing the first two collection crews and me and Nakari killing them back, we had never had time to puzzle out their status.

All of my questions were better answered by Kelen Biolabs, and I was more than ready to drop the entire mess into their lap. I tapped the code into the datapad that would unlock the hatch to the living quarters. No bodies awaited me in the hallway, but I had to step over the fallen body of the human female outside the door to enter it. All the quarters were closed, and I punched in the override for each one, finding the first two on either side empty albeit with signs of recent occupation—papers on desks, half-empty cups of caf, tossed linens, and a carelessly discarded pair of underwear in one case. I found the sixth and final member of the *Harvester*'s crew behind the third hatch on the left. He was a human male, curled up on his bunk, most likely dead, his lips cracked and dry and his skin gone pale. Though his skull was still intact, he hadn't responded to Nakari's shipwide calls when he had the requisite equipment to do so—I checked. The console by the door still worked.

Perhaps he had locked himself in here once he realized the skullborers were loose on the ship and knew that he couldn't venture outside the room without his armor. Several empty water bulbs lay strewn about the floor, but I saw no food packets. Who knew the last time he'd had a drink or something to eat. He'd chosen to die of thirst rather than have his brain sucked up a feeding tube—an understandable decision.

I saw an old-fashioned handwritten diary open on his desk, which would no doubt illuminate his last days. Just to make sure, I knelt beside him and leaned forward until my visor was right next to his open mouth and nose. After a couple of seconds, the glass unmistakably fogged. He still breathed! He had to be near death, though. I had to get him to the medical bay immediately.

Turning off the stun stick in my left hand, I placed it on his desk and then tried to prod him awake with a few finger jabs. He didn't respond, so I turned off the other stun stick and put it down, threw him awkwardly over my left shoulder, then grabbed a stun stick in my right hand before returning to the medical bay.

"Nakari, I found someone," I said as I entered. A pair of robot arms suspended from the ceiling was wrapping up her left hand in a thick protective shroud of bandages.

"Still alive?" she asked.

"Yeah, but he's in bad shape."

"Well, it's finished with me anyway," she said, her words languorous and mellow. The medication must have kicked in. She waved at the medical apparatus hanging above her with her damaged hand. "It can't do the surgery required for something like this. These things are meant to keep you alive, and mending tendons isn't on their list of vital services."

She rose from the examination bed to make room, and I slid the man onto it. "Know him, too?" I asked once she could see his face.

"No." She shook her head. "But I'm sure my father will be glad to get him back."

"Mind looking after him?" I said. "I'd like to clear the rest of the ship."

"Absolutely, you do that," she replied, and plopped herself into a chair resting against the wall. She didn't look entirely lucid, so I programmed the autodoc to begin its work on the man before I left him.

The remaining cabins were empty and the bridge was pristine. I wasn't attacked at any point, so I thumbed the shipwide comm and said, "Nakari, the ship is clear, at least without scanning. I will start up the engines and run preflight, then come back through with a scanner to make doubly sure." She acknowledged, and then the work began. The *Harvester* was okay on fuel and all systems were nominal, except for the profound lack of a crew at the moment. I dragged all the victims into the holding area between the galley and the bathroom, where their unused armor was, then returned briefly to the *Desert Jewel* to fetch a small life-form scanner to scan the *Harvester* thoroughly. It was truly clear, so I asked Nakari what she'd like to do next. "How are we getting this ship out of here?"

"Link it to the *Desert Jewel*'s nav, and you fly us all back to Pasher. I'll stay on board in case this guy wakes up and try to clean up some of this mess."

"Sounds like a plan."

"Yeah. We better get paid *really* well for this."

FAYET KELEN WAITED for us on our assigned landing pad when we arrived on Pasher—waited on Nakari and the *Harvester,* anyway, along with a small throng of his employees. Artoo and I joined them once we'd secured the *Desert Jewel.*

Nakari had evidently given her father a quick summary of events, because as I stepped up to join them, he boomed, "Pilot! Well met and welcome. I am told you distinguished yourself on Fex." That might have been stretching the account a bit far since I had accomplished little beyond my own survival, but his eyes dropped to Artoo and he continued before I could reply. "Your droid has erased all the data provided earlier?"

"Artoo, please delete the files Mr. Kelen gave us." The droid beeped an acknowledgment and Kelen chuckled.

"Good, good. But forgive me if I would like some stronger assurance that my interests are protected." His sausage fingers fished a datachip out of his tunic pocket, and he handed it to me. "I had this prepared for your arrival. It will confirm the erasure of all files

I gave you in your droid's memory and erase any that accidentally remain, nothing more."

Refusing to run the chip would only invite suspicion when I had already promised to erase everything, so I inserted it and Artoo ran the program, spitting it back out in a few seconds. Nakari winked at me, however, indicating that perhaps she had her own backup of the Fexian coordinates stored somewhere.

"Excellent," Kelen said. His hand danced about on his personal datapad and he said, "I am depositing a goodly sum into an escrow account, which your droid may access and distribute to you both, and I thank you for returning my ship, my crew both living and deceased, and alien life that will delight my scientists."

Sensing that he was about to turn his attention elsewhere and dismiss us, Nakari said, "Daddy. Don't send anyone else there until you read my full report. Those things could be sentient. And even if you ignore that, you have to upgrade the armor's mobility."

He placed a hand on her shoulder. "I will digest all you have written before acting further. My primary concern now is that you see a surgeon about that hand. See where my minions come? Go with them."

"What?" An ambulance coasted to a stop near the ship and two earnest medics hopped out, asking Fayet Kelen who was hurt.

"Take my daughter to the finest surgeon posthaste and bill it to me. Go!"

"Daddy, wait! What about Luke?"

"Fear not, your pilot will be allowed to rest in comfort until you are ready to depart."

"Don't leave without me, Luke!" she called over her shoulder as the paramedics led her to the ambulance.

"I won't," I said, though I wondered if she would be able to accompany me on the mission to smuggle the Givin off Denon. She'd be fine eventually, but I doubted she would be 100 percent anytime soon. Admiral Ackbar had given us some slack time in our operation window, but not much.

Fayet Kelen turned to me, his mouth quirked upward in a fond grin. "She will not be long, pilot. You will see. If she is not bandaged and ready to leave in the morning, I will be very surprised." His fingers massaged his datapad again as he spoke. "In the meantime, please stay the evening in Pasher's finest hotel at my expense. I am summoning an escort to take you there. Have your droid search for the file *Skywalker*, encryption key *Jewel Pilot*, and you will find the funds I spoke of, which you may then transfer wherever you please. Thank you for your service to me and my daughter. May the stars keep you safe."

Before I could reply, he turned and strode with impressive speed to the workers unloading the cargo bay of the *Harvester*, bawling out orders and leaving me with my mouth open.

R2-D2 spat out a stream of digital hoots that I imagined to be a wry comment.

"Looks like we get a night off from the war, Artoo. Don't tell Threepio, okay? We'll never hear the end of it."

The hotel was indeed quite a luxurious affair, but once I tried out the bed I didn't find much use for its other amenities. The mattress was so comfortable and I was so exhausted that I fell asleep in my clothes, and Artoo had to wake me in the morning. It didn't bother me to miss out on the excess and splendor, though; a good night's sleep at that point was the height of luxury to me.

A message from Nakari waited for me at the front desk: "Hurry up. I'm waiting at the ship."

"Come on, Artoo, we have weapons to buy." The

money Fayet Kelen had paid us was quite an impressive sum. We'd need all of it for upgrades to the *Desert Jewel,* but the prospect of custom surprises was excitement enough for me: The Alliance rarely had the funds or the will to do anything unusual.

Nakari's left hand, encased in a thin protective sheath full of bacta, waved at me from the ship's loading ramp. "Those must have been some sweet dreams," she said with a smile.

"Yeah, I feel rested. How about you?"

"High on meds and days away from getting back full use of my hand, but otherwise functional and happy to be here."

"Can you still fire your rifle?"

"Maybe not so well on the run. But sniping from a fixed position where I can use my elbow for support should be fine."

"Great. Any ideas where you want to go for upgrades?"

"I was going to ask you."

I considered. It had been a few days since that Imperial alert on the *Desert Jewel.* I doubted anyone in the Chekkoo Enclave would be looking for it now, but just in case, we'd better take steps to throw off suspicion.

"Anyplace on Pasher we can get the *Jewel* painted? We'd have to do it anyway before going to Denon."

Nakari shrugged. "Sure, we can find a place."

"Then how do you feel about outfitting on Rodia? I just set up a contact there and they have everything we need."

"Sounds fine to me."

We found a man obscured in a cloud of cigarra smoke who had a team of friends willing to do a rush paint job on the *Jewel,* finishing it by that afternoon. Nakari had him change the red-and-silver scheme to

blue and gold. Once we were on our way and traveling through hyperspace, I had Artoo display the catalog of Utheel Outfitters in the cockpit, and we picked
out the weapons we thought would come in handy
against Imperials. We checked the prices against the
balance in our accounts and had to dial back our
wish list somewhat, but I thought we'd still have a
fearsome ship when the additions were complete.

The problem was that Taneetch Soonta was not
expecting our arrival, and while we were allowed to
land at the spaceport outside the Chekkoo Enclave,
we were not exactly welcomed. Unlike my first visit,
where I was politely greeted and escorted to Utheel
Outfitters, I was accosted almost as soon as I took my
first breath of reeky Rodian air. A belligerent male
with blue skin and a teal jumpsuit demanded to know
my business from the bottom of the ramp.

"We're here to buy weapons from Utheel Outfitters," I said.

"For a ship like this? No, you're not."

"Of course we are."

"Utheel Outfitters doesn't outfit interstellar ships.
They supply hunters and their small speeders, maybe
some atmospheric craft. You've got the wrong company. Try the Chattza clan on the other continent—
they can take care of you."

"No, look, I need to see Taneetch Soonta. She knows
me and what I'm looking for."

"I don't know anybody by that name."

"Well, somebody does."

He held up a datapad. "See this? It contains a ros-
ter of everyone in the Chekkoo clan, and there's no
Taneetch Soonta here. You're mistaken. You'd best
find your weapons somewhere else, because we don't
have them."

Nakari stepped behind me and her voice floated over my back. "What's the trouble, Luke?"

"I'm not sure of anything except that this fellow wants us to leave. Says my contact doesn't exist and the company I'm to deal with doesn't have the weapons we saw in the catalog."

"Is there any possibility he could be right and you were duped before?"

"I suppose it's possible." That whole business could have been an extremely elaborate Imperial sting with a huge number of agents in on the operation. But it wasn't likely. It was more likely that this particular Rodian had a different agenda. There had to be a way around him without escalating to something unpleasant—and I suddenly remembered that perhaps there was. Taking a deep breath and closing my eyes, I reached out to the Force, and then opened my eyes again, focusing on the Rodian and willing him to accept what I said. "We're here to do business with Utheel Outfitters."

The Rodian's antennae dipped and he chopped the air with his hand. "And I already told you they can't handle interstellar outfitting. You'll have to go visit the Chattza."

That clearly hadn't worked, but I had forgotten something that perhaps would make a difference. When Ben had told the stormtroopers in Mos Eisley that Artoo and Threepio weren't the droids they were looking for, he had used a small hand gesture with it, as if to wave away the trooper's concerns.

"You don't need to worry about us," I said, moving my hand in a tiny arc and rippling my fingers in a wave as I concentrated on exerting my will.

"Poodoo if I don't," the Rodian replied. "I have ships on my list coming in here with legitimate business and I can use the berth. Get going, would you? You're wasting my time."

I had to try again. "You don't need to worry about us," I said, and repeated the hand gesture.

"Look, I know humans are slow sometimes, but I'm starting to think you're exceptional," the Rodian said.

Behind me, Nakari whispered, "Luke, what are you doing?"

"Wasting everyone's time, apparently," I whispered back.

The Rodian's comm squawked a harsh alert at him and he thumbed it, receiving a throaty stream of language that I didn't understand. He replied with a curt acknowledgment and said to me as he put the comm away, "That changes things. Welcome back to Rodia, Master Skywalker. If you would please follow me, I'll take you to Taneetch Soonta."

"What? You said there was no such person."

"And now I'm saying I'll take you to her. Try to keep up."

"Who are you?"

The Rodian didn't answer but turned and walked away, waving at us to follow. Nakari gave me a gentle nudge and I descended the ramp, calling to Artoo to join us. Trailing the rude Rodian in teal, I thought perhaps I would forever associate the color with poor manners. But I realized after I'd had time to cool down that I was more frustrated with my failure than truly annoyed with our guide. I knew Ben had done something to the minds of those stormtroopers, but I didn't know what it was or even what he called it. He said the Force could influence the weak-willed or something like that, but I was so poorly trained that I didn't know if I'd done it correctly and the Rodian was simply too strong, or if I'd done it incorrectly.

It only reinforced how badly I needed someone to train me.

The path we took through the Rodian bazaar was different but the result was the same: We wound up in a dimly lit hidden passage with Taneetch Soonta willing to speak frankly.

"Apologies for the misunderstanding at the spaceport," she said. "For security reasons we keep our illicit commerce on a need-to-know basis, and until your arrival that worker had no need to know who you were."

"It's all right," I said, and introduced her to Nakari.

Soonta greeted her and said, "How may I be of service today?"

We had Artoo play back the catalog entries of the weapons we wanted and flashed a running total of the prices, explaining that we'd like all of them installed on the *Desert Jewel* as soon as possible. "There will be labor charges, of course," Soonta reminded us. She got busy with her datapad and showed me a figure.

I nodded at her and said, "We allowed for that."

"Excellent. And how will you be paying?" We offered to pay half of the total on deposit immediately, the balance to be paid upon completion and inspection of systems.

"Consider it a demonstration of Utheel Outfitters' capabilities to the Alliance," I said.

I authorized Artoo to make the initial payment, and Soonta made a pleased gurgle when her datapad confirmed the transfer of funds.

"Excellent, Master Skywalker. We shall have you armed and airborne before sundown tomorrow."

CHAPTER $\pm 8^2$

$$\sqrt{\sigma^2 + \epsilon}$$

WE DID NOT TRUST THE CHEKKOO completely, of course, and took the *Desert Jewel* to a neutral planet to have the ship scanned for tracking devices and the computers swept for worms and other malignant code. I was as relieved as I was happy when the scans returned clean and we could return to the Alliance without worrying about an Imperial spy lodged among our new allies—for the moment.

The fleet still hid in Orto Plutonia's system, the ships looking like tiny pieces of lint on a black blanket as we approached. Leia was happy to hear of our safe return, and while Admiral Ackbar was somewhat disappointed to learn that Fex was wholly unsuited for a base, he was definitely encouraged to hear that we had upgraded the *Desert Jewel* and tested our new contacts on Rodia at the same time.

He and Leia joined Nakari and me in a briefing room on the *Promise,* along with R2-D2 and C-3PO.

"We now have a contact for you on Denon," Ackbar said. "A Kupohan who occasionally does contract work for the Bothan spynet and others runs a small noodle hut as a front for her intelligence services.

It gives her a reliable location for meetings and the opportunity to conduct operations in an important section of Denon under cover of food delivery. She was the one that the cryptographer used to smuggle out a message to us. You will visit her when you arrive and order something strange. C-3PO, what was it they were supposed to order?"

"It was the Corellian buckwheat noodles with rancor sauce, sir," the droid said.

"Rancor sauce." Ackbar shuddered and the folds of flesh around his mouth flapped audibly. "So glad I don't have to eat that."

Nakari blanched. "I didn't even know that was a thing anybody ever thought of making. We don't have to eat it, do we?"

"No, just order it," Leia said with a smile. "That will let your contact know we sent you."

"Her name is Sakhet," Ackbar continued. "She'll have files for you and scouting reports on the target. It'll be up to you to formulate an extraction strategy from there."

"Where do we take her once we get offplanet?" Nakari asked. She'd missed that part of the previous briefing on the mission.

"She wants to be taken to Omereth," Ackbar said. He clicked a button on a remote and a holo hummed to life, a full-color, high-resolution display of a blue world dotted with small beaded strings of land. "It's a water planet and sparsely populated. Archipelagos of forested islands and an eccentric destination for those who wish to escape the bustle of the galaxy."

"He means it's popular among suicidal anglers," Leia explained. "There are huge hungry things in the oceans there."

Nakari flicked a finger at the holo. "Why that planet? It's nothing like the Givin homeworld."

"That might be the basis of its appeal," Leia said. "We are arranging to have her family meet her there. She will work for the Alliance where the Empire won't be looking."

"Do we have a name for the target yet?" I asked.

"Yes. Drusil Bephorin. She'll be heavily guarded." Ackbar paused and swung his giant eyes back and forth between my face and Nakari's. "You might have to take care of those guards."

Euphemisms for murder make me uncomfortable, but I have always found that one especially disturbing, since killing someone is the opposite of caring for them.

Nakari, however, had no such qualms. She nodded and said, "I'm okay with that."

λ*j*

WE TOOK A BIT MORE TIME preparing for the trip to Denon since it was almost guaranteed that we'd have to deal with Imperial forces at some point. We packed some changes of clothing that might serve as simple disguises, along with some putty and makeup for more sophisticated cover, and gave the *Desert Jewel* new transponder codes to go with her new paint job. The weapons installed on Rodia had interrupted the sleek profile she'd boasted before and that helped alter the appearance, too. Any Imperials on the lookout for the rogue that destroyed two TIE fighters in the Llanic system would have trouble identifying this as the same ship.

We were almost ready to leave when Leia hailed us, rushing onto the hangar deck with 3PO whirring behind her as fast as he could manage. "Luke! Wait! You need to know this." She took a couple of breaths once she reached me. "Glad I caught you."

"What's up?"

"Threepio reminded me of a Givin greeting custom that I'd almost forgotten. You need to know some greeting maths."

"Greeting maths?"

"Yes, it's customary among the Givin to say hello with math. If you can't at least speak the language of math a Givin will have a difficult time trusting you, so you have to demonstrate your ability right away. Almost anything's okay, but I advise you to keep it somewhat simple," she said. "And whatever you do, don't ask them to do linear approximations of non-linear partial differential equations, because they take it as an insult, like you're mocking them."

This was already turning into the strangest conversation I'd ever had with Leia, but I went with it. "Mocking them how?"

"They object to approximations, basically. Asking for approximations instead of precision indicates a lack of faith in their abilities at best, and at worst could be construed as you calling them stupid."

"Oh. I'm very glad you told me that. But like you said, I think keeping it simple would be best." I was hoping she would define *simple* as addition or subtraction.

A tiny smile of amusement played at the corners of Leia's mouth and she nodded. "Good."

"It seems like the list of your talents never ends. Are you a mathematician, too? How do you know this?"

"I had to deal with Givin when I served in the Senate. I have a few equations memorized that you can use."

"Okay, but after I use whatever you teach me, then Drusil is going to reply with an equation for me to solve, right? What do I do then?"

"Well, I suggest you solve it."

"Come on, I can do some easy algebra in my head, *maybe,* but not differential equations!"

"That's quite all right, Master Luke," Threepio interjected. "The most likely answer will be three."

"What? How can you know that?"

Threepio, already ramrod-straight, seemed to grow taller and more proud at the opportunity to be pedantic. "Over the years Givin have grown accustomed to the inability of other beings to greet them properly, so to be polite she will use an equation with the answer of three to follow her traditional greeting customs but spare both of you the embarrassment of your not knowing the answer. But if you want to impress her, you can ask for a *real* greeting and she will give you something random and much more difficult."

"No, no, three's good, I can deal with three."

"Great. Let's get started," Leia said, and she painstakingly taught me and Nakari two different equations and their answers to use when we eventually met Drusil Bephorin. It was definitely not simple addition, and it took us several attempts to commit it all to memory.

When we were finished and finally ready to leave, Leia looked around the hangar, vaguely disappointed at what she saw. If I had to guess, she was searching for the *Millennium Falcon* and unhappy that Han and Chewie hadn't snuck in somehow while she wasn't looking. She was probably worried, as I was, that we'd never see them again. But she always kept fighting for the people she *could* see, the people she *could* save: Hers was the example we all followed. Her farewell was a brief hug and an enjoinder to remain safe, and as usual on such occasions, when we parted I managed a nod and nothing more, turning to board the ship before I said or did anything awkward.

We navigated a sneaky path out of Orto Plutonia to avoid the Imperial division I'd skirmished with earlier, and relaxed once we had a course plotted along well-traveled hyperspace lanes.

Nothing but numbing hours of blurred stars stretched

before us, so I said, "Mind if I ask you something? I hope it's not rude."

Nakari didn't turn her head, but she cocked an eyebrow, her eyes sliding my way. "Well, if it *is* rude, you can be sure I'll let you know."

"Hope you'll forgive me if so. But here's the thing: People who are fairly well-to-do—as you and your father are—rarely get so upset with the current state of affairs that they decide things need to change. Because usually it's the current state of affairs that made them rich, so, you know . . ."

"Why am I involved in the Rebellion?" Nakari finished.

"Exactly."

She looked down, clenched her jaw, and tightened her good hand into a fist, then made an effort to relax and speak calmly. "The Empire killed my mother over a song."

"What?"

"My mother was a songwriter and vocalist. She sang backup harmonies for a band."

"Really? What band?"

"Don't laugh, okay? The name wasn't her idea. They were called Hakko Drazlip and the Tootle Froots."

"The Tootle Froots?"

Nakari sighed with a note of impatience. "I know how ridiculous it sounds to tell people your mom was a Tootle Froot. I don't even know what a Tootle Froot *is,* okay? But anyway, she wrote a political song for the group and they recorded it and it became their biggest hit. Thing is, it got them all sent to the spice mines of Kessel."

"But that means she could still be alive?"

"No," she said flatly. "This was ten years ago. There's no hope she's alive now."

We both knew that life expectancy in the mines

wasn't above a year or two. "Oh. I'm sorry. I totally understand how that would spur you to do something." I paused, wanting to know more but not wishing to pry. Curiosity eventually got the better of me. "That's a pretty extreme reaction to a song on the Empire's part, though. What was it—would I know it?"

"Depends on your access to declared contraband. It was called 'Vader's Many Prosthetic Parts.'"

"Hey, I do know that! Hilarious song! I didn't know the band had been punished for it, though."

"Oh, it happened quickly." She gazed down into her lap, her voice soft. "Mere days after its release. Lord Vader has no sense of humor."

"Yeah, he doesn't seem like the type." I paused a moment, still having trouble saying it. "He's responsible for my father's death."

"So we have that in common."

"Except you know what your mother did. I have no idea why my father deserved his betrayal."

"I'm sure he didn't deserve it any more than my mother did, Luke."

"Thanks. And of course the Empire probably took a long, hard look at your dad after the business with your mother."

"They did. Kelen Biolabs has some Imperial contracts that we would love to burn up, but we can't. My father can't afford to be anything but accommodating to them. And that's also why he can't give money to the Alliance; the Empire has spies in his organization he has to pretend not to notice, and they are watching his finances closely. I don't have such chains around my wrists, though. I'm free to oppose them."

"Free to oppose them—that's a good way to put it. I think lots of people oppose the Empire but don't feel able to do more than secretly despise them. The Empire kind of set me free, too, I suppose. Though they did it in the worst way possible. They were trying to recover the stolen plans to the Death Star and killed my aunt and uncle. There was nothing left for me on Tatooine after that."

Nakari finally turned to look at me, a crinkle between her eyes and her mouth turned down in a concerned frown. "What about your mother?"

"Died when I was an infant. My aunt and uncle raised me."

"Were they the ones who told you about your father the Jedi?"

"They avoided that topic as much as possible. If I asked them about it they would change the subject. It went like this—this is an actual conversation, okay? I said, 'Tell me something about my father, Uncle,' and he had a coughing fit before answering, 'He was concerned about the vaporators on the western slope, like me. Go out there and check them.' It's like they bought the Imperial line that the Jedi were dishonorable."

"What if they were?"

"What?"

"I know the Empire is probably lying about them— don't get me wrong. But what if there was a grain of truth to what the Empire says about the Jedi?"

"A grain of truth won't change my desire to know everything. It's difficult to find anything out since the Empire's done what they can to wipe out all records of the Jedi. But that in itself tells you that the truth contradicts what the Empire wants us to believe: otherwise they'd leave it all accessible."

Mock outrage plain in every word, Nakari said, "You mean you don't think the suppression of information is for our own good? I am *shocked*, sir, shocked, I say!"

Matching her tone, I said, "Not only that, but I

had serious doubts that the Death Star would have brought peace to the galaxy!"

Nakari laughed and then pointed at me with her right hand. "Seriously, Luke, there's your answer. The Empire didn't think of everything when they built the Death Star. And they didn't succeed in getting rid of all knowledge concerning the Jedi, either. It's a big galaxy. I'm sure they didn't erase everything. There has to be something, or somebody, somewhere, that can help you learn whatever it is you want to learn."

"Maybe." I was going to leave it there, but then I realized I had a sympathetic ear and time to talk it through for once, so I continued. "I thought Ben Kenobi would teach me for a while. I've never told anyone except Leia, but I heard his voice in my head after he died on the Death Star."

Nakari turned sharply and watched me to see what further craziness would next spew forth—or perhaps I was misinterpreting her expression. Chances were I was on target, for people who claimed to hear voices in their head were rarely thought sane. I was beginning to have doubts on that score myself.

"Or at least I thought I did. In a way I suppose it doesn't matter—whether it really was him or I was simply imagining it in some kind of stress hallucination during a battle, his advice helped. But after that, I got nothing. I don't know if that means he doesn't have anything to say or if he's faded away or if I'm doing something wrong . . . maybe he's lost interest in me."

A teasing note crept into Nakari's voice. "So you mean it *wasn't* a voice in your head that told you to wave your hand at that Rodian and tell him to take you to Soonta after he'd just told you he wouldn't? Because that would explain a lot."

Heat flushed my face as I remembered my failure.

"No. But I did see Ben do that to a stormtrooper once. He used the Force and somehow convinced the troops to let us pass."

"Was that hand thing a part of it?"

"I don't know. I just did it because he did it. He never explained how exactly it was done, and I was hoping to muddle through on luck and good intentions."

"Tell you what. When we're finished with this, I'll help you find someone to teach you how to be a Jedi."

"Really? I mean, thank you, but why would you want to do that?"

Her eyes flickered over me and her expression turned to something that my imagination would call flirtatious. But then she faced forward and shrugged a shoulder. "You've helped me with my ship. Least I can do."

CHAPTER 10 $= \begin{bmatrix} \Sigma_{11} & \Sigma_{12} \\ \Sigma_{21} & \Sigma_{22} \end{bmatrix}$

DENON IS AN ECUMENOPOLIS like Coruscant, a vast city sprawling over all the landmass and dependent on imports for food and raw materials. Coming from a rural planet with a very scattered population, I wasn't used to seeing an endless vista of buildings all lit up at night and ships buzzing around them like they were flowers to be pollinated. The planet did kind of seem that way, a field of stiff bright plants swarming with alien insects. Except it wasn't nearly as peaceful as a field might be. The visual clutter was dizzying and even from orbit I imagined I could hear the constant throb of it pulsing in my bones.

Our coordinates led us to a rooftop berth on the edge of the Grammill district, which bordered the Lodos district where our target lay. Some arbitrary collection of streets formed the boundaries of Denon's districts, which as far as I could tell were indistinguishable but might hold obvious differences to long-term residents. Our Kupohan contact, Sakhet, had assured Admiral Ackbar that landing in an adjacent district to the target would aid our escape, since each district had its own security and we'd be able to take advantage of the small lag that resulted from any departmental coordination.

Our arrival shortly after sunset guaranteed an aerial slalom through rush-hour traffic as people in speeders and shuttles tried to get home or start the night shift or snag a dinner they didn't have to cook for themselves. Leaving Artoo in our lodgings, we took a conservative droid taxi that was programmed for safety more than speed, and I didn't mind its cautious progress since it gave me more time to appreciate the Lodos district at street level. Glowing signs for businesses were often presented in several alphabets in addition to Galactic Standard, many of them in letterforms that I didn't recognize at all. Once down on the street we were buffeted by a cocktail of noises that ranged from pleasant music to shrill disagreement between a Neimoidian couple in matching gold robes. I felt a headache coming on and I didn't know if it was from a bug I'd picked up earlier or overstimulation. I would put my credits on the latter.

Nakari and I joined a throng of beings coursing down a narrow alley of stalls selling trinkets and flavored ices and stimsticks and all manner of goods that might be desirable but were strictly unnecessary. It broadened at one point to a miniature plaza anchored by a fountain in the middle. Aliens were sitting around the edge of it with food and drink purchased from nearby vendors. One of these on the northwest corner of the plaza sold noodles, and it was there we were supposed to make contact with the Kupohan spy, Sakhet.

"I don't want to think about that nastiness we're supposed to ask for," Nakari said as we took places at the end of the long line. Obviously, Sakhet's noodles were popular with the locals. "You order it."

"What are you going to have?"

She perused the menu above the hut, hand-painted in Galactic Standard and repeated in other alphabets. "Buckwheat noodles and nerf nuggets with onions."

When we got to the window I saw two Kupohans working inside, one taking orders and one in a tiny kitchen area, filling greased flimsicard take-out boxes with noodles, meat, and vegetables. I wasn't sure if I was speaking to Sakhet or not, but I repeated Nakari's order and then ordered the Corellian buckwheat with rancor sauce. The Kupohan gave no outward sign that my order was unusual beyond a small twitch of the primary and basal ears, scribbling on an old-fashioned paper ticket instead of the more common datapad and growling something at the cook, lips curled over her large flat teeth. She took my credits and I began to fear that I would, in fact, be given something with rancor sauce on it. She produced a receipt from her register and she scrawled on it.

"Order number eighty-nine," the Kupohan growled at me, then sniffed wetly through her three nostrils, which did little to stimulate my appetite. "Don't forget your receipt, friend." She shoved it at me and twitched her head to my right. "Pick up your food at the window around the corner."

"Thanks," I replied, taking it from her. Nakari and I shuffled out of the way and I looked down at the receipt. The number 89 was large and circled at the top and then, at the bottom in tiny script, it said, *Return at 0900 tomorrow.*

I showed it to Nakari. "I doubt they'll be selling noodles that early," she said.

"I agree. Should give us plenty of time to talk."

"So what do we do now? I've done some shady things for my dad before, but never something quite like this."

"We follow through and get our noodles. We're just two hungry humans out for a bite."

"Excellent. I'm going to take a holo when you try the rancor sauce."

"Oh, yeah. Right." My stomach turned slightly. "I'm not that hungry, actually."

She smiled. "We can get you something else."

"That might be better," I admitted.

"Order eighty-nine!" a voice called from the pickup window. I flashed my receipt and the Kupohan working there—a third one I hadn't seen before, wearing a red bandanna that draped protectively over the frequency filter organs between the primary and basal ears—took a look at it and thanked me, pushing forward two hot cartons and disposable eating sticks.

"Don't worry," she said in a low voice, her four dark eyes glinting with amusement, "we just gave you two orders of the nerf nuggets."

"Thanks," I said, truly grateful. "See you around."

Tray in hand, I looked back at the plaza area and saw that there was nowhere to sit. Nakari spied a small pavilion farther along the path that had six picnic tables. Most of them were occupied, but one of them had room for two more.

We carried our steaming cartons over to the table in question and asked the nice Gran couple there if they minded sharing some space. Six eyes on stalks swiveled to regard us, and the two Gran grunted agreeably.

"You can have it," one of them said. "We were just finishing." They scooped up their remainders and wished us a good evening. We discovered that the wooden table was well stocked with salt and pepper for our noodles, and the benches offered a wide range of splinters for our backsides.

"So how much do you know already about the—"

Nakari paused, looked around, and lowered her voice. "That special group your father was in?" Using the word *Jedi* out loud probably would not be wise here. It was doubtful that anyone would be interested in our dinner conversation and unlikely that our voices could be picked out in the noise of the plaza, but there was no need to be careless, either. Nakari shook some pepper over her nerf nuggets. "Or should I ask what it is you still need to learn?"

"Practically everything. Right now I can kind of feel the, uh . . ." I waited for Nakari's eyes to look up and then I mouthed the word "Force." When she nodded her understanding, I resumed. "It gives me heightened reflexes in battles, and maybe a tiny bit of predictive ability—like I'm really good at guessing how the other guy is going to move next. But I'm sure that's just the first step into a larger world. There's that suggestive power we discussed earlier, for example, and I don't know how I'll ever make my own . . . weapon."

She squinted an eye at me. "Is that something you absolutely have to do?"

"I suppose not. I already have one. But the ability to make one would mean I have excellent control over the . . . powers."

"How so?"

"You can't construct one without moving the focusing crystals with your mind."

"You mean telekinesis?"

"Yep. I can't seem to get the hang of that, but I should be able to. If this power flows through and around everything, then manipulating it and using it to push and pull physical objects has to be part of the deal. For example, when I'm in a fight, it guides my actions—or at least influences my brain to guide my actions. Still, that's a concrete manifestation of its power, not me simply saying that I believe it's there. If it can physically affect me, then it should be able to physically affect other things, as well. And I should be able to make that happen."

"Have you tried?"

"Yeah. I tried to move something small. I went after a little greasy vegetable on Rodia."

"Did you succeed?"

"Failed. Though in my own defense, I was interrupted."

Nakari pulled out a noodle from her bowl and plopped it on the table between us. It lay there like an anemic grassworm. "Fine. Move the noodle."

"What, here?"

"Yes, here. Look at it, Luke. It is utterly lacking in strength, for it has been boiled into complete submission. It's not going to put up a fight. So move it."

"Aw, you're making fun."

"No, you can do it. Force that noodle to scoot over here. I won't interrupt. I'll just make yummy noises and enjoy my dinner." So saying, she shoved an enormous portion into her mouth and moaned. "Oh yeah," she said around the food, a few noodles still dangling past her lips, twitching like tentacles crying for help. "Mmm. Best nerf nuggets ever. I have no idea what you're doing over there because I'm just eating over here. Being kinda gross about it, too."

I cracked a smile, which was probably her intention. There was no pressure, just friendly encouragement. I did feel encouraged, unlike on Rodia, where I had felt almost overwhelmed at the enormity of all I didn't know. But I did know what everyone knows about noodles: They are not very good in contests of wills. Perhaps this single wet noodle was the perfect object on which to begin. And if nothing happened, no big deal, it was just dinner with a new friend.

I relaxed, closed my eyes, stretched out with my

mind, felt the Force around me, and found the noodle. I imagined it moving away from me and back to the base of Nakari's carton, a detailed animation in my mind, for perhaps half a minute, and I envisioned the Force flowing in such a way as to make that happen. Nakari's whoop broke my concentration.

"You did it!"

"I did?" I opened my eyes and saw a damp squiggly line where the noodle had originally been resting, while the noodle itself lay in a completely different sine wave a few centimeters away from that position. It hadn't traveled all the way back to her carton as I'd envisioned, but it had undeniably moved.

"Yes, indeed! Look at you, you little noodle scooter!"

"Wait, are you messing with me? Did you move it while my eyes were closed?"

Nakari's brilliant smile disappeared and she reached out with her bandaged hand to cover mine. "No, of course not! I wouldn't do that, Luke. I know this means a lot to you, and I swear you absolutely made that happen. It was a smooth undulation, like a snake taking a tour of the neighborhood."

Despite my disbelief in my own success, I sensed that she was telling the truth—it was an absolute certainty in my mind, as if the Force had run a fact-check for me. I didn't feel that way normally when speaking to people, but maybe my recent connection with the Force had something to do with it. It had everything to do with moving the noodle, the reality and significance of which were finally hitting me. "Incredible. I actually did it."

Nakari's smile returned, a bit smug, and she pointed at me with her eating sticks. "Knew you could."

"Did not."

"Your noodles are getting cold."

"Guess you're right about that."

Despite the loss of a few degrees of heat, those were the best noodles I've ever had. To know that telekinesis was possible—not just for Jedi, but for me—gave me better hope for the future than I had enjoyed for a long time.

CHAPTER 11

SAKHET PROVED TO BE the Kupohan in the red bandanna. She was still wearing it when we returned to the noodle hut in the morning. I noticed some additional details that hadn't been so clear in the low light of her stall before. She had six neck torcs circling her throat, indicating her sixth decade of life, and her basal ears practically drooped from the weight of her silver status earrings. The Kupohans wore jewelry with a purpose, never for decoration, and Sakhet's earrings indicated she had earned far more prestige among her people than a food vendor normally would. She pointed to a delivery speeder parked nearby and said, "Get in." It was emblazoned with the name SAKHET'S NOODLES and smelled like cooking oil. There were several bags inside full of cartons that obviously contained fresh food. There was no room there for Artoo and I was glad we had convinced him to stay behind once again. I had a feeling he'd be vital during the extraction, but at the moment he would be an awkward addition to the party.

"What's all this for?" I asked, sitting down next to the cartons.

"That's our cover," Sakhet replied. "We're making a catering delivery. People eat at all hours of the day on Denon." She drove us a short distance to an urban greenbelt that served as a recreational area for the district. We gathered a few bags each, and Sakhet led us to a high walkway that looked down on the park. Similar walkways opposite our position reflected the sun, and our aerial view of the park showed us paths winding through the trees and sculpted hedges, fields of open grass for all-purpose frolicking, and plenty of benches to lounge upon. A few people milled around, tossing balls or ropes for their pets to fetch.

Behaving as if this were a standard delivery and the scenery a bore, Sakhet said, "Every morning the target goes for a walk, and the destination rotates depending on the day of the week. Today she will be in the park below between ten and eleven hundred. Tomorrow she will be at a botanical garden, and the day after that, a café that features live music by some local unwashed aliens. And so on. I'll give you the schedule and a set of maps when we get back in the speeder. Leave your bags here." She set the noodles down on the doorstep of an anonymous address and we deposited ours next to hers. She buzzed the bell once and began walking back to the speeder, not waiting for an answer. I wondered if someone at that address had actually ordered noodles, or if Sakhet was surprising them.

"The upside is that the target has established a routine and makes herself vulnerable in public—on purpose, of course. She's waiting for you to act. The downside is that her security team has also established a routine."

"Who are they? Stormtroopers?"

"No. ISB agents. They know what they're doing, too. They'll have eyes on this walkway and the one across from us. They can get stormtroopers here and air support, as well, with a simple comm call, and that's the case at every location. You can't afford any sort of extended engagement—if you're not successful at the start, you should abort unless you have a death wish. I'd suggest you come back here later to see her because the security team will recognize me. You should not be spotted with me after this."

"What about where she's working? Can we get to her there?"

"Forget it. It's an Imperial death trap even worse than trying to snatch her away from the agents. Don't linger now, you're supposed to be employees helping old Sakhet drop off noodles."

We piled back into the delivery vehicle, and Sakhet steered us back to the noodle hut. On the way, she sent the sum of her scouting on Drusil Bephorin to Nakari's datapad. Local maps and photos, noted security arrangements, placements of Imperial forces within easy reach of each location, and their estimated time of arrival after a request for aid.

"You'll also find an encrypted file in there, which you can unlock with the code phrase *Rancor Sauce*, two words. Don't unlock it unless you need it, and get rid of it once the mission's complete."

"What is it?"

"It's a list of Kupohan contacts on various worlds should you find yourself on the run and in need of help."

"I didn't know the Kupohans had a network like that."

"Officially we don't. We're not organized like the Bothan spynet. But that was you who shot down those TIE fighters in Llanic, am I right?"

"Yeah, that was me."

"My son was on that ship. He was cooking your

nerf nuggets last night and he wouldn't be if you hadn't decided to act. So I'm giving you a place to run if you need it. Contact anyone on that list and tell them you're a friend of Sakhet's on Denon, and that I make the best nerf nuggets you've ever had. They'll give you what help they can."

"Thank you. Hopefully we won't need it. Do we owe you anything?"

"Your admiral has already paid me for these services. Good luck," she said as she exited the speeder, leaving us to our own devices now that her responsibilities were fulfilled.

We returned to our hotel and picked up Artoo before taking a rented speeder back to the park. Besides getting a positive ID on Drusil Bephorin, we needed to see how the security team conducted itself and whether they matched the report Sakhet had provided us. Artoo had plenty of scanning to do, accessing local comm networks, searching for encrypted tight beams and following them to their nodes; he didn't need to know Imperial codes to recognize that beings sending and receiving encrypted transmissions in a public park marked themselves as security personnel every bit as clearly as stormtrooper armor would.

Nakari and I dressed in matching uniforms that suggested we were crewmates of a passenger cruiser enjoying some time together on leave. We both wore caps pulled low over our eyes and had applied lumps of synthflesh putty to our faces to alter the shapes of our cheeks, noses, and chins, and had changes of clothing for later stashed in small duffels. We entered the park on the south side, with Artoo trailing behind. We picked a bench that afforded us a good view of the rest of the park and waited.

A flying security droid, a black spherical number bristling with blasters and sensors, arrived first and swept the area, no doubt capturing our images and checking them against Imperial databases. My altered appearance wouldn't match any files they had on Luke Skywalker. We were also weaponless—I'd been careful to leave my lightsaber behind this once—and otherwise nonthreatening, so it hurtled away from us after a cursory scan to investigate other people.

Nakari caught my attention and with flicks of her eyes directed me to check out the elevated walkways above the park. Two men in loose yet bulky clothing, one on either side, had taken up positions to give them an excellent view of the greenbelt. They might have simply been citizens enjoying the view, except that they had military-style haircuts, alert expressions out of keeping with mere sightseeing, and probably armor hidden underneath their casual wear.

Once I knew what to look for, I spotted a few more walking around the park—four, to be precise: isolated individuals who ignored the charms of the park and instead eyed everyone in it suspiciously. One of them passed near us and squinted in our direction, his mouth a thin slash of annoyance underneath his nose. I guessed we didn't fit his profile of Denon leisure seekers. If his expression was that sour as a rule, I wondered how it would look after we engineered the escape of his charge.

Nakari and I were careful to speak of nothing relating to the operation; we knew we might have long-range audio trained on us. We would talk everything over afterward. In the meantime, we spoke of the crew and passengers of our fictional cruise ship and their behavioral peccadilloes, pretending to let off steam while letting our eyes drink in the habits of the security detail.

Eventually our target appeared, flanked by two obvious bodyguards in black, in contrast with the others scattered about the park attempting to blend in. The security drone we had seen earlier returned to hover above and behind her, though it hung back far enough that she would not be disturbed by its operational hum.

Drusil Bephorin dressed herself in a long, flowing green tunic that dropped below the knees, belted at the waist in brown. I couldn't tell if she was in good health or not.

To human eyes the Givin looked somewhat like sad skeletons, their heads resembling bare skulls with brows sloped up to meet together in the middle, lending them the appearance of perpetual mourning or perhaps dismay at discovering something hairy crawling on their food. The environment of their homeworld was so harsh that their organs were sealed away from the atmosphere and they could survive for a short while in vacuum. That left me without any blush to evaluate; they had no visible eyes and a rather inflexible mouth that betrayed little in the way of expression. I wouldn't know how she was feeling until she told me, and for all I knew, she might express that in calculus.

The bodyguards in black walked behind Drusil a couple of paces, and I noticed that they took care to remain behind her and therefore out of her sight. Perhaps she wanted to pretend that she wasn't being guarded, and the Empire was willing to indulge that illusion. She was a prisoner with privileges, but still a prisoner.

Drusil walked past the benches and deliberately chose a spot in the grass to sit down, legs folded underneath her and long-fingered hands resting on her knees, her back stiff and straight as though it were her mission to model correct posture. She had chosen a view of a family picnic, some adults nursing beverages around a metal table and children playing in the field nearby, tossing a ball around and laughing. It was impossible to tell if this gave her any pleasure.

The two bodyguards kept their position and faced outward, watching for any approaching trouble. The security droid hovered in place and rotated in sentinel mode, colored lights winking as it scanned for threats and bathed the area with radar pings, doubtless securing passive target locks on anything in sight. The plainclothes security maintained a perimeter and rotated clockwise, while the two men occupying the elevated walkways remained stationary.

After a few minutes of this, with Drusil Bephorin keeping perfectly still, it occurred to me that she might not be watching the children at all, but rather meditating. Her eyes might be closed and I would never know.

The eyes of the security droid were vigilant, however, and it was programmed to use lethal force, which was demonstrated when the ball got away from the children and arced through the air on a parabola that might have brought it within the blast radius of a grenade to Drusil's position. The droid whirled, shot forward, and blasted the ball into component atoms before it could touch the ground. The kids screamed, and their parents, roused from their drinking, threw out a few belated screams, as well. Playtime was over.

Drusil jerked at the noise and stood, turning to berate the bodyguards as if they had been the ones to shoot the ball.

"Not so relaxing here in this park," Nakari said, rising from the bench. "I think it best we leave."

"Yeah." As almost everyone else was leaving, too, we would stand out if we lingered. We had all the information we needed anyway: two obvious guards, four in plainclothes, two more up high, and an aggressively programmed security droid. Plus anything else we missed that Artoo managed to pick up; we'd ask him soon.

Returning to the hotel took some time because we employed measures to ensure that we weren't followed. After ditching our rental speeder, we removed our putty faces in the restroom of a public restaurant, destroyed our uniforms and duffels in the incinerator, changed into nondescript clothing, and hid our faces from any security cams as we exited by wearing cowls over our heads. Artoo's identity was rather more difficult to conceal, so we didn't try. We had to take the risk of having him return to the hotel on his own and hope that no one accosted him in the short distance involved. Nakari argued that people would assume he was on an errand rather than wandering around on his own without direction. Luckily he encountered no trouble and waited outside by the door, and we arrived soon afterward. He followed us to yet another establishment since we didn't go inside the hotel; we wanted to be sure we had shaken any tails first, and besides, we had plenty to do.

We ensconced ourselves in a secluded booth of an upscale diner and ordered hot drinks served by a droid. There we pored over the information Sakhet had downloaded to Nakari's datapad and also compared Artoo's observations about security with our own through an interface.

Artoo had identified the same security personnel we had through local comm signals. He'd be able to identify locations again at another site in case we were unable to see them; it looked as if we would not enjoy such an unrestricted view again as we had that morning.

"I don't think we could do the botanical garden tomorrow even if we wanted to."

"No, it's too soon," Nakari agreed. "And there would

be flowers and canopies and tree trunks ruining my line of sight."

"But this café the day after tomorrow looks promising," I said.

Nakari leaned in close and peered over my shoulder, a few wild curls of her hair brushing against my ear. She smelled of citrus and mint. "Depends on where she sits. Can't do it inside."

"Sakhet's notes say she sits outside at one of the tables and watches the world pass by."

"So we try to snatch her on a crowded public street?"

"Well, I doubt it would be very crowded at midmorning. The rush hour will be over, and all we'll see are the people who overslept or who tend to do their business in cafés. Besides, any innocents will work against the Imperials as much as us. And look at this," I said, pointing at a detail of the site holo Sakhet had provided.

"Oh. *Oh!* That might just work."

"Glad you agree." I turned to my droid. "Hey, Artoo. How would you feel about getting an upgrade?"

$$x^{(\lambda)} = \begin{cases} \frac{x^{\lambda}-1}{\lambda} & \lambda \neq 0 \\ & \lambda = 0 \end{cases}$$

CHAPTER 12

AS I UNDERSTAND IT, the human sense of smell is somewhat underdeveloped in comparison with most other species. Sometimes I think that's a shame; there are attractive scents that might be even more alluring when given depth. But when the fragrance slithering into my nostrils is the obnoxious sort, I'm glad we can only smell so much. My trips to Rodia, for example, gave me cause to be thankful for humanity's stunted olfactory nerves. Another time for such gratitude was two days after meeting Sakhet, when I was hunched in a Denon sewer populated not only by waste but also by things feeding on waste and thereby creating their own.

We'd spent the previous day preparing madly for the liberation of Drusil Bephorin, beginning by leaving a message at an Alliance dead drop that Major Derlin's team needed to move the Givin's family to Omereth immediately. We then scouted the location and shopped for necessities, especially for Artoo's upgrade but also some additional layers of clothing for quick changes. After not enough sleep and a quick breakfast, the early morning was spent on new contingencies we had thought of in the night, abort scenarios, and finally getting into position ahead of Drusil's arrival.

Mentally reviewing the Givin "greeting maths" that Leia taught me distracted me somewhat from the fact that I was crouched in slime up to my ankles and could almost feel spores of mold and mildew latching onto all available surface area inside my lungs. It was dark except for the wan light streaming in through drainage grates around the corner, and I could hear creatures splashing in the water or scrabbling among the refuse in search of a meal—or maybe a way out. Something small screamed, cut off abruptly, and then something large belched. I stared at my new comm unit, willing it to squawk to life and tell me to move. Waiting around with nothing to do is terrible, but waiting around with nothing to do in the sewer is worse.

I worried that the signal wouldn't get through the cement above me and I'd miss my cue, bungling everything, despite testing the link yesterday. Technology is always perfectly dependable until it isn't.

But soon I got a chirp that indicated Artoo and Nakari were in their chosen positions, and a second chirp that told me that our target had been sighted approaching the café. These signals were no more than meaningless pings, free of any content that the Imperial security droid could reasonably interpret as a threat. They carried a wealth of information to me, however. The third chirp from Artoo was a ready signal; in less than a minute he would act. I pulled out my blaster and checked for perhaps the fifth time that it was dialed up to its maximum power, and rose from my squatting position, pressing my back against the wall of the tunnel. If the security droid detected my movement below now, that was fine; it would be a distraction from what Artoo was doing, which was opening a tiny hatch on his dome to reveal a small ion blaster we had installed the day before. He would fire at the security droid and disable it, which was really key to the operation's success. Without its recorded memory and transmissions of the kidnapping in progress, the ISB security forces would have to rely on information given to them in real time by human resources, and Nakari was supposed to take care of that.

The final chirp came and I moved, turning the corner to my left and closing on a wide drainage grate located just off the curb of the café sidewalk and outdoor dining area. Artoo must have fired and hit his target, for a sizzle and hiss of electric screams floated down, followed by a loud crash, percussive thumps, and then screams from the throats of various panicked beings. I added to the noise by firing repeatedly at the edges of the drainage grate until it fell away, leaving a hole down which one could fall—or intentionally jump. By the time I was finished some of the voices had faded—the people shouting had moved away from the exploding drainage grate and from droids falling out of the sky. It gave me the opportunity to be heard up above.

"Drusil Bephorin!" I yelled as loud as I could. "I'm from the Alliance and we have your family! Please hurry! Down here!"

The Givin moved with surprising swiftness; I heard her chair clatter to the sidewalk in her haste to join me. Her pale head appeared in the rectangular frame of the hole and her cavernous eye sockets looked down, the slope of the brow suggesting that she was upset with me. I supposed I would never feel comfortable with her expression if it was fixed like that.

"Where is my family?" she called. Her voice sounded

muffled and sticky, as if she were speaking around a mouthful of nut butter. Maybe she was—she had been relaxing at a café, after all.

"On the way to Omereth as you wished! We have to move quickly, please jump down!"

She placed her toes at one edge, squatted, leaned forward until her hands gripped the opposite edge, then dropped down, hanging in the air for a moment before letting go to drop down the last half meter. Her knees bent, absorbing the impact, and then she stood and turned to regard me with those pitlike eyes, adjusting around her right shoulder the strap of a carry-sack that had shaken loose during her swing down. It looked like she had a datapad in there at least, and perhaps some other things.

"I do not normally follow strange humans into dark places," she informed me, "but considering the quick disposal of my security detail, the probability that you are who you claim to be is quite high."

"Greetings from the Alliance. It's a pleasure to meet you. I am Luke Skywalker." It was time to regurgitate the equation I'd memorized this morning. "While we escape the remainder of your guards, would you mind giving me the eigenvalues and eigenvectors for the three by three matrix one, negative three, three, then three, negative five, three, and six, negative six, four?"

"I am charmed, Luke Skywalker. Well met!" I led her around the corner of the first turn, which would get us out of immediate sight of the street's drainage tunnel and into the sewer proper, but had only gone a few steps before her voice said behind me, "To answer your question, the eigenvalues for that matrix would be four, negative two, and negative two, with the associated vectors square root of six over six times the vector one, one, two, square root of two over two times the vector negative one, zero, one, and square root of two over two times the vector one, one, zero—that would be normalized and rationalized, of course."

"Of course," I replied, though I had only a vague idea what she was talking about. It gave me a glimpse at the staggering mathematical intellect behind that blank face, however. Hard to believe she had calculated that in her head so quickly. Leia had offered to walk me through the problem, but I knew it would have taken a quadratic formula and a set of ground teeth to get an answer in five minutes. Drusil had solved it in a few seconds. Hoping to distract her from presenting me with a similar question—I wasn't sure I remembered what an eigenvalue was, even after my crash course—I added, "We need to move quickly through this sewer system to an exit where I have a speeder waiting. We'll take that to a docking platform in the next district where we have a ship ready to take you offplanet. The faster we move, the better chance we have to escape before the Empire tries to shut down outgoing traffic."

The filth grew steadily worse the deeper we traveled into the sewer, as assorted small tributaries of goo gurgled to join our larger sluice. We sloshed our way through the muck at a respectable trot, using a pocket lamp to light our way. I was following the same path out that I had taken to get in, turning at each junction in reverse order. Shouts and echoes of pursuit bounced off the walls somewhere behind us, but Drusil Bephorin ignored that. She was determined instead to greet me properly.

"I will certainly move at my best speed, Luke Skywalker. While we move, can you math something math math for me with something math?"

Drusil used proper terms, of course, and precise numbers, but I don't recall exactly what she asked me or even if I knew all the terms to begin with. It sounded, however, like she asked me a question with a single answer, instead of a set of values and vectors. "Uh, let me see. That would be . . . three?"

The Givin made a phlegmy noise in her throat that might have been laughter. "Excellent."

Yes, it was excellent. Thank the stars for Threepio's and Leia's experience with Givin. A pause in conversation allowed me to hear more clearly. It may have been my imagination, but it sounded as though our pursuers were growing closer. I knew Nakari had taken out at least the two guards closest to Drusil and Artoo had neutralized the security droid—otherwise the Givin wouldn't be here with me—but that still left up to six ISB agents able to pursue and call for backup to capture us. Or, what was more likely, recapture Drusil and execute me.

Before I could ask Drusil anything about her remaining security, she asked a question of her own. "Did I hear you use a first-person plural regarding our transport offplanet? I believe you said 'we' have a ship ready? Might that mean you have confederates?"

"Yes, a droid and a sniper. They'll be meeting us."

"Ah! The two who disrupted my security detail. I see. They will probably be fine if they are vectoring to some point ahead of us on the surface, but I am obliged to tell you that my calculations suggest a high probability of us being accosted before our arrival at your rendezvous point."

"How can you know that? You don't even know where we're going."

"I do not know for *certain*—I did say probability, not certainty. But I can make educated guesses as to our destination based on extant variables, and predict that our pursuit shall catch up to us prior to our exit unless they behave stupidly."

"Isn't that one of your extant variables?"

"The worst possible kind. As you may well know, unlike kinetics or time or distance, human stupidity is incalculable."

"Hey, I—well, yeah. I guess there's no arguing that. Let's see if we can increase our rate and reduce the probability of this confrontation you see."

"That would be wise."

Stepping up our pace increased the noise of our passage and made us more likely to trip and get a face full of something unspeakable, but I'd far rather risk that than getting shot in the back.

Thinking of the ISB agents, however, caused me to forget that the sewers were otherwise inhabited. As we arrived at a junction where we were supposed to take a left, a growl and a flash of teeth warned me in time to keep all my digits, but only just. A squat, four-legged creature cruised past me in the air as I jerked backward, its jaws open for the lamp and crunching down on it, probably taking the tips of my fingers off as well judging by the sharp stab of pain I felt. The light winked out in the guts of the thing, plunging us into darkness. We were deep in the tunnels now, and there were no street-level drainage grates above us.

"Stay back!" I warned Drusil as I heard the creature choke and spit up the lamp. It wasn't working anymore—maybe it was simply in the off position rather than broken, but I wasn't about to search in the dark for it in the bottom of a sewer with something hungry nearby. We needed to see, so I pulled my lightsaber from my belt and hoped it would give off enough ambient light to spot the creature before it attacked again. Holding it in front of me in a defensive stance, I turned it on as I heard the creature snarl and thrash in the filth. The blue plasma blade bloomed up and my eyes, dilated in the darkness, saw the thing open its mouth and bunch its powerful back legs for a spring at my throat. The teeth appeared as slimy, greenish icicles—though perhaps that was an illusion of the poor light—and the beast had large nostrils and ears of pale skin, but only two tiny eyespots. Its lack of fur was doubtless a mercy down here. The nostrils flared and the ears cocked in my direction, and then it leapt at me, jaws agape, certain now that I would be far more edible than a pocket lamp. There was little time or space to do much more than dodge to one side and slash down reflexively at a clear threat; I'm sure my swipe at it would score me no approval from anyone trained in martial arts. But in that confined space it was effective enough. The blade sheared off a slice of its cheek and perhaps a few teeth; its momentum slammed the creature into my shoulder in a passing broadside, but all that earned me was a greasy smear of burnt flesh rather than any injury. Howling in pain and fear, the creature turned upon landing and scuttled directly away from us. Accustomed to ambushing its meals, it had no taste for the kind that fought back.

Unfortunately, its attack and subsequent retreat allowed the ISB agents not only to get a fix on us via the noise it made but also to close some of the distance between us.

"They're down there!" I heard one shout as Drusil said, "Remarkable! Is that a real lightsaber? The odds of encountering a being with a lightsaber in this galaxy now are fantastically low. Why, the probability is so small as to—"

"Come on!" I said, "Follow the lightsaber. We're turning left here."

Instead of following immediately, Drusil shook her head, which I barely perceived by the pale blades of her cheekbones dancing from side to side. "There is no need to worry, Luke Skywalker. My vision is some-what better than that of a human. I can see well enough to avoid obstacles."

A blaster bolt zipped by us, and the sound of its fir-ing echoed and amplified in the tunnel. Pinpoints of light down the tunnel indicated pocket lamps like the one I'd recently lost.

"I assume you saw that, then? Let's go."

"With alacrity, yes." We turned the corner as our pursuers fired again, but this time the sound was different—the warped electric flutter of a stun blast. In the small diameter of the tunnel it would spread out to fill the entire area, making it impossible to avoid. Except that we had already turned the corner and it passed behind us, weakened and close to dissipation after traveling such a long distance. The flare of it briefly illuminated my path, for which I was grateful.

Drusil asked, "Are we growing closer to your planned point of egress? The probability of your death in-creases with every second we remain subterranean."

"Yeah, we just need to take one more right turn and then we should start seeing some drainage lights. Find-ing the turn itself might be tricky, though, with only a lightsaber to see by. Don't know how I'm going to find it in the dark."

"Is it the first right turn down this passage?"

"Yeah, why?"

"You just passed it."

I tried to stop too quickly, slid in the slime, and prepared myself for a graceless landing while trying to make sure I didn't slay myself with the lightsaber. The impact was much softer and squishier than I an-ticipated. I didn't want to think about what kinds of substances might be providing the cushion. Getting up involved squelching noises that would haunt my dreams later, and the odor was nearly enough to make me retch. I probably would have let it happen had we not been in such a rush.

"Hurry. They are coming," Drusil said. "Shall I lead you? I can't see fine detail but I can see more than well enough to navigate."

"Yeah, go ahead," I said, stretching out with my left hand. It was covered in muck and was also the one that had been scraped and bitten by that creature, but the Givin grabbed it and pulled me along into a passage that I had completely missed in the dark. Just before we left the tunnel in which I fell, I saw the beams of ISB pocket lamps off to my right and heard their urgent footsteps. They were very close.

"We should see some light from above soon," I said, "and a ladder on the left leading up to the surface. There's a service access door set in the street between two buildings. We climb that and there should be a speeder there waiting for us."

"Yes. I see the light. That should help us both. Can you run faster?"

"Yes, I can manage." This particular passage wasn't cursed with the muck and buildup of the others; it was used for rain drainage and access to the deeper tunnels, so the floor was only slick with the remaining dribble of the previous night's light showers. Up ahead, I saw shafts of sunlight spearing down into the gloom from the street; that oriented me, gave me more confidence in lengthening my stride. Behind us, voices and splashes grew quite loud and I looked back to see the eyes of two pocket lamps pass by our position, then a third in the rear paused, swung our way, and the person holding it shouted to the others to come back. I probably should have turned off my lightsaber as soon as I saw the sunlight; that might have fooled them a few more seconds before they realized their mistake and doubled back. But since we'd been spotted, I was glad I had it ready. I switched it from my right hand to my left, because that would allow me to wield it defensively as I climbed the ladder. My fingertips still stung and my hand was covered in slime, but it functioned well enough.

"You go first, fast as you can," I told Drusil. "There should be a human woman with dark curly hair and an astromech droid waiting. Go with them."

She obeyed and began to climb but called down, "What about you?"

"I'm following right behind you."

The agent who'd spotted us had waited for his backup to join him before plowing forward together. The beams of three pocket lamps approached, no doubt held by agents whom Nakari and I had seen circling in the park two days before. I wondered if they had ever met Darth Vader and seen what he could do with a lightsaber. If so, they might know more about lightsabers than I did. If they shot blaster bolts at me, I might be able to catch one or two of them on the blade as I had with that training remote back on the *Millennium Falcon*, but I doubted my weak skills in the Force would allow me to deflect repeated fire from three blasters at once. But if they shot stun blasts—well, I didn't know exactly what would happen, but following a hunch, I activated the stud to lock it into the *on* position.

Drusil was three-quarters of the way up. I began to climb behind her in an awkward three-limbed process, holding my lightsaber out behind me in an attempt at misdirection. In the dark, the agents' eyes would naturally focus on the light source, and since they would probably be firing at me in seconds it would be wise to make sure my body wasn't behind where they would be aiming. I figured I would gain only seconds or fractions of seconds by it, but that might be enough to get me out of there.

One thing I didn't consider was how difficult it would be for them to judge distance in those conditions. I could hear them arguing about how close I was because they didn't want to shoot too soon, and that gave us another couple of seconds. When Drusil opened the access door, however, and a square of natural light fell down and illuminated us both, they realized we were much closer than they thought—and we were about to escape.

"There they are!"

"I see them!"

"Stun 'em now!"

This might be it—I hoped Drusil would get away and give the Alliance an edge in the war, regardless of what happened to me. She was pulled bodily through the opening by Nakari, giving me a clear path up and out. I wouldn't make it before the ISB had taken their shots, though. They raised their blasters at me and fired, expanding blue halos of energy that would disrupt my neural system and drop me unconscious—or maybe even kill me, considering I would be getting three blasts at almost the same instant. Choosing to stun instead of shoot plasma bolts at me, however, indicated that they would like an interrogation before my execution.

I held my lightsaber in front of me, blade aligned horizontally but pointing slightly toward the agents so that the tip would meet the oncoming wave first. There was no dodging to be done and no great skill with the Force required—either the lightsaber would save me or it wouldn't. And it did, sort of. There was a crackle as the blasts hit the blade, and a blue spiderweb of energy that shimmered outward as the blasts dissipated, leaving me conscious and the ISB agents flabbergasted. But before it dissipated, some of the energy kissed the fingers I was using to hold the hilt of the lightsaber; they went numb, and I dropped the weapon. Perhaps against a single stun blast that wouldn't have happened, but against three, something got through. Now the agents could simply fire again and I'd be knocked out.

"Nakari! Help!" I yelled as I leapt down from the ladder, grabbed my blaster, and fired at the agents, who were slow to recognize that the tactical situation had abruptly changed. They recovered quickly after the first one cried out with a charred hole in his chest; whatever armor he was wearing wasn't up to deflecting the heat from my blaster turned up to maximum. The second one standing in the middle fired a stun blast a split second after my shot rocked him and the charge sailed harmlessly into the ceiling. The third one, however, had a clear shot at me, and he took it, his blaster pointed down so that the center of the blast would slam into me.

One of the features of stunning someone is that you don't have to be a very good sharpshooter thanks to the spreading footprint of the blast. But in this case that worked in my favor: The lower edge skimming the wet floor ran into the blade of my lightsaber, still glowing and lying prone on the floor, and as soon as it did, the blade dissipated the blast with the same crackle of electricity as before.

Nakari shot the last agent before I could, her bolt coming from above. I looked up and saw her head and right arm dangling down the access hatch; she'd fired accurately upside down.

"Thanks," I said.

"No problem. Hold on." She calmly fired again into the body of each agent.

"Why'd you do that?"

"Need to make sure. You'll be vulnerable for a few seconds while you climb up here, and if one of them is still alive we can't have him taking a free shot at you."

It was a valid point but not one I had considered. Even if I had thought of it, I'm not sure I would have followed through and shot them again. Something about it struck me as bloodthirsty—or simply not quite right. I'd have to think about it some more. I kept all such thoughts to myself as I holstered my blaster, retrieved my lightsaber, and returned it to my belt after turning it off. It was my first opportunity to get a good look at my left hand; there was skin missing around the knuckles and a bit off the tips, and it was still bleeding. It was also completely soiled and horrific and I needed to get it scoured and dipped in an entire vat of sanitizing solution.

But we weren't out of trouble yet; I imagined we wouldn't be for quite some time. I longed for time enough to make myself presentable before ascending into public, but we had to get to the ship as fast as possible. I climbed up quickly and immediately began to strip off my (formerly) white outer tunic. We had planned to change later anyway, but I couldn't wait. The dark tunic underneath was wet and probably smelled awful, but at least it wasn't encrusted with waste. Nakari wrinkled her nose.

"Ugh, Luke, what is that all over you? Did you slip and fall into—"

"Let's not talk about it, okay? If we don't say it out loud then maybe I can forget about it in a few thousand years."

"Hey, everybody has accidents." She was fighting hard to stifle a smile but appeared to be losing the battle. I'm sure I was blushing: I felt the heat in my face.

Nakari kicked the access door shut and we crammed into an enclosed speeder with a dark-tinted cockpit. Artoo and Drusil were already waiting inside and I shoved the repulsors to maximum thrust, heading for a parking structure at the edge of the district. Nakari and Drusil exchanged equations courteously and Drusil thanked us for the continuing rescue attempt.

"I do hope to reiterate my gratitude after a successful escape," she added, her words emphasizing that we still had a long way to go.

We had another rented speeder waiting in the parking structure and we took the time to change clothes completely before getting out into the view of security cams. We had a cowled hood for Drusil to wear so that her face would be completely hidden, and Artoo would attempt to jam local transmissions for the few minutes we were inside the garage, since we could do little to disguise him. When we had planned the operation the day before, I'd thought this part was an excess of caution and sacrificed speed for skullduggery, but Nakari insisted; she was convinced the ISB would be scouring all security feeds in search of us, and if they picked us up before we got offplanet we'd be hard-pressed to fight off the reinforcements they could summon.

Artoo had programmed a course into the speeder's rudimentary navigation computer that would take it out of the garage and fly a random pattern in the Lodos district. It was a ruse that wouldn't hold up forever, but like everything else we did, it was designed to give us a bit more time—we just needed enough to jump out of the system. Let them go ahead and piece everything together, Nakari said, just as long as they did so too late to stop us.

While Artoo's jamming program operated, we clambered into another speeder, also with an opaque cockpit, and drove that out of Lodos while our decoy drove deeper into it. We saw local and Imperial law enforcement vehicles dart overhead along vectors that would place them in the neighborhood of the café, and Nakari looked faintly smug.

"Any predictions on the probability of them catching up with us, Drusil?" I asked.

"I don't have enough data to perform the calculations," she replied. "It would be an equation filled entirely with variables and few real numbers at this point, resulting in little more than a guess."

"Oh, sorry."

"Perhaps you could tell me if you have solid proof that my family is safe, or if you were speaking of probabilities?" she asked.

"Probabilities," I admitted. "We let the Alliance know that we would be attempting to snatch you today, so a separate team should be extracting your family now." I hoped Major Derlin had succeeded, or we would have an extremely unhappy Givin on our hands.

"Or they may have already done so," Nakari said. "We won't know until we get to Omereth, unfortunately."

"Why Omereth, if I may ask?" I said to Drusil.

"It is insignificant and of little interest to either the Empire or the Alliance. Negligible infrastructure, no sentient life-forms, and poor mineral prospects have condemned the planet to a vacation destination for adventurers. It cannot support a large population or indeed many modern conveniences without significant offworld imports. No one would suspect a cryptographer would live someplace so cut off from active networks of trade and military staging areas. It is among the least probable places to find me—I have done the math, I assure you."

Smirking, I said, "I don't doubt it. We'll talk more once we get out of the system."

I guided the speeder to a soft landing on our docking platform a short distance from the *Desert Jewel*. As with the previous speeder, we sent it flying away on a preprogrammed course as soon as we disembarked. There was a chance this one wouldn't be found right away, so Artoo had programmed it to land safely before it ran out of fuel.

"I sure hope the Imperials haven't begun to check outbound ships," Nakari said as the ramp descended and we boarded the craft.

"How many of my security team survived?" Drusil asked. "Two were slain next to me. Three in the sewer. That leaves three more, unless you killed them later?"

"No, that's right," Nakari confirmed. "Three survived and are no doubt coordinating the attempt to reacquire us."

Artoo rolled into the starboard quarters to hook up with the *Jewel*'s nav computer. He already knew our first jump but needed to fine-tune calculations for our earliest possible exit. I headed straight for the cockpit to get the *Jewel* fired up while Nakari and Drusil continued to talk in the corridor. The Givin was listing gaps in Imperial knowledge—primarily due to taking out the security droid—that all added up to time.

"They know you and your astromech droid were involved but may not have seen Luke until he emerged from the sewer behind me. I assume by now they have discovered that site by homing in on comm units of the three slain ISB agents. They will be scouring the city and looking for that first speeder for sure. The question is not whether they'd be willing to activate their orbital resources and anger the civilian population for the chance to prevent our escape; the question is how long they'll delay before giving that order."

Trying to lock down traffic here would be a tall order, since Denon rested at the intersection of two of the galaxy's most well-traveled hyperspace lanes.

"They might not realize we're with the Alliance," I called back as I checked the systems and was gratified by a row of green lights. "We could be mercenaries working for the Hutts or something."

"That is true, but it will probably have no bearing on their decision making. They wish me to remain under their control and will exert themselves to ensure that happens."

"Understood, but if they think we're with the Hutts, they might waste time searching for us in the criminal underworld here." Perhaps I was overthinking it; I could see how pondering the possibilities might slow down command decisions. Up to now, I had been given little freedom to plan and execute operations on my own. Mostly I flew where the Alliance told me to fly and shot what they told me to shoot. There's an undeniable pleasure in ruining the Empire's day with blasters, but planning and anticipating enemy moves had a different appeal that I was beginning to appreciate. I released the brakes and said, "Better strap in somewhere. We're taking off, and this could be an exciting trip."

Nakari showed Drusil into the starboard living quarters and then joined me in the cockpit, taking the copilot's seat and flipping on an intercom channel to the quarters so that both Artoo and Drusil could hear us.

The *Desert Jewel* lifted smoothly from her berth and sliced through the atmosphere without any Imperial pursuit. Once I set the course, I asked Artoo to monitor security channels as a subroutine while maintaining our hyperspace jump as his top priority. We were going to jump Coreward along the Hydian Way to Exodeen, and from there we would take a smaller hyperspace lane called the Nanth'ri Trade Route that would eventually offer several different ways to reach Omereth.

The sky burned away and stars replaced it as we left Denon's atmosphere with no trouble. Commenting on it drew a wry chuckle from Drusil.

"You should hear of trouble soon enough," she said. "The probability is almost certain."

Artoo blurted an alarm and a stream of characters appeared on our heads-up holodisplay, translating his words: EMPIRE HAS ORDERED A SYSTEMWIDE BLOCKADE TO SEIZE REBEL SPIES. INTERDICTOR CRUISERS EN ROUTE. ALL SHIPS THAT DEPART PRIOR TO IMPERIAL INSPECTION WILL BE NOTED.

Drusil's prescience made me want to spend more time studying math. "Let them note it! Do you have the course ready? Jump if you do."

JUMPING.

I had hoped we would get out of the system without being tagged for pursuit, but that plan was slagged now. We had to hope that our ship would move faster than any dragnet the Empire put together.

THE FIRST THING I DID while in hyperspace was visit the bathroom to wash off my hand and take a quick shower to sluice away the filth of Denon's tunnels—it was a public service as much as a personal wish to be clean, because I still reeked even after shedding the filth-encrusted layer of clothes outside the sewer. I took some strong antibacterials as a precaution. My cuts would scab over and heal soon enough, but they'd probably sting for a while.

Scoured, bandaged, and finally presentable, I rejoined Nakari in the cockpit with a few minutes to spare before entering the Exodeen system. She smiled as she took in my fresh clothes and damp hair.

"Bet that feels better," she said.

"Unbelievably so."

"I'll do the same after the next jump."

"Intercom still on?" I asked as I strapped into the pilot's seat. "Can Drusil hear me?"

"I hear you," Drusil's voice said.

"Great. I wanted to ask you why the Empire and Alliance are so interested in you specifically as a cryptographer. What sets you apart from others?"

"What interests the Alliance is that I have written some slicing programs that will easily cut through low-level routine Imperial encryption, which I will hand over as soon as I'm reunited with my family. I can also slice through some of the higher-level codes when supplied with sufficient time."

"Begging your pardon, but how do we know that, exactly?"

"Did not the Kupohans assure you of my capabilities?"

"They assured the decision makers in the Alliance, and they believed the Kupohans well enough to send us to get you. But it's a fact that the Alliance has yet to see any proof that you can do all that you claim. It isn't that I doubt you; it's just that I prefer to confirm your abilities."

"What would you suggest?"

The stars snapped into focus as we exited hyperspace into the Exodeen system. Our scanners immediately detected the presence of several Imperial ships, including a heavy cruiser and a Star Destroyer. Their images were a few minutes old, owing to the speed of light, and they wouldn't see us for a few minutes yet.

"Calculate the jump for Nanth'ri, Artoo!" I said, and after he chirped acknowledgment, I added to Drusil, "Perhaps you can pick up some Imperial communication here and decrypt it for us while we wait?"

"If it's low-level communication, certainly. If you will scan the system for some of their communications while I set up my hardware, we will see what can be accomplished."

"Your hardware is in that sack you brought with you?"

"Yes. A datapad I assembled myself with associated couplers for interfacing with most alien dataports. It is . . . unique." A note of unmistakable pride crept into the Givin's voice, which still sounded as if it were being muffled by a mouthful of something chewy.

Nakari's right hand shot forward and switched off the intercom. Her eyebrows tracked upward on her face as she waggled her head, muttering, "Well, aren't we special?"

I laughed. "We really should find something for her as a test. It'd be good to know we're not getting conned here."

Nakari's fingers flipped a couple more switches and turned a knob. After a few seconds of white noise, a stream of unintelligible syllables filled the cockpit and she reestablished the intercom link with the starboard living quarters so that Drusil could hear it.

"Ah! Just a moment," Drusil said. "Calibrating . . . feed established. Decryption running." The babble paused for perhaps thirty seconds before starting up again in a short burst, most likely a standard receipt of the prior transmission. Drusil's voice spoke into the silence. "Success! The Empire has transmitted orders through their HoloNet originating from Denon. We missed the beginning of the transmission, so I must begin reading in midsentence: . . . *small custom ship, inbound from Denon, search for two humans, one Givin, one droid, highest priority, report sighting immediately to ISB, bounty offered for capture, do not destroy.* And then what follows is simply an acknowledgment."

"Thanks, Drusil," Nakari said. "Please hold a moment." She flicked off the intercom so that she could talk to me privately. "You know she could have just made that up, right?"

"Yeah, I know. That's going to be difficult to test. We would have to keep going toward the planet, let the Imperials spot us, and then see if they chase us."

"We'd get away easily," Nakari pointed out, "but

then they would have a sighting to report and a good idea of where we're headed. Right now they've broadcast that everywhere and don't have any idea where to concentrate their forces. If we give them a clue we could run into a whole lot of trouble ahead. Is it worth it to stick around here just to confirm that she can decrypt standard orders?"

"No, I don't think so."

"They're going to know we were here soon because we can't conceal the reflected light of our entry, but if we leave now we can prevent them from getting a deep scan and confirming three life-forms aboard—assuming that her decryption is true and they're looking for us. And note that if it *is* true, the Empire knows about your specific involvement after you got out of the sewer. They've definitely seen security footage from somewhere."

"Agreed. I don't like the idea of sticking around anywhere until we drop her off at Omereth. I'm curious to know if she's for real, but it's really not our job to determine if she's telling the truth or not. We're just a lightly armed taxi service now."

Nakari winced. "Can we call it a *heavily* armed taxi service? I like the sound of that better."

I shrugged. "Sure."

"No argument, huh? That's nice." She turned the intercom back on.

"Artoo, can we jump?" I asked. "Let's go if you're ready."

JUMPING, came the reply, and once we were safely in hyperspace Nakari unbuckled and rose from her seat, imitating her father as she headed aft. "Pilot! Refreshment is in order! Fly responsibly in my absence!" She trailed a finger along my shoulder as she passed by, and I couldn't suppress the grin her touch inspired. I liked her and was starting to think maybe she liked me back.

Nothing I could do about it now, however. Flirting on a mission is one of the best ways to ensure mission failure—and most likely romantic failure. I'd seen Han Solo get in trouble too many times while he was trying to charm Leia to doubt it, and he hadn't exactly won her good graces yet.

We had five planets to skip over before we got to Nanth'ri and decided which way to go from there. We could swing to the galactic north, which had the benefit of being a shorter transit route to Omereth but the drawback of more Imperial worlds, or dart south for a short distance and then east again, traversing Hutt Space and avoiding the Empire while risking who knew what in the seedy side of the galaxy. One thing was more likely near Hutt Space: bounty hunters. If the Empire had rebroadcast that message about a bounty on our heads on unencrypted channels, we'd have all sorts of beings on the lookout for us who didn't need to abide by Imperial protocols and procedures. They also didn't need to do all the other things Empire forces needed to do—patrol vast areas of space and guard against the Alliance, police smugglers, and so on. Bounty hunters could devote 100 percent of their attention to finding us. Thinking about that made me nervous, but I'd rather face a single bounty hunter's ship than the heavy firepower the Imperial fleet could bring to bear. Turning south was probably a better decision.

"Artoo, when we get to Nanth'ri, begin calculating a jump that will take us through Hutt Space. If you can do a jump all the way across it without stopping, that would probably be best."

The droid's agreement showed up on my holoscreen as Drusil's voice came through the intercom. "Would you like my assistance in calculating these jumps? It should not be terribly taxing—indeed, I would find it refreshing."

I searched for a diplomatic way to say no. If, by some awful chance, Drusil was in truth an Imperial spy and this was all an elaborate sting, then the coordinates she fed us might lead directly to an Imperial fleet position. And I wasn't sure I wanted to trust the ship's navigation to calculations done in someone's head, anyway. What if she forgot to carry the one or something like that?

"Thanks, Drusil, but Artoo's already wired in and familiar with the ship specs, so I'd like to have him take lead. Perhaps you could check his work, though?" I winced, hoping she would not take my reply as a slight on her abilities.

"That would be fine," she said, and then a silence settled over the cockpit. Presumably both Artoo and Drusil were lost in pure math and had nothing more to say. With Nakari gone for a while, I had nothing to do except remain in the pilot's seat in case something went wrong.

It was an ideal opportunity to meditate and see if I could strengthen my bond with the Force. When I'd first felt the Force on the *Millennium Falcon,* it had been the barest tickle of a presence in my consciousness and in the air around me that wasn't attributable to my five senses. Since then I had reached out to the Force on numerous occasions, and each time it grew marginally easier to make that contact and feel the Force swirl and coalesce around me, a not-quite-tangible but very real sensation, sort of like exercising and discovering over time that the same routine requires less effort because your strength and endurance have increased.

I didn't have any goal in mind other than increasing

my awareness of the Force; there were no vegetables or other objects to nudge around in the cockpit, anyway, and I figured a greater grasp of the Force would help me perform such tasks more quickly later on, and perhaps allow me to move larger objects, or accomplish any number of other Jedi exercises.

The streaming starlines of hyperspace were excellent for clearing my mind. No distractions, just visual white noise. I remembered training with the remote, wearing a helmet with the blast shield down and feeling the Force as a power within and without that worked with me and yet was not me. That had been a twinge, a tiny awakening of a new part of my mind, like a half-glimpsed dawn through sleep-encrusted eyes. I knew I wasn't fully awake yet; I think part of me wanted to go back to sleep. But the dawn comes whether you sleep through it or not, and I think the Force might be like that—always there, but unseen until you make the effort.

My breathing slowed and deepened, and soon I became aware that there were others breathing on the ship. Drusil was nearest, sitting in an attitude of prayer or perhaps meditation like myself, attempting to soothe away her worries. Perhaps the activity of her mind was pure math. Farther back and to the left, Nakari felt happy, though I didn't know about what. Her breath was uneven and sort of purred—was she humming to herself? I couldn't hear that to confirm it, of course, but I felt through the Force that it must be true.

And what about . . . beyond the ship? There was nothing else breathing nearby, that's for sure. But I knew the Force could tell me of things beyond my immediate surroundings. Ben had shown me that. When the Death Star destroyed Alderaan, he had felt it, even in hyperspace, when we were still light-years away. I wondered if I could sense anything outside hyperspace.

I opened myself more—or perhaps I should say that I lost myself more, let go of my five senses and focused only on what the Force could show me. Nanth'ri waited ahead, and around it . . . some kind of danger? Anger? No, nothing so personal. More like antagonism. Aggression. But I couldn't see who was feeling such things, or against whom they were directed.

Artoo's warning bleep was a sharp tug on my hearing that broke my trance. I blinked and saw his words stream in the holofeed: ONE MINUTE TO ARRIVAL IN NANTH'RI SYSTEM.

Nakari returned and took her seat as I acknowledged Artoo. I remembered feeling through the Force that she had been happy and humming about something, and now I tried to confirm visually that she was in a good mood. She had pulled her curly hair back into a ponytail and I admired what that did for her profile, the line of her neck, and—uh-oh, she caught me. When my eyes came back to her face, one eyebrow and a corner of her mouth were quirked up as if to ask, *What are you looking at?* That sent me into a brief panic—if I admitted I thought she was beautiful that would be flirting, badly, but if I said nothing I'd look slow-witted.

I cleared my throat and said, "I wonder if the Jedi had any secret tricks to keep them from feeling awkward."

Amused, she asked, "Didn't Ben Kenobi have anything to say on the subject?"

"Well, he kept telling me to 'trust my feelings,' and I trust that I feel awkward right now. Sorry about, you know. Staring."

Nakari snorted. "Relax, Luke. You're not the first

man I've caught in the act—and this isn't the first time I've caught you, either. It's just the first time I let you know you're a little obvious."

I winced. "Is it possible to be a *little* obvious?"

"No. I was trying to be nice. You were obvious."

I was grateful that we dropped into the Nanth'ri system a moment later, because it drew our attention to something else. An alarm pinged in my brain—*danger, there*—and without thinking, I banked the ship tightly to starboard and accelerated, even as a small fleet of ships appeared on our scanners that decidedly weren't Imperial. It wasn't the Alliance, either, so why were there more than twenty ships flying below us to port in a loose formation? Most of them were small fighter craft escorting a large cruiser capable of docking them all. Some of those fighters on the trailing edge of the formation were close enough to engage us if they wanted, and within seconds they demonstrated that they wanted that very much. The others turned to pursue, as well, but they would never have time to get involved unless I flew at them; my quick assessment was that I only had about five to worry about, but if I had waited those extra few seconds for them to appear on the screen, and then assessed the information before acting, I would have flown closer and drawn within range of a few additional ships.

Throwing up the deflector shields, I accelerated even more, to about three-quarters full, and their first shots never landed, but Nakari still saw the bolts zip past the cockpit and realized belatedly that we were under attack.

"Whoa, who's firing at us?"

"Most likely pirates," I said. "Right now they probably just think our ship is slick and carrying something valuable. When they find out we're traveling without any goods, though . . ."

"They'll take the ship and sell us into slavery. Or ransom us to my father."

"Or give us to the Empire, if they find out about the bounty on our heads."

"I liked that thing you did a few seconds ago where you made the ship go faster," Nakari said. "I think you should do it again."

"I'll consider it, but I think we're okay for a little while." Their cannon fire was coming faster and starting to concentrate but still hadn't hit us; the *Desert Jewel* was a slim target and I had run evasive patterns before. We did have room to push the engines, but I didn't want to pull away too quickly because the pirates might decide to use missiles if they saw us widening the gap; our deflector shields should be able to withstand some blasterfire but might be overtaxed by missiles.

"Artoo, how long until you can take us to hyperspace?"

FORTY-FIVE SECONDS . . . MARK, his reply read.

"Okay, take us as soon as you can; don't wait for my order."

"Forty-five seconds is a long time when people are shooting at you," Nakari pointed out, tension clear in her voice. I stole a quick glance at her and realized that she hadn't been in many firefights like this. Her comfort zone was in atmosphere with a slugthrower cradled against her shoulder and a backup blaster; piloting was something she did to get to the next planet, and her evident worry told me she'd flown in few if any combat situations. Her experience working for her father had taught her the shooting usually didn't start until she landed.

Not that I wasn't a little concerned myself; five

against one is a poor scenario, especially when the five have fifteen more behind them, but the fact was we had a better ship and the enemy didn't know it yet. I was willing to bet these sublight engines could match the speed of a TIE interceptor. The *Jewel*'s sensors told me that the pirates firing on us flew Cloak-Shape fighters and a couple of B-wings, and while they were no doubt customized to some extent, it was improbable that they could match the *Desert Jewel* once I went to full burn. But I didn't want to use that fuel if it wasn't necessary; we had a long trip ahead and friendly ports would be scarce when we got into trouble, so if the shields and our Rodian upgrades could handle this, I would let them.

"I think we'll be okay," I said, and of course as soon as the words left my mouth we took our first hit on the bottom of the starboard wing. The shields prevented any damage, but the impact spun us around and changed our vector. I had to fight the ship back on course to present the smallest target.

"That's *not* okay, Luke! What are you waiting for? Go faster!"

"The shields are still fine. Most of their shots are missing us."

We got hit and spun again, and this time the shield energy readout dipped noticeably.

"It's the ones that hit us I'm worried about!" she exclaimed.

"Every time I try to reassure you we get nailed, so I'll just fly, okay?"

Before Nakari could retort, a growled message from one of the pirates fed through the comm system. "Unidentified ship. Surrender for inspection and we guarantee your personal safety. Continue to flee and you will be destroyed."

Nakari snarled and took out her frustration on the

speaker. She jabbed the comm button and said, "Unidentified hole, please shut it and inspect yourself. Continue to talk and you will be ignored."

Her rebuke worked in one sense: They didn't talk anymore. But all three of the CloakShapes decided to let heat-seeking missiles do their talking for them, a development for which I was prepared but which still surprised me. A ship blown to fragments wouldn't yield them any profit.

Maybe they'd had a rough day of piracy, or maybe they were trigger-happy; I didn't dwell on it since surviving the six missiles was more important than discovering why they'd been fired. I'd hoped to avoid dealing with missiles altogether, but we'd had some flares installed on Rodia that would be useful now.

Phosphorous flares can burn much hotter than the engines for a brief time and draw the heat seekers away, but timing their release is crucial. Deploy them too early and you risk them dying out and allowing the heat seekers to reacquire the sublight engines; deploy them too late and the explosion will damage your drives anyway. Thinking of that made me reevaluate the pirates' strategy: They weren't trying to kill us—they were merely trying to damage our engines. They were gambling that we had flares and hoped we would either deploy them poorly or at the very least deplete the number of flares at our disposal. If they damaged us, their objective was achieved; if not, fire another volley and repeat until we were crippled. If they gambled poorly and we were destroyed after all, they wouldn't lose any sleep over it, because they'd given us a chance to surrender.

If Drusil were in the cockpit she might be able to look at the vectors and speeds of the incoming missiles and calculate the optimal release time for the flares, but I had to rely on instinct—or rather instinct aided by the Force. We wouldn't be jumping to hyperspace before the missiles reached us, and trying to outrun them was the sort of idea that would have C-3PO pronouncing our doom, so it had to be the flares.

When I closed my eyes and reached out to the Force, it was as if I had never left it a couple minutes ago; the awareness was still there, a rush of it filling my head like an additional sense that spoke to me of my surroundings, inside the ship and out. Nakari was worried and willing to let me know; Drusil was also worried but keeping silent; Artoo was simply there, and I assumed he was busy working with the nav computer on our jump. I felt the five closest pirates and the six missiles, adjusted the course of the *Jewel* in response to their positions and pattern of fire, and waited for the right moment to set off the flares.

When it came, I opened my eyes to check that my finger really was hovering over the correct button on the newly installed Rodian weapons system panel— a moment of self-doubt, I suppose—and pressed when my eyes confirmed it. The flares deployed and attracted the heat seekers; explosions rocked the space behind us, cannon fire continued to streak past, and the pirates launched another round of missiles.

"Are we okay? Did you get them all?" Nakari asked.

"I got the first six, but six more are inbound."

"Do we have enough flares for that?"

"I think we have enough, but we won't need them."

"Why not?"

I grinned at her. "Because it's been forty-five seconds now." The stars streaked past like raindrops on a window as Artoo jumped on schedule.

Nakari closed her eyes, clenched her fingers on the armrests of the copilot's seat, and took a deep breath.

When she exhaled, she relaxed, tension draining out of her shoulders and fingers, and she opened her eyes and looked at me. "I'm sorry for yelling, Luke. You obviously knew what you were doing, and I wasn't helping."

"Don't worry about it," I said. "People tend to yell in combat. It's high stress. Was that your first time being chased like that?"

Nakari nodded, her lips pressed tightly together.

"If we'd been in the *Harvester,* you'd have had cause to be worried," I told her. "But you made a good decision to spend all your credits on those engines. A fancy bunkroom wouldn't have saved us."

"Thanks." She took another deep breath and then made an effort to smile. "You know, we never did get to finish our earlier conversation."

Uh-oh. "We didn't?"

"No, we were interrupted." She unbuckled herself and moved close to me. Her right hand raised to my left cheek and I flinched minutely, wondering if I had crossed a line with my staring earlier and now I was going to pay for it, but something else happened. She rested her hand lightly there, and then she planted a soft kiss on my right cheek. She murmured in my ear, "I was going to say I don't mind if you're obvious. But since I think you missed all my subtle hints, this is me being obvious."

"Oh" was all I could manage to say, overwhelmed by surprise. Nakari didn't remove her hand from my face, but she reared back to look me in the eye, her expression incredulous. "That's all you have to say? 'Oh'?"

I made a completely unnecessary throat-clearing noise and said, "I liked that thing you did a few seconds ago where you kissed me. I think you should do it again."

CHAPTER 14

DRUSIL'S VOICE CARRIED over the intercom, interrupting a kiss that was more than a peck on the cheek. "Quick thinking, Luke Skywalker, and admirable piloting. But be advised it is now probable the Empire will know where we are."

We broke apart and Nakari chucked me once on the shoulder and whispered, "To be continued." She returned to her seat and buckled in while I responded to Drusil.

"Why is that?"

"That small fleet was patrolling the sector of space that would come from Exodeen."

"So? That's what pirates do."

"Do they normally waste fuel by having their escorts launched and spread out for fast attack when they could simply have scrambled to catch an unsuspecting and slow-moving cargo ship? Most of their normal targets would not suspect anything of that cruiser until it launched fighters at them, and by then it would be too late. Catching a fast ship piloted by a crew anxious to avoid capture, however, requires different tactics, am I correct? Hence the fighters already in position. Few fleets would be so wasteful of their resources otherwise."

"You mean they'd already heard about the bounty on us and were patrolling in case we showed up," I said.

"Yes. And now they can profit merely by reporting that they have seen us and telling the Empire which direction we fled."

"They had plenty of time to scan us, Luke," Nakari said. "They would know we have three life-forms aboard. If the pirates get a message to them quickly enough we could be running into Imperials sooner rather than later."

Drusil chimed in. "A message from the pirates isn't necessary to make an Imperial encounter likely. We're near a frequently patrolled area of the galaxy. I happen to know the Empire has been inspecting—and thereby harassing—all traffic going into Hutt Space in an effort to cut into their trade and reduce the Hutts' ability to remain independent."

"That's a recent development? How old is your information?"

"Very recent. For the past few weeks the Empire had me working on encrypted messages they intercepted in those sectors."

That sounded like a bad omen, but there was nothing I could do about it, so it was pointless to waste time worrying about it. "Well, nothing's happening right now except recharging the deflector shields. I could use some caf." I unstrapped myself and rose from the pilot's chair. "Would you like a cup?" I asked Nakari.

"I'm not sure," she said. "Do you make your caf like your nerf steak?"

"I'll try not to burn it, but no guarantees."

"Okay, I'll risk it, then. It'd be an equal risk if I made it."

I felt almost giddy heading back to the galley because I thought that the automatic brewer in the galley would produce something drinkable, but it turned out to be fair-to-middling horrendous, a fact that I remembered belatedly from our trip to Fex. Since it was the same type of brewer one saw almost everywhere, it was likely that the problem lay with me and perhaps with Nakari also, not the appliance. I gave up and decided to mask my incompetence with lots of cream and sugar.

A shrill alarm from the cockpit and an accompanying explosion of digital dismay from Artoo was my first clue that something had gone very wrong. A lurch in the ship caused me to spill all the hot caf on myself, and that was my second clue. Nakari followed that up with, "Luke, get back here! We're in trouble!"

Slapping at my tunic and pants to wick away some of the caf, I dashed back to the cockpit, where a battery of red lights winked at me and the infinite black of realspace darkened the view.

"We've been pulled out of hyperspace. Fail-safes came on in response to a mass shadow."

"What? But Artoo plotted a course using established— oh." We'd been pulled out of hyperspace by an Imperial Interdictor cruiser—shaped like a Star Destroyer but much smaller, with four gravity-well projectors. One of those projectors had pulled us out of hyperspace, and no doubt the others were blocking our exit from the system. We couldn't leave without dealing with the Interdictor. So be it.

"Shields up and arm everything we have," I said to Nakari as I strapped in. "Artoo, where are we?"

DAALANG SYSTEM, came the reply.

"Okay, I need a way out of here. We can't go back

because of the pirates. If we keep going on the route we already chose, we'll probably run into more Imperial resistance. Is there another lane out of this system?"

YES. TRADE ROUTE TO KUPOH.

The home system of the Kupohans. Perfect—or at least the best option at the moment. Since the Kupohans were superficially cooperative with the Empire, they wouldn't have an Imperial fleet parked in their orbit to bully them into good behavior.

"All right, I need you to prepare us to jump for Kupoh and tell me which gravity projector on that Inderdictor is blocking our path to it right now."

"Wait, are you suggesting we attack the Interdictor by ourselves?" Nakari said.

"It's either that or let them catch us. I don't think they'll respond to a polite request to stand down. And this is one of the old models. We should go before they have time to get reinforcements here. Right now it's unescorted and only has twenty-four TIE fighters."

"*Only* twenty-four? We're one ship with a couple of blasters and a few missiles!"

"That's all we need. And the TIE fighter pilots might be on lunch break or something, so we should be clear for a minute or two. We have speed and surprise on our side." I probably sounded more confident than I actually felt, but that is the only way to engage the enemy—something I picked up from Han. He told me, "Never go into battle saying, 'Well, I *guess* I'll fight for my life now, if I really have to.' Once committed, kid, you have to commit fully, or you won't survive." I pointed the nose down toward the Interdictor and accelerated for the first time to full attack speed, and it was breathtaking. The *Desert Jewel* was definitely faster than my X-wing.

"Luke, they've seen us by now! You can't surprise them."

"I'm talking about the surprise we picked up from the Chekkoo clan on Rodia. And the surprise that we would attack them at all, considering their advantages."

The Interdictor's batteries swung up and began spraying green bolts from quad laser cannons, but most of it was for show, since only a couple of them had the proper field of fire. The first squadron of TIE fighters, which must have been on alert or else eating lunch in their cockpits, began to swarm out from underneath.

"Let's get out of here!" Nakari insisted. "This is insane!"

I didn't think so; I wasn't simply charging in with the hope that things would work out in my favor. I had a plan, and crazy people rarely had them. "I prefer to think of it as *risky*," I said, and saying that reminded me of the conversation I had with Leia on the *Patience*. Surely this wasn't as dangerous as going after the Death Star. "Artoo, which gravity projector should I target?"

ITS PORT SIDE, OUR STARBOARD.

"Both of them?"

YES.

"That complicates things."

"They weren't complicated before?" Nakari asked. "That cruiser has to be shielded."

"It is, but this is one of the Immobilizer models, and we've been studying them since the Empire has been using them against us on our raids. They have twelve shield generators—some of them ray shields, some particle shields. We take out the particle shield generators for the port side first, then go after the gravity projectors with whatever we have left."

"While dodging TIE fighters and quad laser fire. Do you hear yourself?"

Both were coming at me now, and I sent the *Jewel* into a spin away from an aggressive TIE pilot. Nakari missed seeing it, so focused was she on convincing me to flee. "I did say it was complicated."

"Luke, let's just run to the edge of the interdiction field! The *Jewel* is fast enough!"

I'd thought of that already, and perhaps it would have worked if I'd been in the cockpit instead of trying to make the caf machine produce something drinkable, but we'd lost too much time and space in those ten to fifteen seconds while I was unable to do anything. "No, they sucked us in too close. The TIEs are already on us."

Nakari turned her head, saw the vast assortment of death heading our way, jerked in her seat, and exclaimed, "Gah!" She didn't press her point after that, seeing that it was too late. Situations develop fast when fighters close on one another so quickly. We wove through the first six TIEs, avoiding their fire and head-on collisions; I managed to wing one of them with our laser cannons—we had three now, not just one—and it careened into another, taking both out. I didn't bother firing at the cruiser, since there was no way our lone ship could weaken the shields enough to punch through, but I would gladly pull the trigger on the TIE fighters whenever opportunity afforded.

The Empire had stopped making these particular Interdictor cruisers because of their vulnerabilities, but while they weren't making any new ones, there were still plenty of them out there. The Alliance kept running into them, so we had been training recently on how to eliminate them before our raiding parties got wiped out by their escorts of destroyers and cruisers. The Empire was putting gravity projectors into

Star Destroyers now, much more difficult to take out for a group and impossible for a single ship to damage. To my knowledge no one had ever taken out an Immobilizer with a single ship before, but I'd theorized about the possibility with Wedge. I wouldn't be trying it except that we were desperate—and we also had a bonus weapon that we'd picked up on Rodia. The Empire must have been frantic to find us if it had sent this one Interdictor to the edge of Hutt Space without any escorts.

Already in touch with the Force, I opened myself more to it and slipped into a nonthinking state of awareness, anticipation, and reaction, sliding the *Desert Jewel* into an attack vector that minimized my profile to the Interdictor's gunners and led us straight to the portside shield generators.

We were slightly faster than the standard TIE fighters. After the first half of the squadron passed by and then banked around for another pass, the second half emerged from underneath the ship, coming up on either side of the cruiser and moving at me in a pincer formation, albeit behind me so as not to catch themselves in a crossfire. Their shots were sloppy and they didn't care about hitting the ship, depending on the shields to ward off the stray bolts. The *Jewel* handled well—this was her first test at full speed under heavy fire—and we took a couple of hits that reduced our shields to 70 percent. I was glad they had fully recharged before we encountered this situation.

"Artoo, light up their particle shield generator for me on the targeting holo." A small rectangle flashed and blinked for me on the bladed edge of the cruiser, and I assigned two of the *Jewel*'s six concussion missiles to it while also locating it with the Force. If I didn't bring the shield down, nothing else would work; the missiles had to get there. The TIE fighters would do nothing about them, but the cruiser's gunners would probably attempt to shoot them down. Spinning and juking my way down and feeling the ideal moment approach, I took two more hits from TIE fighters before launching the missiles. Cruiser fire aimed at me ceased and shifted to the missiles, which gave me more leeway to dodge the TIEs. I pulled the nose of the *Jewel* starboard so that we would dive past the shield generators shortly after the missiles hit. The sensors could pick up whether we scored a hit or not.

The cruiser itself represented a blind spot. The hangar that spat out the TIE fighters was underneath the ship and I couldn't see what lurked underneath. I squeezed the blaster trigger and held it down as we approached the edge; two TIE fighters emerged from beneath the ship—the vanguard of the second squadron—caught bolts in their cockpits, and exploded. Four down, twenty to go—though the second squadron was still in the process of scrambling into action.

The concussion missiles struck one after the other, the first weakening the generator's own shield and the second following up, penetrating and destroying it. Before we passed it, another hit took our shields down to 50 percent, and then we were briefly hidden from line-of-sight as I pulled the *Jewel* up to skate underneath the cruiser, just a meter above the shields to make it impossible for the TIEs above the cruiser to track me—to their scanners I was invisible now, lost in the shadow of the Interdictor. I planned to come up over the opposite side and take a shot at the newly vulnerable gravity projectors.

I didn't hold my course, however; the TIE fighters above the cruiser's plane would be waiting for me in a direct line from where I disappeared, filling the space with ambush fire. I drifted aft so that I would reappear on the back starboard corner, and from there I'd fly up and over the bridge before attacking the projectors. Three TIEs pursued me from behind but couldn't get a lock. Their wings wouldn't allow them to get as close to the underside of the cruiser as the *Jewel,* and they couldn't line up a decent angle in the brief time they had before I cleared the other side. They took a few shots anyway to make it look like they were trying, and the bolts dissipated harmlessly against the cruiser's shields. The Interdictor's gunners either didn't see me or were holding their fire to avoid tagging the TIEs; a couple more launched out of the hangar and soon they would all be after me.

As I cleared the starboard edge and climbed up, green bolts zipped past forward of my position where the topside TIEs had predicted I would emerge. The shooters followed too close behind that to correct course once they spotted me—they had to bank around for another pass. But some of the trailing fighters spotted me and banked to intercept. One of them banked right into a TIE that shot up from under the ship—two more down. I kept hugging the structure of the cruiser to make a firing solution difficult for their laser cannons, and as soon as I cleared the bridge I targeted the twin bulges of the port gravity projectors and sent two concussion missiles each at them. That wouldn't necessarily set us free; with two of its projectors still working, we'd have to clear the Interdictor's simulated mass by a good deal before our hyperdrive could engage, and the cruiser would have plenty of time to redirect those starboard projectors toward Kupoh if its crew was alert and operating efficiently. We needed a kill shot—and we had one on board, purchased at great expense from Utheel Outfitters' secret catalog. The problem was that it might kill us in the bargain. There was no time to think it over; if it was going to work at all, I had to use it now, before the missiles hit, because the physics demanded it. I couldn't expect to get another pass with only 50 percent of my shields remaining—the TIEs were forming up and responding to the surprise of my attack, the other squadron would be fully deployed any second, and when it was eighteen against one, they would surely deplete my shields before I could take my shot.

So I armed and released the Utheel Rockcrusher Compact Seismic Charge, letting it fall toward the rearmost gravity projector from the bracketed housing on the bottom of the *Jewel*. It didn't have a guidance system or any propellant, so it followed the *Jewel*'s trajectory upon release and would detonate on a proximity trigger. It fell in an arc rather than continuing straight on our course because the gravity projector was still working.

Nakari sucked in a breath and whispered, "Uh-oh," when she saw me press the button, but I couldn't spare a glance in her direction.

As the gases inside the seismic charge mixed prior to detonation, I pulled up and leveled out, streaking past the batteries of lasers. Then I kept going in as straight a line as possible, thrusting past the Interdictor as the concussion missiles hit and running for all the *Jewel* was worth, and my path was like a needle pulling a string of TIE fighters behind me. They spread out in the back into a cone so they could all try to blast me.

I stole a quick look at Nakari now that I had the time to do so, and she was breathing heavily, her eyes wide and her hands clutching the armrests—or at least as well as she could. Her left hand wasn't up to clutching anything yet, but it looked tense. The *Jewel* took a direct hit on the rear deflector as a result of my distraction, and our shields fell to 20 percent.

Right afterward, the seismic charge dropped into the open, unshielded wound of the gravity projector and detonated, its massive shock wave shredding the structure of the cruiser from the inside so that the huge ship bulged and came apart in a mess of bodies and metal, shearing the front half from the rear completely and rendering them into lifeless hunks of space debris heading in opposite directions. We picked up a tiny bit of speed as all the simulated gravity ceased to exist. We were clear to jump to hyperspace, and I reminded Artoo of the fact.

But the shock wave continued in our direction, too, plowing through the trailing TIE fighters behind us and shuddering them apart. We watched on the scanner as the red triangles representing the enemy disappeared one by one. They kept firing green bolts, as if they were determined to see us dead before they died themselves. Almost all of it sailed past our cockpit into the void, but the concentrated fire was too much to dodge forever and another bolt clipped us, essentially wiping out our shields except for a courtesy veil of energy as sheer as a negligee. The fire eased up as the TIEs were destroyed, but the closest one with the best angle landed one on the rear starboard and, a fraction of a second before it was obliterated, took out the sublight engine there, which spelled the end for us.

Having nothing else to distract me from approaching death, I felt a spike of fear shoot through me, cold and unforgiving. We'd never outrun the shock wave now, and though I'd overcome daunting odds to this point, I wouldn't get any points for almost surviving. I was about to turn to Nakari and apologize for getting us killed when Artoo bleeped in triumph, flipped the hyperdrive, and we shot forward into a white blur, leaving behind a puzzle of wreckage for Imperial late-comers.

"We . . . we made it? We made it! *Woooo!*" Nakari pounded her armrests and stomped her feet on the floor until she ran out of breath. "Three kinds of dragon dump, Luke, I don't ever want to do that again! I *hate* space battles, you hear? All I can do is sit here and clench and pucker and hope I don't die."

"I know. I'm sorry."

She rounded on me, her relief disappearing as she remembered that I had been the one to leap into that battle. "Charging that cruiser was stupid, Luke! We should be dead!"

I shrugged. She was right, but coming out of the battle fugue, I was beginning to feel something that was two parts relief, one part euphoria, and one part smug. "It worked."

Realizing she couldn't second-guess success, she said, "Yeah, but . . . yeah." She broke into a grin. "Okay, that was some pretty good piloting. Maybe even legendary."

"Don't tell your dad."

She laughed. "I won't."

"I'm going to go check on Drusil."

"Okay, I'll yell if we're pulled into realspace again."

Entering the quarters, I wrapped my arms around Artoo and told him he was the best droid in the galaxy, but he couldn't tell Threepio I said that or I'd have to deal with passive-aggressive complaints for the next ten years. "Thanks for the save."

R2-D2 burbled happily, and I turned to Drusil and inquired after her health.

Her spine looked even more rigid than normal as she sat, and her voice was thicker, more muffled. "I am recovering from glandular excitement, thank you for asking."

"Well, I . . . I beg your pardon? Is this a bad time?"

"I am told it is a biological phenomenon not unlike the aftereffects of adrenaline in humans."

"Oh, *that* kind of excitement! Good. No, I mean— I'm sorry I worried you. Er. We're safe for the moment, anyway, en route to Kupoh."

"We should have perished. Mathematically we had almost no chance of survival once we attacked. How did you accomplish this?"

I shrugged. "Artoo got us out of there."

"The droid did his job adequately," the Givin said, a dismissive summation to which Artoo belched an electronic burst of outrage, "but I speak of the piloting prior to that. Are you a Jedi in fact, Luke Skywalker?"

"No," I snorted. "Not even close."

"You refuse the title yet dress yourself in the trappings. You carry a lightsaber. And you used the Force to aid in the piloting of the ship, correct?"

"Yes," I admitted, wondering where this would lead.

"Astounding. I have never thought of it before, having had no occasion to do so, but the Force must be a fulcrum variable. Yes, I must give this more thought."

"Sorry—a fulcrum variable?"

"A variable around which improbabilities can be turned to probabilities, or vice versa. The impossible becomes possible—at which point one might as well not even do the math. But of course I can't help myself in that regard."

I was relieved that her line of questioning only looped her back into another math trip, but I couldn't resist asking about the path ahead. I still had my doubts about Drusil's value to the Alliance, and her questioning about my connections to the Jedi was disconcerting, but she might prove useful to us in the short term while her interests and ours coincided.

"Listen, since you appear to enjoy it, could you

maybe think about the likelihood of us making it to the surface of Kupoh without running into any more Interdictors—or other Imperial contact? If you think it's improbable, we should abort now and see if we can reach somewhere else, because we can't make another escape like that with an engine gone and nothing to shoot but laser cannons."

Drusil's mouth widened in what I supposed must be joy. She grabbed her datapad and woke it from its sleep. "A task! Excellent! You have my thanks. I will report soon." Her face turned down and I realized that I had just been dismissed.

CHAPTER 15

THE KUPOH SYSTEM WAS BEAUTIFUL in that it was free of any Imperial fleet ships. "This is good. We're going to have to land and make repairs," I said. "The *Jewel* couldn't outrun a bantha right now."

"Do you have someplace in particular in mind?" Nakari asked.

"I will in a minute. Remember that list of Kupohans that Sakhet gave us back on Denon? She probably didn't expect us to wind up on her home planet, but maybe there's a name there we can contact."

"Oh, right! The file we're supposed to decrypt using *Rancor Sauce*. Hang on."

She left the cockpit to retrieve her datapad, and I set a course for a smaller city on the opposite side of the globe from the capital. I'd adjust as necessary—and thanks to the peculiarities of the planet, I was looking forward to the challenges of any adjustments.

Kupoh had achieved a somewhat legendary status among pilots. It was supposed to be constantly buffeted by howling winds—seriously loud, dangerous winds, not gentle breezes—that not only made piloting difficult but also interfered with hearing. So much white noise whipped around on the surface that most offworld beings had to communicate via helmet intercom—either that, or shout. Or use sign language. The Kupohans had evolved their frequency filter organs to screen out all the noise and detect voices, and of course it helped them hunt as well. There was an entire ecosystem of creatures that lived in the wind, animals that rarely if ever landed, spending their entire existence in the air. Pilots had to go in with their shields up or risk taking damage from the larger beasts. And then hope the winds didn't toss them into the ground like poorly flown kites.

Out of necessity the Kupohans had built tall baffles to help pilots land on the surface rather than crash. They had dozens of recommended atmospheric entry points where the wind patterns were merely annoying rather than terrifying, and you had to ride them out until you could drop down behind a mountain range or one of their baffles and settle down. Even then you'd have to worry about rogue gusts and eddies, but they had the approach routes to most places worked out to at least a modicum of safety.

Nakari returned, datapad in hand. "There's a contact here listed in the city of Tonekh on the eastern continent. Name is Azzur Nessin. Hold on a second, let me see if we can bring up some more information." Switching from her datapad to the ship's computer, which could access Kupoh's infonet maintained by satellites and orbital platforms, she typed in a query and growled at a mistake that forced her to delete it and redo, punching the keys and showing that word who was boss.

There was a lag in processing due to the distances involved, but the net worked well and an information dump appeared soon enough. Nakari summarized:

"Azzur Nessin is founder and head of Nessin Courier and Cargo. He has facilities scattered about the planet, but its headquarters matches the location that Sakhet provided in her files."

"All right, we'll head there. Good business to be in for a spy, eh?"

"Yeah. Gives him a legitimate reason to go anywhere."

"And if he has his own fleet, that means he could have his own repair facility." I changed course in accordance with the recommended atmospheric entry point for Tonekh and asked Artoo to attempt to reach Nessin via comm using the number Sakhet had provided. Meanwhile, several different ships in orbit and entities on the ground were trying to reach us, all of them asking for our names and business.

"Inquisitive lot, aren't they?" Nakari remarked after the third time she told someone we were "tourists, here to enjoy Kupoh's windsurfing."

Though the Empire strictly controlled the interstellar HoloNet, the Kupohans had a local system infonet set up almost of necessity to exchange weather information and help ships land safely. We received a call from Azzur Nessin within minutes of Artoo's comm request. He popped up on our holodisplay, a stocky individual wearing a vest, his arms folded across his chest. At some point he'd lost a bite-sized chunk of his left basal ear and had never had it surgically improved. The fur hanging down underneath his jaw was long, braided, and beaded, which struck me as unusual for a Kupohan because it would make distracting noises when he moved. I didn't know if it meant he belonged to a secret society, or if it was a fashion he had chosen to offend society as a whole.

"Yes? What news?" he asked.

"Hello, Azzur," I replied, perhaps taking liberties

by using his first name when we were strangers, but strangers were almost certainly listening in, so we couldn't tell him we were Alliance operatives desperate for help.

"We just came from Denon and tried Sakhet's noodles like you suggested. But you didn't tell me how good her nerf nuggets were! I'd say they're the best in the galaxy."

Azzur Nessin cocked his head to the side; the movement made his mutilated ear more noticeable, and I wondered if he did that on purpose. "Nerf nuggets, eh? I don't suppose you brought me any?"

Sakhet hadn't told us how to respond to additional questions; if it was a test or a code of some kind I didn't know the answer. Maybe it was a roundabout way of asking if our mission had been successful. Deciding to go with that, I said, "Of course! Sakhet made a batch especially for you."

The Kupohan righted his head and showed his teeth in a broad grin. The movement made the braids of his beard sway like vines in a gentle breeze. "Cannot wait. My place of residence has changed since we saw each other last. New coordinates at the end of transmission. See you soon."

His image winked out, replaced by a series of numbers that I asked Artoo to input and execute into the autopilot. They were only slightly different from the course I had already set.

"Oh, and Artoo, since we're going to be limping in there with only one engine, can you give me an estimate of our arrival time?"

Drusil Bephorin replied instantly over the intercom. "Three hours and forty-three minutes, twelve seconds, give or take a few minutes depending on the point that you take manual control and other variables."

"Thanks, Drusil," I said, then added, "We're going

to try to resupply while we're here. Is there anything you want or need to add to the list?"

"My basic needs are being met. I would not want to request anything else that might delay our eventual departure. My primary desire is to be reunited with my family."

"Okay, we'll do our best."

Almost four hours to planetfall would give the Empire time to catch up to us if they knew where to look. It would also give all the spies in the system a nice long look at us, and maybe they'd pause to wonder why we were currently diving toward the planet more like a dead bird than the rich windsurfing tourists in a custom yacht we were pretending to be.

"I'll tell you what I want," I said to Nakari.

"You mean besides another engine?"

"Yeah, besides that. Before the Empire interrupted, I was back in the galley trying to make caf. I could really use it now."

Her eyes flicked down to my tunic. "That first cup looks great on you, Luke. That's some seriously forward-thinking fashion you're wearing."

"Oh, come on—"

"Not everyone can make their spills look like art. Did you use the Force to get that pattern right there?"

"Guess I'll go change while I'm at it."

As I stood, Nakari dropped her teasing manner and said, "Luke? We used up almost all our money getting those upgrades."

"Good thing, too. They did the job for us."

"I know. But how are we going to pay for a new sublight engine? We have some credits to take care of food and such but not nearly enough to finance these repairs. I can't imagine the Alliance is suddenly flush now, even if we could get hold of Admiral Ackbar from here."

"Maybe we could trade a future favor or do a job of some kind for this Azzur Nessin. Not all transactions need to be in cash."

"I don't know. He looked like he was a cash-money kind of operator."

"What makes you say that? The beads in his beard?"

"I thought they might be a clue, yeah. I know you can't see colors well on my cheap holoprojector, but they seemed to me like they might be gold."

"I bet they clack together when he's chewing food. Probably makes all kinds of racket."

She gave a short courtesy laugh and then said, "Be serious."

"All right," I said, leaning against the cockpit hatch and folding my arms in a futile attempt to cover my stained tunic. Nakari turned in her chair to look at me as I spoke. "I think we're in trouble. We can't trust this Azzur Nessin not to sell us out the moment someone from the Empire offers to buy him some more beard beads. And it's not just him we can't trust: It's this whole system. Information is currency, and right now the Empire is offering plenty of credits for information on our whereabouts. You can bet all those people asking us questions have noted that we have three life-forms aboard, and that labels us as an interesting contact already. They'll pry closer for sure. And we can't be a hundred percent sure whose side anybody's on, regardless of what they say"—here I jerked a thumb at the living quarters and rolled my eyes to indicate Drusil, who could still hear me through the open intercom—"but we have no choice but to attempt to complete the mission. Can't go back to the fleet until we do."

"Do you have any ideas about how to convince him to help us?"

"I'm hoping to come up with something before then."

I couldn't think of anything, though. I knew plenty of Alliance secrets, but those weren't for sale. The *Desert Jewel* herself might make us a fair bit of money, enough to trade for another ship, but I couldn't imagine breaking even on any kind of deal like that, much less coming out ahead. We'd never get a ship that could manage the same speed, and I wouldn't dream of suggesting it out loud to Nakari.

After I'd cleaned up and changed, I visited Drusil and Artoo in the living quarters. The Givin was sitting up straight in a meditative position on the top bunk, her long tunic flowing down from her shoulders like draperies. Her datapad lay on top of her crossed legs, but she wasn't using it when I entered. She was staring at the ceiling for some reason—or maybe her eyes were closed, I don't know. Her chin was tilted up, and I got the idea that she was praying or meditating rather than searching for defects in the ship's construction.

"Drusil? Mind if I speak with you?"

Her head dropped and turned, and those black eye sockets regarded me with an unreadable expression.

"If it's convenient," I amended. "I hope I'm not interrupting."

"You are no bother. After our earlier conversation regarding the Force, I have been entertaining myself with cascading probability ladders. I can always return to them later."

"Great," I said, having no idea what she meant. I edged into the room and passed Artoo, patting him on the dome and telling him that I appreciated his work before taking a seat on the lower bunk opposite Drusil. I explained that we needed a new engine and fuel at minimum to leave the planet once we landed on it, and whoever sold them to us would need money or valuable information in exchange for that. Drusil volunteered to share what little she knew of Imperial operations in the sectors surrounding Hutt Space, and I said we'd certainly make the offer, but the Kupohans probably knew much of that already and wouldn't place much value on it.

"I could, perhaps, avail myself of some information in this system," the Givin mused, gesturing at her custom-built hardware. "If our host wishes to raid a particular data cache and rifle through its contents in exchange for an engine, I am confident that I can slice our way to an accommodation."

"You'd be willing to do that?"

"Of course." For once, her voice rang clearly, free of the thickness it usually contained. "I will do whatever needs to be done."

I believed her and felt unnerved, for it had occurred to me that she might have made the same promise to someone else—someone in the Empire. Her long tenure under the "protection" of the Imperial Security Bureau could very well mean she was working for them even now. Leia and Admiral Ackbar hadn't shared with me any details on Drusil's background. How did they know she was legitimately an enemy of the New Order? The ISB could be using her to infiltrate the Alliance.

Our escape from Daalang had me suspicious, as well. How hard had the Empire really been trying? They had certainly seemed intent on killing us at the time, but strategically that cruiser shouldn't have been there by itself. The Empire knew of the Interdictors' vulnerabilities or else they wouldn't habitually surround them with escorts. So why send one in alone this time to pull everything out of hyperspace in the hope of catching us? They might have caught something a whole lot meaner than a single fugitive ship. It reeked of desperation—or a sacrifice.

But a sacrifice to what end? Would the Emperor sacrifice an entire cruiser and all its crew to bolster the credibility of one operative? I didn't know if he was heartless enough to throw away lives like that. Vader probably was, but we hadn't had a whiff of his involvement yet.

I shook my head to clear it. Maybe it was all an elaborate plot and someone had planned their holo-chess moves far ahead of time, but if so, I couldn't see the shape of their attack yet. It was far more likely that the Empire never thought a single ship would have the ordnance or guts to successfully attack an Interdictor solo, and that was it. Then again, Drusil could be playing both sides for some other agenda of her own—she was certainly intelligent enough to do so.

Regardless of the true situation, our best bet was to get the *Jewel* refitted and out of the system as fast as possible. And a tiny twinge of paranoia probably wouldn't go amiss here; the Kupohans weren't quite as renowned for spying as the Bothans were, but for my money they were a close second—or in a way, even better precisely because they *weren't* renowned for something that should be conducted secretly. Their extraordinary hearing made them excellent eaves-droppers, able to catch snippets of whispered conver-sation across a busy cantina by using their sonic filters to isolate the voices they wanted. Rumor had it that Kupohans who trained in law enforcement could iso-late your heartbeat and detect stressors in your voice that betrayed when you were lying. And because it was almost impossible to sneak up on them, they made a game of it, becoming naturally stealthy as they grew up; they would make excellent assassins. Maybe they *were*—so good no one ever caught them at it—but in any case, we would have to assume that anything we said on the planet could be overheard. I reminded Drusil of that because we could easily reveal in an unguarded moment who we were and what we were doing—and that would be valuable information to sell.

I told Artoo to stick close to me while we were on the surface. "Don't ever be alone. Someone could try to mess with you to get at your memory." The droid rocked back and forth on his support arms and chirped and whistled in outrage at the very idea.

"Thanks for your time, Drusil. I'll let you get back to your probable ladders or, uh. Yeah."

The Givin nodded once in reply and tilted her chin at the ceiling before I left the quarters, but her voice called me back.

"Yes?"

"One of the probabilities may interest you. It is almost certain that this ship's system has been remotely sliced since we arrived in this sector."

"What? How?" Artoo added several indignant beeps to that. "Don't you think my droid would have noticed?"

"I imagine he will find something if he looks now." Artoo's socket jack whirred in the computer and his dome light began to wink as he worked. Drusil continued, "It will not be an invasive burst of code. It will behave more like a mynock, attaching itself inconspicuously and going along for the ride. But it will see what you see, know where you go and who you talk to. Were we tourists this would be of little consequence and the information unworthy of trade. However, we are not tourists, are we?"

"No, we're definitely not."

Artoo spat out a long warbling stream of annoyed

chirps and the top of his dome rotated in extreme agitation. I'd have to go back to the cockpit to get a translation of the noise; Nakari was already reading it and her loud reaction sounded unhappy.

"I'll be right back," I said.

Nakari scowled as I ducked my head into the cockpit. "Luke, who could be slicing into the *Jewel*?"

"Hold on, let me see what Artoo said." The message read, MALICIOUS CODE FOUND AND NEUTRAL-IZED. SURVEILLANCE PROGRAM, ORIGIN UNKNOWN. INSERTED RECENTLY.

"It would have been almost as soon as we entered the system and accessed their net," she said. "When I did that search for Azzur Nessin. I can't believe we'd get tagged so fast or so easily."

"Well, we already know that some of them do contract work for the spynet. This is probably their way of saying hello."

"It's rude."

"To them it's business as usual. They probably figure if we can't protect ourselves, then we deserve to be spied on."

"I obviously need to upgrade my firewalls. Lots more fire, I think," she said. "Could it have been Nessin himself who did it? Or one of his employees?"

"Sure." I shrugged. "It could have been almost any-one in the system, though." I jerked my head to indi-cate the living quarters. "I need to get back. Keep an eye on the scanners, and yell if anything develops."

"Yeah, all right."

I was trying not to fall into the trap of conspiracy theories. Once you start looking for them you see them everywhere, but they're usually just mirages, nothing more. And yet this was quite a coincidence. I returned to the quarters, thrust my hands in my pock-ets, and looked up at the Givin.

"You know, Drusil, I think we should talk."

"You say that as if we had not been talking in the very recent past, or as if we are not in fact already talking."

"Sorry, that was sort of a human idiom. I said that to suggest we should talk about matters underneath the surface."

"The surface of what? Oh!" She nodded to herself. "I understand. We have arrived at the time when you search for the politest possible way to accuse me of being an Imperial spy."

"How do you— Do you have equations that predict human behavior?"

"I would be the Emperor if I did. But there is no need. Human faces are expressive, and yours is not a difficult one to interpret. And I can hardly fault you for being suspicious. You do not know me well—or any Givin, I would wager—and I was most recently in the employ of the Empire for an extended period, however unwilling. A certain amount of suspicion is warranted. I take no offense."

"Well, I suppose that's good. I'm glad you're not offended and that you're willing to discuss it so frankly. But I'm not reassured. The invasive code you predicted would be there—and *was* there—could have been placed in the ship's system by you far more easily than by someone else in the system who barely had time to realize we were here."

"You are assuming that someone is manually inserting the code rather than the code existing on the net and executing on an automatic trigger, but as you are speaking of mere possibilities rather than likelihoods, you are correct, Luke Skywalker. I also could have taken over the entire ship whenever I wished, for your security is laughably easy to circumvent. Do you see the flaw in your reasoning? If I had wanted to ensure that we were captured by the Empire, why did I not move more slowly in the sewers on Denon? Or shut down the ship in the Nanth'ri system so that we would be captured by pirates, or disable us in Daalang, and then simply wait for the Empire to pick us up?"

"I never said you wished us to be captured by the Empire."

"Ah. So you believe I have some other goal in mind. What might that be?"

"The theory I favor at the moment is that you want to learn the location of the rebel fleet—that's the only intelligence goal that would justify an elaborate plot like this. By tracking our communications you hope to find out something useful. You're waiting for us to contact Alliance personnel."

Drusil Bephorin nodded. "I see. Your reasoning is sound; the Empire would indeed do almost anything to discover where the rebels are hiding. And if I already know the location of the rebel fleet, would that allay your suspicions about my loyalties?"

My guts turned cold. "Are you posing a hypothetical question about my reaction, or are you saying you actually know the location?"

"I do not know its precise location, but I can make an educated guess based on my insider's knowledge of current Imperial fleet deployments, then subtracting the majority of occupied worlds, and continuing to eliminate other such variables until we arrive at a manageable number. The rebel fleet is in the Outer Rim."

A relieved chuckle escaped my throat. She didn't know anything dangerous. "Of course it is. Everyone knows that. All those unoccupied systems to hide in makes it obvious."

"But a large number of unoccupied systems can be

eliminated through modal reasoning matrices, logistics loop theory, and the high probability that the Alliance would use only known hyperspace routes."

"Uh, you lost me in the middle there."

"Then I shan't dwell on the methodology. But had I wished the rebel fleet discovered, I would have already told the Empire to search the Zaddja, Kowak, or Pantora systems. My analysis points to one of them."

The cold feeling returned. If she had told the Empire that, they would have indeed found the Alliance around Orto Plutonia in the Pantora system. I didn't bother to dispute her analysis. I have no talent for lying; my best option was to keep silent and confirm nothing.

"Your silence is telling, Luke Skywalker."

"Are all Givin capable of analyzing fleet movements the way you are?" I asked. Because if so, the Empire could ask any of them for help. Or coerce them, which was more likely.

"Most are capable of the basic functions, but I hope you will not think it immodest if I proclaim myself to be unusually accomplished in probability theory. It has useful applications in cryptography. And I cannot imagine that anyone else would be privy to the secrets that I was during my ersatz employment with the ISB. I have knowledge of where the Empire has searched and can guess where they will search next with a high degree of probability, since they lack imagination and distrust the power of randomization."

"That would be useful information."

"I will be delighted to share it with you when I am successfully reunited with my family."

"You can predict Imperial fleet movements, but you're keeping it to yourself? Sharing it now could save lives!"

"And if I have nothing to trade, I could lose mine."

I understood her position, but it was frustrating to run up against self-interest when a team effort would serve everyone better. Still, I could press her regarding the math she had willingly taken on earlier. "Did you finish your probability calculation regarding Imperial pursuit before we get to Kupoh?"

"I did. It's possible they will appear but unlikely. We will make it to the surface. Getting off it again without Imperial efforts to find us is much less likely."

I nodded, privately thinking that she might spur those Imperial efforts herself. We were headed to the residence of a Kupohan spy who, if he did not work with the Alliance, was at least referred to us by one that did. Pulling on the thread of Azzur Nessin might unravel quite a bit for the Empire. I would have to make sure Nakari hadn't hooked her datapad into the ship's computer at all, because Drusil—or I supposed anyone else in the system if we were now exposed—would then be able to slice it and access the entire list of contacts given to us by Sakhet.

As if she could read me again, Drusil said, "If I may make a general observation: The problem with conspiracy theories is that they have their own gravity: They are black holes from which one rarely escapes. Caution is advisable at all times, of course, but recognize that sometimes the beings you meet truly are good."

"Noted," I said, and I made an effort to smile. "And I agree. Think of me as cautious."

"I do, and approve."

Nodding once and excusing myself after asking Artoo to continually monitor all systems for data invasions, I returned to the cockpit and caught Nakari up, advising her to keep her datapad isolated and in her possession until we no longer needed that list of contacts.

Drusil's calculations proved accurate again, as we were able to bite into atmosphere and land on Kupoh without active pursuit by anything except the wind.

The "mild" winds of the entry point gave us the most harrowing ride I've ever experienced, though, and I was grateful that the *Desert Jewel* was all one piece and we didn't have to worry about wings shearing off. The descent was a bone-shaking ride even with the benefit of acceleration compensators, and it was still rough going after we dropped behind the first baffle. The chop of the air didn't reduce significantly until after we dipped over a second and third baffle, and then we were guided via Tonekh's traffic control through a sort of slalom of towering stone wind traps, which not only served our purposes but also provided some shelter to the pale grassy flatlands below dotted with herds of pahzik.

Using the *Jewel*'s upmarket scanners, I took a close-up holo of the pahzik because I'd never seen one before. They were broader and shorter than nerfs, coated with a dense mat of black fur, and their horns were strangely aligned on the tops of their heads as if someone had rested a giant scroll on top of them, facing forward. These were supposed to be hollow, allowing the wind to pass through, and by angling their heads into the wind or placing their backs to it they created various sounds to call to others at much greater volume than they could manage with their vocal cords. Since most of the planet was an unbroken windswept plain, the pahzik had plenty of room to roam and multiply, and the Kupohans seemed happy to let them breed, since they were supposed to be delicious.

The wind traps did their job, improving conditions until we had smooth air on our final approach to Tonekh, which, like all the Kupohan cities, was nestled inside a protected mountain valley. To reach it we had to fly through a tunnel bored into the great range of the eastern continent, and when we emerged, we saw the Kupohan city stretched before us, resting in between the peaks as if the buildings had tumbled there after a landslide.

Nessin Courier & Cargo sprawled along one side of Tonekh's busy spaceport, boasting rows of warehouses, hangars, and freighter ports. Our contact had done very well for himself, and we soon discovered that he was not the sort to lounge in an office and take long lunches that consisted mostly of alcohol. Like Fayet Kelen, he took an active role in the daily business of his company.

Uniformed crew and flashing glow panel lights guided us into a vacant space in a large hangar. When we disembarked, the air possessed a mysterious animal tang, like wet dog or feathers on fire. I wasn't sure if it was Kupoh's natural odor or specific to this area— or if it was borne here by the wind. Even in the sheltered confines of the city, the wind whistled and moaned and ruffled our hair, though I suspected the moaning was caused by the passage of air through pahzik horns.

There was a light freighter under repair in the berth next to ours, and I noticed that the crew was not entirely Kupohan, but of mixed species. One of them was a Wookiee, which made me miss Chewbacca. Azzur Nessin was waiting for us at the bottom of the *Jewel*'s loading ramp, dressed in the same gray-and-green uniform as all the other workers.

That's not to say he displayed no hint of his elevated status. In addition to the earrings on his basal ears, his beard beads turned out to be gold, as we'd suspected, and his braided strands swung and clacked together like an abacus when he spoke. It was a mesmerizing display, and I gradually became aware that it was purposeful. One became so absorbed in his

animated chin fur that his other movements went
largely unnoticed—such as the discreet tapping of
his finger against a miniature datapad strapped to
the inside of his left arm, or the way his gaze would
lose focus briefly as his attention fixed on something
scrolling past a display lens he had suspended over
two of his four eyes. He hadn't been wearing that
when we spoke via holo, but now he was obviously
dividing his attention.

"Welcome to Kupoh, friends. If you are fond of
Sakhet's noodles, you might also enjoy something I
can provide for you. How may I please you today?"

He wasn't running any kind of restaurant here, so
his phrasing was peculiar. I wondered when or even if
we would begin to speak plainly about who we were
and how we had come to be there. Were we being
observed by unfriendly eyes even now? I decided we
didn't have time for roundabout speech and baldly
stated what we had come for.

"We need to refuel, rearm with six concussion missiles, and we also need to either repair or replace one
of our sublight engines, depending on the damage."

"The first two items should be no trouble," he said,
already moving to the back of the ship and speaking
as he walked and typed, "but engine damage may
require some time to remedy—days or even weeks,
depending on specifics—and, of course, significant resources. Let us see what needs to be done."

He made a whistling noise that secured the attention of a uniformed mechanic who detached himself
from the light freighter detail and came over to exam-
ine our ship. He was also Kupohan, but he only had
two neck torcs, a single earring on his basal ear, and
an entirely ordinary beard. Azzur introduced him
as Ruuf Waluuk. He greeted us amiably, but it quickly
became clear that Ruuf's expertise would not be needed;

the engine was a total loss, half melted to slag by that last TIE fighter that had chased us out of Daalang.

"Inconvenient" was the sum of Azzur's commentary on the subject. "What kind of engine is it?" Nakari told him and he tapped out a search on his datapad and waited for results. All four eyes blinked when the information came in. "That is—or was—an outstanding engine. Unfortunately, there aren't any of those available on the planet." He shook his head and set his beads knocking together. "It is the curse of beautiful custom ships, yes? They are superior to all other ships until it comes time to repair one. We could order that engine offworld, but I am unsure if you have the luxury of time to wait for it."

"We don't," Nakari confirmed.

"Then we must choose an available substitute. Your ship will not be as fast, of course, and you will lose efficiency as your system compensates for thrust differentials."

"It'll still be faster than flying on a single engine," Nakari said. "Tell me about our options."

"Certainly. If you will follow me, I have a holotable where I can display specs for you." He led us past the light freighter to a suite of administrative offices. I noticed that the hangar was equipped with several offices on one side; on the other, near the *Jewel*, was a kitchen and dining area for the crew's break time, along with restrooms and lockers.

As soon as the door closed behind us, Azzur Nessin's facade of polite professionalism sloughed off to reveal a snarling Kupohan. He rounded on us and curled his hands into fists at his sides. "I don't know who you are, but you had better not be bringing the Empire behind you! Tell me true: Do I have to worry about stormtroopers coming in here and burning down my life around me?"

"Maybe," Nakari replied, "but how is that different from any other day in the galaxy? The Empire will be there until we destroy it."

"I know they could come for me anytime," Azzur growled, "but rebel spies are more likely to bring them sooner rather than later. That engine didn't melt down spontaneously, and I'm assuming you launched your six concussion missiles at someone."

Nakari matched his tone. "Hey, we don't want to be here, either. If we had a choice we wouldn't be, but Sakhet gave us your name in case we needed it and she said you'd help us. So will you help us, or was her faith in you misplaced?"

Azzur snorted in derision. "She doesn't have faith in me. She knows I hate the Empire and that is all."

"So we shouldn't put our faith in you?"

"Definitely not. But I do hate the Empire and I like money. You can trust in that. Can I trust that you have money?"

"No."

The Kupohan said nothing for a few seconds, tension building as his face twitched, his ears flattened, and he stared at Nakari in disbelief. Finally, he exploded. "Then why are you here? You expect me to furnish an engine for free?"

"We have information. The lucrative kind."

Azzur visibly calmed, his primary ears returning to their customary position. "Oh, then that's different. You could have said so before I lost my temper. What is the nature of this information?"

Drusil offered up her knowledge of Imperial maneuvers outside of Hutt Space first, and when Azzur inquired as to how she came to possess this intelligence, the answer renewed his agitation. "You're the ones, aren't you—the ones they have a bounty on! Half the galaxy is looking for you, and you fly into my hangar!"

"The information's good, though," Nakari said.

"It's the worst kind!" He pointed a rude, thick finger at Drusil. "If I sell anything that this particular Givin woman knows, then the Empire will come ask me where I got it! I can't risk it, I'm sorry." His finger flew across his miniature datapad keyboard. "As it is, I have to send my family away on an emergency vacation so that there's an outside chance of their survival. If I ever see Sakhet again, I'm going to kick her kneecaps backward. Because you know my whole crew out there saw you and your ship. If any of them figured out who you are, your presence here could already be sold to the Empire."

"How likely is it that mechanics are information dealers?" Drusil asked.

"I don't know. I don't spy on my employees—there's no money in it."

"Out of curiosity," Nakari said, "how much money is on us? I mean in giving us up—what's the bounty?"

Azzur had the grace to look uncomfortable speaking of us as commodities. He sniffed, shrugged, and avoided specifics: "There's a goodly sum for information leading to the capture of the Givin, but a much greater one for directly delivering her to the Empire."

"Really goodly, then?" Nakari asked, her tone solicitous but clearly mocking.

"There is another alternative," Drusil said. "I am an excellent slicer and cryptographer; indeed, that is why I am so closely pursued by the Empire. Should you wish to acquire any data available here on Kupoh, I am almost certain I can procure it."

Azzur Nessin began to shake his head before Drusil even finished. "No, no, no. I am an honest businessperson."

"You're also a spy and trade in secrets all the time!" Nakari pointed out.

"I *trade* in secrets, yes—there is a certain commerce there and mutual consent to the exchange. I do not steal secrets, nor do I extort them or do anything but provide value for value, lest I dishonor my family and lose one or more of these." A finger drifted up to point at his status earrings. "So while I thank you for the offer, I must decline. What else do you have that might offset the expense of an engine?"

Silence stretched and took up all the space in the room, and Nessin waited. His beard beads remained perfectly still, gleaming and predatory like a cat before it pounces.

"Have you heard of Kelen Biolabs based on Pasher?" Nakari asked, her voice pitched low and dull with defeat.

"Yes, of course. A vastly profitable enterprise."

"I am Nakari Kelen, daughter of Fayet Kelen. I can provide you with firsthand knowledge of what my father called 'the most significant biological find in decades' and furnish coordinates to find the source."

"Nakari, what are you doing?" I said.

"Getting us an engine," she replied.

Azzur Nessin narrowed his eyes, flattened his ears against his skull, and reared back. "What is this? You expect me to believe the heir to Kelen Biolabs conducts espionage operations for the Alliance?"

"I expect you can independently verify my identity with that datapad strapped to your arm. And rumor has it that Kupohans can hear the ring of truth in human voices anyway. The question is whether such information will earn us what we need."

"I imagine so, if it is truly the best discovery in decades."

"My father knows his business and likes money just

as much as you do, sir. When he says the development potential is vast, you may rely upon it."

"You say you have firsthand knowledge of this . . . discovery? A planet?"

"A moon. And yes, we have been there. So far, fewer than ten beings have set foot on the surface, almost all of them in the employ of my father."

Azzur Nessin turned his gaze to me. "And who are you, exactly?"

"He's my pilot," Nakari said before I could answer. It was the truth, if not all of it, and Nessin responded by turning his gaze back to Nakari, his ears twitching in agitation. Deciding to drop the question of my identity—for which I was relieved, since I doubted that my name would ease his worries—Nessin pursued a different line of questioning.

"Why would you sell this information and betray your father?" I thought that was an excellent question. I wanted to hear the answer to that myself.

"It's not a betrayal. He gave me full permission to deal his business a setback in an emergency, and since we can't expect to complete our mission without an engine, I believe this qualifies. And it's not like he owns that moon or exclusive rights to exploit it. It was inevitable that other people would find out about it eventually. It might as well be now, when we can profit by it." She hooked a thumb back at Drusil, adding, "And when the Empire can lose a valuable resource in the process. My father hates the Empire, too, you know. He'd gladly give up all the profits of this moon if it means a victory for the Alliance. And my survival." She tacked on a wry smile at the end of this. Azzur Nessin's ears continued to twitch for a few seconds, and I saw some movement of the gilled fins inside his frequency filters—he was probably listening for irregular heartbeats or stressed breathing, indicators of dishonesty, and finally he nodded once, curtly, which set his beads clapping together as if in approval of a bargain made.

"Very well. Provide me the details. I will sell the information immediately and order you an engine of your choosing, together with the concussion missiles and the fuel you need."

Nakari pushed back a little. "We will keep the coordinates in reserve until you have a buyer."

Nessin had no problem with that. "Of course."

"Begging your pardons," Drusil said, "but assuming a buyer is found quickly, how long will it be until the engine can be installed? I wish to know the earliest possible time we may resume our journey."

"It will be a few days, even if I order one this instant," Nessin replied. "But it could conceivably be weeks. It all depends on how fast I can find a buyer."

The Givin's shoulders visibly slumped. "I see. Thank you for your candor."

"I assure you I'll move as quickly as I can. In the meantime," the Kupohan said, "I will find you some discreet lodging. And I think it might be a good time to begin spying on my employees."

"I thought you said there's no money in it," I said.

"There isn't. I want to make sure there's no Empire in it, either, until you're gone."

"I might be able to render assistance in that regard," Drusil said, pulling her custom hardware out of her carry-sack. "If you provide me the names of your crew, I will effectively block their access to the Empire until we leave."

"How? You're just going to cut them off from the 'Net?"

"No, nothing so crude. I will reroute all their messages to a temporary account where we may screen it first before allowing it to pass on."

"What about holocalls?"

"A mysterious outage in service will plague them for a brief time."

Nessin flicked his gaze to Nakari. "Can she really do that?"

Nakari shrugged. "Think of the goodly sum the Empire is offering to recapture her and you tell me."

"Very well," he said, "I suppose I can trust you in this, since your self-interest and mine coincide." Once he gave Drusil the names and received assurance that he would get regular reports from her, he clapped his hands together and sank into a plush office chair behind his hardwood desk. "Now," he almost purred, gesturing to some other, less comfortable chairs across from him that we had ignored until now. "Please be seated and tell me more about this fascinating moon."

CHAPTER 16

AFTER HIS BRIEFING, Azzur Nessin felt sure he could monetize Nakari's information about Fex—brainsucking skullborers and all—and allowed us to pick the fastest engine available on the planet that would fit the *Jewel*.

"The engine won't get here for a couple of days at least and you must be exhausted," he said. "Let's get you a place to lie low while this gets sorted out. I will be in touch."

We ducked back into the ship to get hooded cloaks before departing to a hotel near the spaceport. I worried that Artoo was probably recognizable, but he could plausibly be any astromech droid of his series and not necessarily the one involved in the operation on Denon.

Utterly exhausted after a day that began in another part of the galaxy, I fell asleep almost as soon as I crashed onto the bed. After a night's well-earned sleep, we ordered room service and ate together in my room. We thought it wiser than showing our faces in the hotel's buffet—or anywhere.

Drusil hadn't slept much; she'd spent most of the

night slicing into the accounts of Azzur Nessin's employees.

"The Wookiee was completely clean," she reported, "as one might expect. They are not a species prone to sympathizing with a regime that commonly enslaves them. Another of the mechanics, a Duros, supplements his income by selling powdered pahzik horn offplanet as an aphrodisiac, but otherwise has no interest regarding us. The other two may present problems."

"Which two are they?" Nakari asked.

"Ruuf Waluuk and Migg Birkhit—both Kupohans." Glancing across the hangar at the light freighter next to the *Desert Jewel*, I noted that neither of the Kupohans was there; only the Wookiee and the Duros had shown up for work today. Drusil continued, "I was able to stifle the initial efforts of the former, but unfortunately the latter got off some communication to the Empire before I could interfere."

"What kind of communication?"

"A general insistence that we are somewhere on Kupoh and he might be able to narrow down the search and point them in the right direction for a fee. He didn't give our precise whereabouts, but the Empire is capable of tracing his transmission to this city and presumably to his place of work. I erased the file, but they could have read it and acted before I did so."

"Acted how?"

"They may be en route even now, looking for Migg Birkhit and additional details. Or they may have contacted confederates already on the planet. They may have reached him already."

Nakari cursed. "We can't stay, then."

"We have no place else to go," I pointed out. "And leaving now before we get repairs will only cause the rest of the crew to get suspicious. It would be better and simpler if Migg Birkhit wasn't around to be questioned when the Empire comes looking for him."

"So you're saying we should make him disappear?"

"Temporarily," I said. "Not permanently. Maybe a couple of days tied up in a hotel room. He can be Azzur Nessin's problem after that."

"And if the Empire's already found him?"

"We may have to resort to permanent disappearing if that's the case—but only because he'll probably be shooting at us along with Imperial troops."

The Givin shook her head. "I doubt a single unconfirmed message would mobilize troops. More likely it will mobilize an investigator or a lazy electronic request for more information. I will intercept any messages sent to Migg and Ruuf, of course, but I cannot control his personal interactions."

"That gives us a project for the day, I guess," Nakari said. "Can't do anything without the replacement engine and we'd have to hide out in our rooms instead. Actually, Drusil, that's probably what you should do in any case. Any Givin seen on the street right now might draw more curiosity than we want."

"I have no objections," she replied. "I need to monitor communications in any case. But what will you do?"

"We'll go looking for Migg Birkhit," I said.

Nakari frowned. "Look where?"

"His house first," I said. "I bet Drusil already has his address." She nodded. "Failing that, we'll check the local cantinas."

"You mean the places where anyone would sell us out for a drink?"

"We can go in disguise underneath our hoods. Should be fine."

"The investigator could be almost anyone," Drusil

cautioned. "The ISB won't advertise themselves by wearing a uniform."

"We'll be careful."

"Will you also try to discover if the Alliance successfully extracted my family?"

"Yeah, we'll look into it. We have a dead drop on the planet. Not sure if we'll get an answer before we leave, but it's worth a try."

Drusil gave us Migg Birkhit's address and we walked her to her room. We left her with strict instructions not to open her door for anyone unless they used a passphrase.

"Oh! Can I give you one?" Drusil asked as we stood in the hallway and she stood at the threshold. Her mouth stayed open a little bit, and that might have signaled a smile. Since she seemed excited about it, I said sure, but before she could speak, I motioned us into her room and then shut the door in an attempt to keep us from being overheard. There hadn't been anyone in the hallway, but you couldn't be too careful on Kupoh. I suggested she keep her voice down before giving it to us.

"Excellent," Drusil said in a whisper. "Knock however you wish and then say, $(p + l)(a + n) = pa + pn + la + ln$." She left her mouth open a bit wider this time, expectant, but I didn't know why.

"Okay, that's a little long for a passphrase, but we'll do that."

Her mouth closed. "Wait. Don't you get it?"

"Get what?"

"I foiled your plan!" At our blank looks, the Givin's head drooped and stared at the floor. "Oldest joke in the galaxy and it's completely wasted on humans. I miss my husband." She pressed a button on the wall and the door slid open behind us in a clear invitation to exit.

Once we were out in the hall, Nakari snorted. "I get it now. It's a basic algebra thing. You have to picture it written down in High Galactic instead of listening to it. She must think we're unforgivably slow."

"I guess we are in that area. But you and I have other redeeming qualities."

"Oh, you mean our cooking skills?"

I snorted. "No, definitely not that."

Plugging Artoo into a public terminal and using him to encrypt our message, we requested an operational update on Drusil's family and left it in an Alliance onetime account, setting up another one for a reply. If the Alliance was on alert here, we'd hear back. We then did what we could to disguise our appearance and hailed a droid taxi to take us to Migg Birkhit's address.

It was a short ride through the streets of Tonekh to a slum, where Birkhit's home turned out to be a boxlike economy space crammed into a large cube of similar spaces. The block of apartments had probably gleamed at one time, but that was long past and it now possessed a lived-in look, except the people here obviously lived with sickness, addiction, and despair. No children playing outside, just hooded figures like us, loitering, watching, hiding intentions as well as identities. It was little wonder that Birkhit would jump at the chance to buy himself a better life.

"I guess a ship mechanic doesn't make much here," Nakari said.

"Maybe not, but it shouldn't be this bad," I said. "He might have gambling debts or a checkered past."

We felt eyes on us as we moved to Birkhit's door and pressed the visitor chime. The console politely informed us that the room was currently unoccupied.

"That was a waste of time," Nakari said.

"Well, we know he's not missing work due to illness. Had to eliminate that as a possibility." Turning around, I met several dark hooded stares that mirrored my own. "And he'll be told someone is looking for him if he comes back." I knew that the Kupohans could hear me say that just fine, even though I didn't raise my voice.

We visited two stale and smoky cantinas next where no one had ever heard of Migg Birkhit, but if we needed some information on Azzur Nessin we could have had it for a price. At the third cantina, the bartender had heard of Migg and was willing to tell us where he spent most of his time for "a small consideration." We accepted, paid him, and he directed us to a fourth cantina that was only a kilometer away. We decided to walk, since the wind was mild and the sun was out, and the outdoor market in the district promised a journey surrounded by colorful stalls and loud sales calls.

"You know, if we weren't on a mission, I'd really enjoy this," Nakari half shouted in the wind. "I might be getting used to the smell, whatever it is. You think it's the pahzik?"

"That's a good guess."

"It's kind of nice in a way—I mean the strangeness of an alien world when you're not worried about anything but experiencing it."

I agreed. Traveling through the galaxy would be perfectly pleasant were it not for the Empire trying to kill us.

We'd never gotten a really good look at Migg Birkhit back at the hangar, so as we approached his alleged favorite spot I wondered how we'd recognize him.

Turned out he made it easy for us; he walked out of the cantina wearing his gray-and-green Nessin Courier uniform when we were still twenty paces away. Unfortunately, he recognized us, too—even though we were somewhat disguised, we stuck out a little in Tonekh as two humans. Hoods and robes were great for concealing details, but they couldn't hide the fact that we weren't built like Kupohans and didn't move like them. And it was tough to confuse us with other humans when there were so few others around in the local area; most offworlders stuck to the vicinity of the spaceport, and we were deep in the native part of town. With a snarled curse, Migg bolted around the corner and we gave chase, Artoo blatting a stream of noises that probably asked us to wait for him.

I discovered in the space of five steps that Nakari was a much faster runner; she was taller and had a longer stride than me, but she was also in outstanding shape. She was faster than Migg, too; before he could escape the alleyway and lose us in another crowded market street, Nakari pulled out her blaster and stunned him.

She turned to me, licked her finger, and made an imaginary tally mark in the air. "Chalk up one Imperial snitch for me. He won't be talking to anyone now."

"Good job. Shall we take him out to the street, pretend he's a drunk friend coming out of the cantina, and get a droid taxi back to the hotel?"

"Yeah, sounds good."

We hoisted Birkhit up between us, Nakari on his left and me on the right, an arm draped over each of our shoulders, letting his feet drag behind.

A chirp sounded from up ahead. When I looked up the alley to locate Artoo, I saw that he was coming, but another figure strode with purpose in front of him. It was a Gotal with sienna skin and yellow eyes, thick brows supporting the sensitive horns that allowed his species to detect electromagnetic fields of all kinds. It made them excellent hunters, empathic to some extent with many species, and dangerous in confrontations, since they often sensed what you were planning to do before you did it. Han had warned me that many of them sympathized with the Empire.

"Excuse me," the Gotal said. "That's my friend you have there. I was just about to meet him when he ran down this alley."

"He's our friend, too," Nakari said, smooth and smiling. "Poor Migg had a few too many drinks and ran back here to be sick. We're taking him home."

"He's not unconscious from drinking," the Gotal said, gesturing at his horns with a thumb. "I can tell. He's been stunned. And you stunned him."

Nonplussed, Nakari said, "Whatever, friend. He still needs to be taken home. You want to come along?"

"No, I want you to let him go and tell me where the Givin woman is."

"What are you talking about?" Nakari asked, exasperation in every word. But she lifted Migg's arm and ducked her head to obey at least the first part of it, while with her right hand, hidden behind Migg, she pulled out her blaster.

She never got a shot off, though. Moving far faster than I expected, the Gotal's left leg whipped out in a straight kick aimed at the side of Nakari's midsection, and it knocked the blaster out of her hand just as she was squeezing it between her body and Migg's to target the Gotal. As she staggered backward, Migg's entire weight dragged on my left side, and without replanting his foot, our attacker cocked his leg back at the knee, pivoted slightly, and kicked at my face. He connected and I supposed I should be grateful he hadn't stepped into the kick: My nose remained unbroken and I kept my teeth, but the impact dropped me—and Migg—to the ground.

Nakari lunged forward, weaponless, and I heard more than saw blows being traded, smacks of fists on flesh, and grunts of pain and exertion. Rolling over and pushing myself onto unsteady feet, I managed to stand just as Nakari fell, her legs swept out from under her by the Gotal. He wasn't in immediate kicking distance this time—he'd have to reset and take a few steps to get into range—and I remembered that I had a blaster. Couldn't remember if I had set it to stun, though. He had a blaster, too, and he was remembering that at the same time I was.

R2-D2 had an arm capable of delivering an electric shock, and the Gotal never saw the strike coming from behind, having forgotten about the random droid he'd passed in the alley and probably never expecting a droid to get involved. He screamed and clutched at his horns, which due to their electric sensitivity made such shocks doubly painful, and collapsed twitching to the ground until he subsided, carried off into oblivion for a while.

I breathed a sigh of relief. "Thanks, Artoo." I wasn't sure I would have beaten him to the draw.

"You all right?" Nakari asked, rising and knocking dust from her pants.

"I'm a bit woozy and I think I'll be bruised and sore, but otherwise okay. You?"

"Some bruises for sure. That," she said, pointing at the Gotal, "is a dangerous individual. Coming at us like that barehanded, with complete confidence? Crazy."

"He had good reason to be confident. We weren't doing so well."

"We have to take him with us. You heard him ask about the Givin."

"Yes, you're right. The story will be the same to any passerby—we just have two drunk friends we're escorting from the cantina back to our hotel."

We lugged Migg and the Gotal up the alley to the cantina entrance, making sure our hoods were back in place, and Artoo summoned a droid taxi to take us back to the hotel. We got a few stares, but no one wanted to make our business theirs. Since it was only a short distance to the hotel, we were able to get our captives up to my room and stretched out on the large bed before they began to stir. Nakari promptly stunned them again.

"We need something to bind them," she said. "And a guard."

"Right. Be back soon."

The hotel concierge was a silver protocol droid to which someone had hilariously applied a fake mustache. I made sure to keep my hood lowered to prevent him scanning my face for later download and pitched my voice higher than normal to ask his help.

"Say, do people around here enjoy mountain climbing?"

The droid whirred and clicked before answering. "Absolutely, sir, it is quite the popular pastime in Tonekh. Would you like some directions to nearby cliffs?"

"No, I know where I want to climb, but I'm a little low on supplies. Might you know where I can find ropes, rock hammers, that kind of thing?"

"Certainly, sir." He gave me the address of a specialty vendor, and I hired one more taxi to take me there. The rope I bought wouldn't be foolproof binding, of course, but I could hardly ask the concierge where to buy stun cuffs without raising suspicion. I bought four coils along with some lunch and returned to find our prisoners conscious but lying very still, since Nakari and Artoo both had weapons pointed at them.

"What did I miss?" I asked.

"Nothing. I told them to be quiet until you got back or I'd stun them again."

"Great. I'm here now. Hello," I said to the Gotal, "we haven't been formally introduced. Who might you be?"

The Gotal said, "You have made a huge mistake. I'm not some info sleek to be rolled over."

"Do tell."

"I'm an agent of the New Order. When I don't report in, the Empire will come looking for me, and when they do they'll find you."

"I don't think you're all that important," Nakari said. "We know all the Imperial agents in the area, and I don't remember seeing a Gotal on the list." That was a lie so casually told that I almost believed it myself.

The Gotal sneered at her. "I'm not with fleet security. I'm with the ISB."

Nakari narrowed her eyes at him and then looked at me, her cool mask of control slipping into uncertainty. "The ISB list we have isn't sorted by species. He might be telling the truth."

I shrugged, playing along with this charade of lists. "It's possible."

"What's your name?" Nakari asked.

"Barrisk Favvin."

"That's the name you use with the ISB?"

"Yes. And the ISB is waiting for my report. Let me go and I'll make sure they treat you well once you are captured."

Ignoring him, Nakari turned to me and said, "Will you check his name against our list?"

"Sure thing," I replied, and exited the room to go visit Drusil across the hall. Instead of trying to remember the equation she'd given me earlier, I just knocked and said, "I foiled your plan," and she let me enter.

"Luke Skywalker. Your face is contused. Did you not capture Migg Birkhit?"

"We did. We also have a Gotal in my room who claims to be an ISB agent. Caught him trying to meet up with Migg. His name is Barrisk Favvin. Any way to figure out if he's an informant?"

"Let us see." Moving to her custom hardware, Drusil tapped a series of commands at her keyboard and stared at the results. She repeated the process several times before finally saying, "Yes, he is. Dispatched to meet with Migg Birkhit and investigate his claims, which means they saw that message after all. His orders are to report as soon as he knows anything."

"So he's not supposed to report on a schedule?"

"I'm in his personal files and looking at the orders from his superior. There is nothing about a schedule here."

So he had lied about that. "That's perfect. We can just hold on to him and the Empire won't pursue it. But keep monitoring that account. If you get any queries on his progress, tell the Empire that Birkhit is currently unavailable and you—or he—will report as soon as you have solid information one way or the other."

"Should we not simply say that Birkhit's information is faulty?"

"No, because then the ISB will reassign Barrisk and we want them to think he's occupied for a couple of days. We are just delaying them, so we tell them that Favvin is following leads or confirming suspicions, but nothing specific."

"Understood."

Returning to my room, I let Nakari know that Favvin was indeed ISB but we didn't have to worry about scheduled reports. "Basically we can hold on to him here."

"So you *are* the fugitives!" he said. "Where's the Givin?"

"Elsewhere," Nakari said, and then she stunned them both so that we could bind them easily. We tied up their wrists and ankles and enjoyed lunch together while we waited for them to wake up again. I recruited Artoo to be their sentry, since I didn't especially want to spend any length of time in the same room with an ISB agent, and neither did Nakari. I had no desire to kill him, but it didn't seem wise to let him see or hear anything more about us than absolutely necessary, and we didn't want to listen to an endless stream of threats and Imperial propaganda, either.

Hotel rooms aren't ideal prisons, but knotted ropes can make decent restraints and a tireless droid capable of delivering electric shocks makes a pretty good guard.

"Don't complain too loudly, guys," Nakari told them when they woke to find themselves bound. "You each get a soft bed, we'll bring you food, and you can watch whatever entertainment holos you want. Try to move from the bed or call for help and the droid will knock you out. If you need to use the bathroom, tell the droid and he will contact us via comm. Behave and you'll be alive and free in a few days. And if you want a beating at the end to make it look to your superiors like you didn't enjoy yourselves, I'll be happy to administer one." She smiled winningly. "All you have to do is ask."

THERE WAS A TIME WHEN I thought of war as an exciting prospect and maybe even desirable—compared with the unrelenting dullness of my early life on Tatooine, almost anything else was attractive. But I have discovered since then that there is precious little comfort to be had by anyone during war; the constant stress and loss of friends is like getting lost in the dunes of my homeworld, slowly drying up the tissues of your life until all that remains is a crispy shell of a person. But sometimes—I should say, very rarely, but it happens—you encounter a range of rocks in the sand, and hidden away somewhere among the crags is a spring nestled in a crevice, a lifesaving oasis that is all the sweeter for its unexpected appearance.

Nakari was like that.

After isolating the threat represented by Migg Birkhit and Barrisk Favvin, we had an afternoon and evening of free time until the new engine arrived the next day, and Nakari surprised me by inviting me to relax in her room, a suite with a couch and table and a holoprojector. I accepted, and an afternoon of trading stories about the desert extended into a dinner of room-service pahzik meat, which was in my opinion tastier than nerf and a significant point in Kupoh's favor. At some point about halfway through the meal she laughed about something and her smile was so charming that I forgot not to stare and she caught me again—she literally had to snap me out of it.

"Hey." *Snap*. "Hey." *Snap*.

"What?"

"If you're looking for your food, Luke, it's down there in front of you," she said, pointing with her fork.

"Sorry," I said, dropping my head and feeling the heat rush into my face, trying to think of a time when I'd felt more embarrassed and coming up with nothing.

She chuckled softly. "You're not what I expected, you know," she said, and waited until I looked up. Seeing my raised eyebrow, she reassured me with a nod. "That's a good thing. You weren't what I pictured from the very first moment we met on the *Patience*."

"You had a mental picture of me before we met?"

"Well, yeah! You hear about someone blowing up the Death Star—someone painted as a hero of the Alliance—and you think, *That kid's head is probably so swelled it has its own gravity by now.* Or you think someone like that is all about duty and righteousness and wears super-tight underwear. No sense of humor, you know. Because when they prop up someone as a hero they're not promoting you as a real person: You're this ideal of political zealotry."

Simultaneously amused and horrified, I said, "So in your head I was a stuck-up ideologue with no room in my shorts?"

She gave an embarrassed laugh. "Maybe something like that, yeah."

"Wow. I've never been so glad to defy expectations."

"I'm glad to be proven wrong."

Thinking of the aftermath of Yavin, I sighed, dinner forgotten. "If I'm honest, though, I probably did let it go to my head for a while."

"Ah, so I just caught you at a good time?"

"Kind of. I mean, have you ever looked back at who you were two years ago or even six months ago and shook your head at how stupid you were back then?"

Her expression brightened in recognition. "Yeah! I know that feeling. And you want to go back in time, armed with what you know now, and tell her how it is."

"Exactly! Two years ago I thought I'd never escape Tatooine and I complained about everything." I grimaced at the memory of how I'd behaved. "I'd definitely have some things to tell that kid now. And then everything changed. I met a Jedi, joined the Rebellion, and almost instantly had this tremendous success. I saved a princess and blew up a superweapon, got a medal from the same princess, fireworks in my honor and everything. That could turn your head into a planet really fast."

"Mm-hmm."

I thought that was just a polite noise and my cue to continue, but Nakari drummed her fingers on the table to stop me and then asked a dangerous question couched in a coo. "Tell me, Luke, am I mistaken in thinking you have feelings for that princess? Because I thought I heard a note of yearning there."

My eyes shifted to her face and found hers waiting, studying my expression carefully. After a couple seconds of terror, I remembered a widely held policy about honesty and how it was probably for the best.

"No, you're not entirely mistaken," I said. "But we're just friends."

"Uh-uh, pilot, that's not going to fly. I'm talking about what you *want*, not what you *are*."

I couldn't believe the conversation had gotten this uncomfortable this quickly. I wasn't any sort of expert on relationships, but I felt certain that I had already said too much, and it was unwise to speak to one person about your desire for another. Honesty, I reflected, might not always be the best policy. Sometimes you need to take evasive action.

"I think it doesn't matter what I want. I'm a farmboy and she's a princess. Being her friend is about all I can hope for."

Nakari shook her head slowly as she spoke, not letting me get away. "She's not all that inaccessible for you. You're not a farmboy anymore."

"All right, maybe I'm not, but she's never shown any interest in me beyond friendship and what I can do for the Alliance. I hope we're not going to fight about her."

Nakari's eyes hardened and her lips pressed together in a thin line. "Hopes are fragile things, Luke. Especially right now. Because it sounds like who you want and who you're with are different people."

For a fleeting half second I was elated that she thought I was *with* her, but I squashed that feeling because that might not be her thought for much longer. "No, that's not it at all. Why are you angry? You asked if there was a note of yearning and I was honest and admitted one, but it's nothing beyond that."

Nakari held up her good hand to quell any further words and then used it to pinch the bridge of her nose as she shut her eyes and took a deep breath. After she exhaled, her hand dropped away and her eyes opened. "Honesty is usually good, Luke, you're right. But sometimes it's not what people want to hear."

"Oh. Well, I wish I could go back to the Luke of two minutes ago and tell him how it is."

Much to my relief, she snorted and her mouth split in a wide smile. "Don't be too hard on him. His first impulse there was a good one."

Allowing myself a cautious grin, I said, "All right, I'll go easy on him. But I do apologize for encouraging any doubts with my honesty. The honest truth you should remember is that I'm glad we met."

"Attaboy," she said, encouraging me. "You bring me the sugar now. Go on."

It took me a moment to realize she was speaking metaphorically, but I was glad I caught myself before I moved to search for a sugar packet in the hotel room. "Right. Sugar. Well, you are so . . ."

"I'm so what, Luke? Don't stop now."

"So . . . how do people do this? Everything I can think of to say sounds trite and insincere in my head."

"Don't worry. You just earned all these sincerity points with the too-much-honesty thing. That's not saying you shouldn't strive to be original; I'm just saying that if you blurt out something I've heard before, I might believe you."

"Ah, but no pressure, right?"

She winked. "Right."

"Well, actually, that's something I really admire about you. No pressure."

Nakari narrowed her eyes. "You sure this is sugar?"

"Definitely. I guess this is a roundabout compliment, but I'm going for originality."

"All right, dazzle me."

"Well, I don't feel the crushing weight of your expectations. I mean you had them—you just shared them with me—but I never would have known unless you said something. And believe me, that's refreshing. Important."

Nakari prodded me to clarify. "Important how?"

I struggled to find the right words. "Ever since the Battle of Yavin, I feel sometimes that people expect me to top it and wonder why I haven't yet. What I feel from you is *encouragement* to top it—which is very different—and rare." The other person who habitually encouraged me was Leia, but I thought it best not to elaborate on that.

Nakari leaned back in her chair. "Whoa. I'm not encouraging you to top the Death Star thing."

"I know—that probably didn't come out right. Let me try again. The secret about the Battle of Yavin was that I succeeded because of the Force, so to me, topping what I did there doesn't mean a bigger explosion or killing more stormtroopers. It means taking another step along the path to becoming a Jedi. And I've made more progress in the Force since I met you than any other time after I lost Ben. I actually have hope that I can learn to use it now and it's because of your encouragement . . . So, you see, you're . . ." I flailed for some kind of original phrasing and nothing came to mind. Panicked that I would clam up and let loose another awkward silence into the world, I finished up with a simple fact: ". . . You're good for me."

Nakari waited a few beats to make sure I was finished. "Hmm. That was some pretty complex sugar," she said, her mouth teasing up to the left, "but you wrapped it and put a neat little bow on it at the end." She leaned forward again, pushed her plate out of the way, and propped an elbow on the table, resting her cheek against her good hand. Her half smile bloomed into a wide one. "That wasn't bad, Luke. Full points."

I felt giddy and exhausted at the same time, the way you feel after a narrow escape from death. I was glad she didn't seem intent on fanning the flames of jealousy. I didn't doubt for a second that she still thought of Leia as competition, but at least for the moment she was content to let it slide. And I had better not push my luck any further. Having negotiated one minefield successfully, I'd be a fool to step back in and dance around.

Reaching across the table to snag her plate, I placed it on top of my own and rose to clear away dinner.

"You know what?" I said, as I moved to the kitchenette. "If I could go back to see that old Luke—the one right after the Battle of Yavin with a medal around his neck, still riding high after sinking proton torpedoes down an exhaust port that must be history's greatest design flaw—I don't think I'd be angry with the way he felt back then. But I'd tell him it wasn't always going to be that easy. Because the Empire's obviously still out there. A huge victory for us was only an inconvenience for them. They still kill and enslave people—well, I don't need to remind you of that. We're hiding in the Outer Rim like the vermin the Empire says we are, and running missions like this one where we don't know if it will make a difference or not, or if anything we do really matters."

"Oh, it matters, Luke," Nakari said. When I turned to look at her she had a crease between her eyes and was regarding me intensely. "We are the thorn that pricks the Emperor's finger when he looks at the galaxy as his personal garden. And you know who he punishes every time we get away with something? Vader."

"What? How do you know that?"

"Because poodoo rolls downhill and Vader's not at the top. He passes it on to everyone beneath him, for sure, but he gets it first every time the Emperor is displeased. And the fact that we are still out here displeases him plenty, I bet."

"You want Vader to get what's coming to him, eh?"

"Sure. I mean, it's not *all* I want. But I wouldn't pass up a chance to take a shot at him if the opportunity presented itself. He took my mom from me and betrayed your dad. Don't you want him dead?"

"I want him defeated."

"Dead qualifies as defeated," Nakari pointed out.

"Yeah, but I guess I'd like to know how he became the thing that he is so I would know what *not* to do. You can't get answers from a dead man."

"Hold on. You think you could turn all evil like that? You think you have that inside you?"

"No, no, that's not what I meant. Ben said he'd been seduced by the dark side of the Force, almost like he didn't have a choice. I need to know more."

Nakari's voice deepened along with the crease between her eyes. "He chose to send my mother to the spice mines and let her die there, Luke. It wasn't some metaphysical dark side that made him do it. He chose to do that, just like everything else he's chosen to do. He's not helpless. He's responsible."

Seeing my mistake, I hastened to reassure her. "Yes, he is, absolutely. I'm not saying I agree with Ben—I simply don't know what he meant. There are mysteries about the Force to which Vader might know the answers."

"True, but you couldn't trust anything he said anyway, so why talk?"

"Like it or not, he's one of the few people remaining in the galaxy who can even discuss it with me."

Nakari blinked. "So what are you saying? You want him to teach you?"

"No, of course not. I just think I could learn something from him."

She made a noise like steam escaping a pressure valve. "I don't think you'd like anything you learned. He's not going to make you happy."

"No, I suppose not."

"Vader probably doesn't even know what happiness is. You know what? I bet he's never had a slice of cake."

The abrupt change of subject startled me. "What, cake is happiness?"

"Absolutely. You want to ask him something when he's defeated, ask him that." Her voice changed this time, not to imitate her father but to imitate me. "'Lord Vader! Have you ever had any cake? Answer me!'" She sounded strange and kind of nasal.

"Hey, I don't sound like that, do I?"

"Don't get distracted! We're discussing Vader's dessert preferences. If he says yes, he's had cake, then he was human at one point and remembers what it was to be happy, and you can continue to talk because there's some common ground there. But if he says no, he's hopeless. Chuck him out the air lock and end his misery."

We started laughing, and even though it wasn't that funny, we laughed until our stomachs hurt and tears streamed from the corners of our eyes. When you laugh at something that scares you, it's not so scary anymore, which is probably the reason Vader had Nakari's mother sent to the spice mines. He wanted to be feared and couldn't bear to be mocked.

I never told Nakari, but I thought those stolen moments with her in a Kupohan hotel were so much better than cake.

WE CHECKED ON OUR PRISONERS in the morning, and aside from being annoyed with us they were fine. Room service provided berries and a selection of strange cheeses, and after eating we let them use the facilities one at a time, making sure the bathroom had no avenue of escape and keeping them in blaster sight to and from. We got them settled, bound yet comfortable, and made sure Artoo was fine on power. Nakari hooked up an interface with her datapad so he could download a report for us. Favvin had attempted to get up and hurl himself at Artoo at one point in the night and received a debilitating shock as a result. He had been perfectly docile since then, and Migg Birkhit had enjoyed a day of rest and entertainment in a hotel room that was no doubt far nicer than his apartment.

"Just one more day on vacation, guys," I said. "We'll let you get back to work tomorrow." Favvin scowled, but Birkhit waved as we left the room.

That visit was quite friendly compared with the reception we got across the hall from Drusil. The Givin never let us in the door; she simply spewed math at us through the comm and threw in the words "Go away" at one point, so we gave up and said we'd be at the garage if she needed us. She must have been involved with something complicated if she couldn't stop to talk.

At the Nessin Courier & Cargo facility, we spent the remainder of the morning and the entire afternoon helping Ruuf Waluuk, the Duros, and the Wookiee remove the totaled engine from the *Desert Jewel*. When the Wookiee warbled something to Ruuf, the Kupohan shook his head and said, "I don't know where Migg is. Could be sick, or he could be off playing around with one of his girlfriends. Good thing these people are willing to help us; I don't think we'd get the job done otherwise."

I didn't know where Nessin was, either, and it was mildly worrisome. So was the fact that we hadn't heard anything positive from the Alliance regarding Drusil's family. On the plus side, we had the old engine out and the chassis prepped for the new engine by the time it arrived at the end of the workday.

Drusil finally joined us shortly after its arrival, hooded. Her arms were laden with food containers; she took them over to the dining area, where she laid them on the table and invited us all to dig in. Nessin's mechanics took some of the containers at her urging but begged off sitting down.

"Mr. Nessin has a policy about us fraternizing with customers," Ruuf explained. "We'd love to stay, but we can't. Thank you kindly for dinner, though," he said. "Wish all our customers were so considerate."

The Wookiee grunted in agreement and added a nod of gratitude, and they bade us farewell for the evening after promising to return first thing in the morning to begin installing the new engine.

"Hey, Nakari, it's quitting time," I called, and her

curly head popped out of the *Jewel*'s engine bay to reply.

"Not quite for me. I still have a couple things to do. Go ahead and start; I'll be there in a few minutes." She disappeared.

I turned to Drusil. "Well, I'm hungry enough to start without her, and she gave us permission, so let's see what you brought."

"Yes, please, be satiated," Drusil said. The containers held an assortment of meats, vegetables, and noodles that could be combined with several different sauces.

"Ah, in addition to the pahzik meat, we have nerf nuggets! Nakari will be so pleased," I said. In a lower voice, I asked, "How are our guests doing?"

"They continue to be well, though the Gotal is a surly creature."

I began dishing out some noodles and nerf with a clean fork from the utensil drawer. "You sound like you're in a better mood than when I spoke to you through the comm. Did you work out whatever was bothering you? The math, I mean?"

"The source of my agitation remains—I am separated from my family and worried about their fate. When you interrupted me, I was involved in probability ladders supporting the idea of further Imperial encounters before our departure, and the results were less than pleasing. Still, I have had only one request for status from Barrisk Favvin's superior, and I believe they are content and free of suspicion for now. And I restored a sense of personal balance after dwelling for an extended period on experimental geometries."

"How does that work?" I asked. "I mean, not the geometry itself, but how does that restore your balance?"

"Have you never meditated before, Luke Sky-walker?"

"I have," I said, thinking back to my exercise in the cockpit on the way to Nanth'ri.

"Do you find it centers you and restores your focus, grants you new perspective on matters great or small that trouble you?"

"To some extent, yes. I wouldn't say I'm really skilled at it yet."

"Presumably you focused on something to take you outside your routine patterns of thinking. I use experimental geometries. What do you use?"

"Visual noise helps," I said, "but mostly I focus on my breathing."

"Excellent. That is a common method employed by many beings. Regardless of how we achieve our alternative state of consciousness, it allows us to shift our perspective and reassess our challenges so that they appear manageable rather than insurmountable."

I had never thought of it that way—I was simply trying to forge a stronger connection to the Force—but her ideas had merit.

"I am unsure how to interpret your current facial expression. Are you upset?" Drusil asked.

"No, just thoughtful." I searched for a phrase to express my appreciation. "Your ideas are giving me the benefit of a new perspective without the meditation."

"Indeed? Why were you meditating, then, if not for a different perspective?"

I considered whether to trust her with the truth. She was either my ally or my enemy. If the first, then trusting her couldn't hurt. If she were my enemy, then telling her wouldn't make her any more or less so, and since she'd already seen me use a lightsaber and pilot us through some challenging situations, my talents weren't exactly a secret anymore. "I was reaching out to the Force."

"Ah, the Force! The Jedi font of miracles. I find it a wholly mysterious subject."

"I find your mathematics pretty mysterious, too."

The Givin leaned forward and whispered. "Is it not wondrous that we have found common ground in our alienation?"

I chuckled and Drusil's mouth dropped into that open smile as she made hoarse wheezing sounds that must have been laughter. But even her joke provided me with an insight into how people must see me: The quick, casual way in which I and many others dismissed her expertise as "math stuff" applied equally to how others must view the Jedi. I wondered if I could duplicate my small success with the Force on Denon here without Nakari around.

"Would you mind terribly if I tried something?" I asked.

"Try what?"

I scooped up a single noodle on my fork and let it fall with a wet smack onto the table. "I want to move that noodle using the Force."

"I would find it vastly entertaining if you did. As long as you don't plan on moving it into my mouth. I have doubts about the sanitary condition of this table."

"Don't worry. I just want a witness if I'm successful."

I concentrated on the noodle and summoned the Force, but it didn't answer. Examining why that might be, I realized I wasn't as relaxed as I had been on Denon with Nakari. Then, I'd felt no pressure; now I did, which was silly, since I'd been the one to initiate this. Maybe it was the pale, implacable face of Drusil, which said to me that she had already calculated to fifteen significant digits how much of a fraud I was.

But I recognized that it was precisely such petty concerns that prevented me from connecting with the Force—a host of insecurities and stresses that acted like shielded blast doors against its flow. Keeping my eyes pointed down at the noodle, I pretended that it wasn't Drusil sitting across from me but rather Nakari, her encouragement and confidence in me replacing the skepticism of the Givin, her smile and dark eyes gazing at me instead of Drusil's skull-like visage. And then, when I reached out to the Force, it met not a barrier but a warm welcome, and I embraced it and felt a modest measure of its strength course through me. When I willed the noodle to move, it did, sliding across the table in a damp, uneven slither until I released it near the Givin's bowl.

"Remarkable," Drusil said, pointing a finger at the noodle. "Moving that may be a trivial feat to you, but it is an impossible one for almost every being in the galaxy. Do you realize how small your demographic is, Luke Skywalker? Statistically nonexistent, yet here you are." She leaned back, crossed her arms, and tilted her head to one side. "The Force has never been mathematically described," she said. "There are stories, of course—legends, really—of a few Givin who became Jedi in the past, but they refused to share their insights with the rest of our species. They did their best—and it was quite adequate—to keep the workings of the Force an enigma. Therefore I do not know precisely what you did. I only know what you did not do."

"What?"

"You did not move the noodle with your mind. Physics prevents it, so it would be more accurate to say that you moved something else, and *that* moved the noodle."

"Oh!" The Givin had a talent for uttering sentences that altered the way I looked at a problem. Her observation made it clear that I'd been moving the Force, not the noodle, but I hadn't perceived it that way until she said it.

"Have you tried this exercise on anything larger?"

"Not yet."

"Shall we experiment? Attempt to move the fork in your bowl."

"I don't know. That's quite a bit heavier than a noodle."

"Are you speaking of the Force as being heavier? Or the fork?"

"Well, I . . ." Her words stunned me again. I'd been looking at it from the wrong angle—which only underscored my need for help. "I meant the fork, but I guess that's not what I should be worried about. You've made me realize I'm in a mental rut and it's going to take some effort to get myself out of it. If I'm moving the fork, I'm manipulating the Force instead of the steel. Okay, I'll give it a try."

I unconsciously stretched out my fingers toward the fork and stopped, taking the time to consciously note it. Why had I done that? My fingers wouldn't move the Force; that was a task for my mind. But perhaps that unconscious gesture reflected the focus of my mind. Since my attention was directed at the fork my hand naturally followed, being used to doing my bidding. Maybe that's all there was behind Obi-Wan's gesture at Mos Eisley, then, when he did something to the minds of those stormtroopers. The hand movement wasn't key to the procedure but rather an unconscious reflection of Obi-Wan's mental focus. I felt foolish again, remembering my failure to influence the Rodian at the Chekkoo spaceport, waving my hand in his face like an idiot.

But even that small insight was easy to second-guess. If I ever had the good fortune to be trained by a real Jedi, he or she would probably tell me that hand motion was vital, serving a function I couldn't even fathom, and all my halting progress was little more than staggering drunk in the dark and taking the wrong road home.

I refocused, took a couple of deep breaths, and reached out again to the Force, urging it to lift the fork out of the bowl. It didn't twitch so much as shift lazily in the soup, like a teenager who, commanded to get up out of bed, rolled over instead and went aggressively back to sleep.

"I do not mean to presume, but perhaps you should close your eyes?" Drusil suggested. "The Force is an unseen power, so it is plausible that your sight may be interfering somehow, occupying a part of your mind that should be focused elsewhere."

Of course she was right. I wasn't flying an X-wing now, and Artoo's translated words weren't scrolling past on a screen; I didn't need to see. And I knew from recent experience that I felt the Force more clearly when I minimized visual distractions. "Okay, I'll give it another try that way."

I shut my eyes and let my awareness expand, and the Force took on a stronger presence, as if it were giving me its full attention now. It was probably the opposite—my full attention was on the Force. It built within me and I coaxed it to lift the fork out of the bowl, not a jerk or a leap but a slow, sustained levitation, laden with noodles that dripped noisily as they cleared the puddle of juices in the bowl, redolent of garlic and peanuts. To give Drusil credit, she made no noises that might distract me during the process. I was about to smile and savor the victory when a voice that was decidedly not Drusil's whooped nearby.

"That's right, pilot, feed your partner with magic noodles!"

Startled, I opened my eyes, lost my concentration, and the fork plopped down into the noodles with a loud *glop* and splashed me with what must have been half the broth.

"Aw, not again," I said, looking down at the mess.

"Now, that's a useful skill, Luke!" Nakari said. She pulled out a chair next to Drusil on the other side of the table and slid into it, her eyes sparkling behind a lock of dark curls. "I'm just going to sit down over here, and you can Force-feed me from over there, okay? Congratulations on the new stain, by the way. You really look like you smell good."

Her smile was infectious, but I asked her, "Are you finished?" in an effort to cut off her teasing.

"Not even close. You know, you should exhibit your tunics on one of those fancy art planets. What do you think, Drusil? Does he have a decent chance at making it as an artist if the piloting career doesn't work out?"

The Givin looked disturbed as she flailed about for an answer. She might have thought that Nakari was asking seriously instead of merely taking the opportunity to give me grief. "There's no accounting for taste," she finally muttered.

My embarrassment must have shown, for Nakari said, "Hey, Luke. Comparatively speaking, a little spilled broth is no big deal. Remember, I've seen you covered in poodoo and I still think you're fine."

NAKARI AND I DIDN'T waste any time in the morning. After checking on our prisoners, we were back at the hangar at daybreak, anxious to get the new engine installed. It proved to be more time consuming than we'd hoped; it was a surplus job from Kuat Drive Yards, plenty of power but not designed with a sleek housing in mind, so we had to make some rather ugly modifications to the *Jewel*'s clean lines to make it work, ripping up some plating and welding on basic gray replacements. Nakari wasn't happy about it at all and it would make the ship tougher to fly in atmosphere—especially Kupoh's—but she spoke to the *Jewel* as she worked, telling the ship it was only temporary and vowing to return her to her former beauty.

When Drusil entered the hangar midmorning brandishing a large carry-sack and holding her datapad like a weapon, I suspected that she had bad news for us, though I could not imagine how she would look different if she had good news. Nakari and I took a break from working on the *Desert Jewel* and met her at the metal table that constituted the staff dining area.

"Hey, Drusil—"

She held up a hand to stop me and shook her head once. Then she pointed to the carry-sack and beckoned us closer. Once we stopped next to her, she pulled out some thick fishbowl helmets with electronics inside. "Put these on," she said, "and seal them before speaking."

It was a strange request and I didn't see an oxygen system, but I took the helmet anyway to humor her, figuring I'd take it off after a few minutes. Once we were all under glass and sealed up, Drusil's tinny voice came through the built-in comm.

"I've been assured that these are soundproof. We need to speak now and cannot risk being overheard by Mr. Waluuk over there, or anyone else."

"Where did you get these?" Nakari asked.

"That is unimportant," Drusil said, her voice curt. "I have been monitoring Imperial communications while taking care of our charges and we are faced with a quandary."

"What's that?" I asked.

"The Empire has blockaded all outgoing traffic from Kupoh. They are almost certain we are here."

Nessin hadn't mentioned that to us. "How did they become so certain?"

"I have not calculated the probability that they deduced it on their own versus the probability that they received intelligence from other sources like Migg Birkhit. Is it vital that I do so?"

I supposed it wasn't, so I shook my head. The vital question would be how to escape.

"Intercepted transmissions indicate they are inspecting all ships leaving the system, looking at passengers and crew only, not cargo."

"That's disappointing. I guess we could try to hide you in some cargo," I ventured.

"That won't work. They are using life-form scanners."

"I can't believe the Kupohans are putting up with that," Nakari said.

"They are protesting, to be sure, and are demanding the immediate departure of Imperial ships, but the Empire is stalling them for now. Their story is that they are looking for certain criminals only and have no other interest in Kupohan affairs. So far that seems to be true. They are not holding anyone, just inspecting and then having their Interdictors turn off their gravity projectors at intervals to allow cleared ships to leave. All incoming ships are left unmolested. Since the net result is an inconvenience only to outbound ships and it is in pursuit of 'criminals,' the Kupohans have little cause to push the Empire too hard—especially when the appearance of rebellion would bring an even larger force in system."

"Okay, thanks," I said, not knowing what else to say. This would require some thought.

"I was not finished," Drusil replied. "I have a recommended course of action."

"Oh, sorry. Go ahead."

"Our best options for achieving our goal rest in taking two steps: One, abandon the *Desert Jewel* and secure alternative transport offplanet. The *Jewel* is too recognizable now, and we would attract attention as soon as we left the hangar. However, a repaired ship can be traded or sold for another. Two, forge an entirely new hyperspace lane between here and Omereth— one that the Empire cannot possibly be blocking."

"Can we even do that?" Nakari asked. I was surprised she hadn't immediately vetoed the idea of abandoning her ship.

"Yeah, I've done it before," I said. "With the *Jewel*, in fact. It was just a short trip to throw off any pursuit as I was returning to the rebel fleet, but Artoo is brilliant that way. How long a jump are you proposing, Drusil?"

"I am in favor of executing several short jumps until we are well outside the Empire's probable containment. Then we can use a safer, well-established route to get to Omereth."

A few days earlier I would have questioned Drusil's suggestion as a genuine one, but despite many opportunities to betray us—especially here on Kupoh—she had never taken advantage. Her assistance in keeping our presence here a secret had been invaluable, in fact. I was willing to believe now that she just wanted to reunite with her family on Omereth. And aside from that, I just *felt* that she was telling the truth; whether that was attributable to my Force sensitivity or not, I didn't know.

"What about the Interdictors in this system?" Nakari pressed. "Aren't those gravity projectors going to keep us here?"

"They would keep us from using any established lane out of here," the Givin replied, "but of course we will not be using any of them. We will be exiting the system in another direction, where their simulated mass will not hinder our hyperdrive. May I show you?"

"Please do," I said. I cast an uncertain glance at the surface of the dining table. It was decorated with brown caf rings and assorted sandwich crumbs, which we didn't notice when we were going to add to it, but looked mildly horrifying if you wanted to place anything valuable on top of it. Drusil didn't care, though; she approached the table and put down her datapad so that we could see it easily without peering over her shoulder. It displayed a map of the system that had been marked with glowing yellow dots and blue circles around them as if they identified orbits.

"The Empire's Interdictors are blocking egress here, here, and here." She pointed with a pale finger to the three yellow dots. "I have indicated the mass shadows of their gravity projectors with blue lines. So to escape, we must plot a course out of the system in between those mass shadows and travel a goodly distance offplanet before the hyperdrive can engage. And you see that there are several options available to us—but our interest would be to move to the galactic east, correct?"

"Yes," I admitted, "but there's almost nothing mapped out in that direction."

"Precisely why they won't consider it a possible avenue of escape."

"You're right, nobody would consider it, including me. I'm all for the element of surprise, don't get me wrong, but what are you using for a navigation point? Not Gamorr, right? Because there's an entire sector of space between here and there, and that sector is largely unexplored. There might be uncharted brown dwarfs or planets or any number of things we could run into if you just pick a direction and go."

"Ah. One moment." Drusil dismissed the system map and called up a second one, which was a much larger view of several sectors, except that it had math symbols written all over it. "We will use this star here." She pointed to an equation below and left of center, and I failed to see any indication of a star. The marks looked indistinguishable from any other set of scribbles on the map. I had no idea what she was talking about.

"I'm sorry, which star again? You pointed to an equation."

"That's the star."

"I . . . what?"

"Unexplored space does not equate to unobserved

space. An analysis of the movements of other stars around it prove that it must be there. No one has viewed it yet except through the lens of mathematics, but such a lens is frequently better than mere glass."

Nakari and I exchanged a glance with widened eyes, each wondering if the other had heard the same thing. "Except that I can reach out with my hand and verify that the glass is there!" I said.

"Your senses can be fooled. Math and physics do not lie."

"No, no. I'm not suggesting that you did the math incorrectly. I'm wondering how you can be sure that you've considered everything or didn't accidentally miss a variable. Your senses can be fooled as well, right? How do you know you've accounted for everything?"

"I cannot be a hundred percent certain, of course, but I am confident that I have extrapolated correctly based on the stars we do know about."

"Well, on the positive side, the Empire certainly won't be looking there," Nakari said. "On the negative side, if you're wrong we'll most likely be dead."

"It's a pretty big risk, Drusil," I said.

"It is far less risky than remaining here for an extended period. How long can we expect to remain hidden and unreported to the Empire—and to keep Migg Birkhit and Barrisk Favvin in captivity? The variables are too numerous to consider, except for the significant pressure the Empire will put on the Kupohans to surrender us." Her eyes flicked over to the *Jewel,* where Ruuf Waluuk and the Wookiee continued to work in our absence. She lowered her voice, even though we were supposedly wearing soundproof helmets, and continued, "Even if Azzur does not betray us, one of those other crew members will. You have already seen how unreliable they are. This astrogation, however, is based on quantifiable and verifiable data. I can walk you through the math if you wish."

"No, that's okay, I believe you," I said. "It just seems like we're jumping blind."

"Propose an alternative method by which we may escape this planet and make it to Omereth before my family gives up hope and departs."

"Give me some time to think about it."

"How many units of time?"

"Until the repairs to the *Desert Jewel* are finished. I know that's nonspecific, but at least it's a deadline."

"Will we not take another ship?"

"I wouldn't want to take another ship than the *Jewel*. Even as patchwork as she looks now, we're not going to find another one like her, and we need every advantage we can get." Nakari gave a thumbs-up to indicate her agreement.

"What advantages are necessary?" Drusil asked. "Once we go around the Imperial forces and make it to the Omereth system, we should have no trouble. The Imperials are spread too thin to watch everything."

That didn't sound like her. She should have rattled off a statistical probability of precisely how thin the Imperial fleet would be at any given point in the galaxy. But I think her desperation to get offplanet and reunite with her family was clouding her usual clear thought. "Stakes being what they are, they might have pursued your family," I said. We still hadn't heard anything from the Alliance regarding that part of the mission. "There's no knowing if Major Derlin got them there or not, and if he did, whether he did so without detection. If he was followed, we could have some bounty hunters watching the planet, waiting for you to show up, all with their own custom ships. The Empire might even be there. We don't want to be in a standard slow bird in a situation like that."

"Can we not contact the Alliance, then, and enlist some more robust assistance?"

"I've already tried that, too," I admitted. "Aside from using the dead drop, I asked Azzur to get a message through to the Alliance, requesting more help. They're probably lying low right now with the Empire here in such numbers."

The Givin's tone turned morose. "Under such circumstances as these, that would be a delay of indeterminate length with no guarantee of aid."

"I'm afraid so."

Using crisp movements, Drusil cleared the maps from her datapad and made a conscious effort to ameliorate her tone. "Barring unforeseen complications, then, we shall forge a new path through the silence," she said, "but in the *Jewel*."

"Yes," I said. Work had proceeded even faster than anticipated, and I thought that we could technically get the *Desert Jewel* ready to fly by that evening, but I didn't want to try managing such a journey without a good night's rest first. We'd have hazards enough without compounding them with a logy pilot. "We're going to put in a new transponder identifying us as one of Nessin's couriers, and we should be able to leave tomorrow." When I tried to nod for emphasis, I smooshed my nose against the inside of the helmet, and it hurt because even that tiny impact reminded me of the blow I had taken from Favvin. Nakari seemed to find my pained reaction endlessly entertaining.

DRUSIL NEARLY QUIVERED with eagerness as she watched us eat our breakfast in the morning. We still didn't feel comfortable eating in the hotel buffet area where anyone could spot us but we were sick of our rooms, so we had brought our breakfast to the relative privacy of the staff kitchen area in Nessin's hangar. It was gloppy and half-cold; we'd ordered some for our captives in the hotel, immobilized them completely and gagged them after they'd finished, and then brought our own meals down to eat by the ship. Claiming that she had no need of sustenance at the moment, Drusil stared at us as we ate, most likely willing us to chew faster and idly computing how long it would take us to finish at our current rate of consumption. What had been a pleasant interlude for me and Nakari had been a festival of impatience for her.

"Please let me know if there is anything I can do to speed our journey," she said, and uttered two similar statements to that effect as we shoveled eggs in our mouths and poured caf down our gullets. Even though we were wolfing it down as fast as we could, Drusil appeared ready to inject us with a nutrient solution and pronounce us able to fly. To take her mind off the fact that we weren't currently on our way to Omereth, I asked her a question.

"Is there a chance you could slice through Imperial comm traffic and let us know if any of them are interested in us as we leave the atmosphere?"

"Certainly. Are you planning to head directly to the galactic east as discussed?"

I'd made more detailed plans with Nakari earlier, but Drusil had been absent for that discussion. "No, I thought we'd behave like a law-abiding courier ship at first, angling toward one of the Interdictor choke points, and then turn sharply spinward and move at top speed to get to jump range before they can redirect their gravity projectors to stop us. That'll take them a few minutes, and we should be able to outrun the Imperial decision-making process. After that it's up to you and Artoo to get us safely to Omereth."

"That shall be as trouble-free as quadratic equations," Drusil assured me. "I have rechecked my math twice, and your remarkable droid has checked it thrice." It amused me that Artoo was now *remarkable* where earlier he had performed only *adequately*. "We can program the first jump into the nav computer as soon as we leave the surface, and a few moments of recalibration and safety checks at the end of each jump will allow us to make the others shortly afterward."

"Good. Do that, and as soon as you finish—before we escape the atmosphere—I want you and Artoo both to check the system and the ship for any spyware or tracers that the Kupohans may have placed on the *Jewel*. And don't forget to program a call to the hotel checking us out just before we jump to hyperspace. The cleaning staff will find Migg and Barrisk and they can go on with their lives, and we can go on with ours."

Nakari nodded. "I'll go get the preflight started and then I'll go over the hull, as well." She chugged the last of her caf and rose from the table. "Better get started."

"I'll help," Drusil said, and the two of them left together, with Nakari dropping a "Hurry up, pilot!" to me in a perfect imitation of her father.

I looked at Artoo, whose cam eye swiveled from their retreating forms to my face. "I guess chewing your food is overrated, huh?" It was the wrong thing to say to a droid. His eye rotated back to Nakari and Drusil and his body followed, a few beeps chiding me for being a slowpoke. With the three of them headed to the *Desert Jewel* and the pressure off, I took my time finishing my breakfast and clearing off the table.

Azzur Nessin found me by the sink while I was recycling my plate, partly to wish us a safe journey but primarily to give me one last update. "After some thought, I changed the transponder signal to the fleet code of a competitor last night," he said. "They're called Polser Couriers. The story you'll tell the Empire as you leave the planet remains the same: You're still bearing important diplomatic pouches to Rishi. But once you turn and run, the Imperials might inquire afterward why a courier would behave so strangely and jump into nothingness. I'd prefer not to answer such questions."

I shook his hand and thanked him for his help. He bobbed his head, setting off one last clacking party among his beard beads, and said it was a pleasure conducting business with me. His primary ears twitched, his mouth turned downward, and he began to turn, saying, "Someone—"

Then his skull exploded in a bolt of superheated plasma, spraying me with blood, bone fragments, and brain tissue. Another high-powered blaster bolt followed close behind it, but I had already ducked instinctively, and it sailed over me and Azzur Nessin's fallen body. I yanked my blaster out of its holster and spied the assassin from a squatting position. It was the mechanic, Ruuf Waluuk, and he had company—a horned Devaronian dressed in black and laden down with weaponry. They had come in from the hangar entrance and were squatting down by the engines of the *Desert Jewel,* firing at me from under the wing. The bounty hunter loudly called the Kupohan an idiot for his poor aim, which told me that I had been the target.

I squeezed off a couple of shots in their direction to disrupt their focus and dived for the dining table. I flipped it on its side for a makeshift shield and crouched down behind it as fresh bolts slammed into the top. The table wouldn't hold up for long, and I knew it was tactically a terrible idea to let the enemy pin me down with no place to run, but they had timed their ambush well and it was either use the table or let them shoot at me in the open.

Drusil might have stymied Ruuf's direct attempts to communicate with the Empire, but she couldn't have stopped him from going into almost any cantina and looking for help. He could have reported—and probably did—through an intermediary that we were on the planet, thereby corroborating the story of Migg Birkhit, but he wanted to make sure he collected that full bounty himself, hence the blaster and the Devaronian bounty hunter. He probably figured even half the price on our heads would be a good haul—assuming he survived his partnership with the bounty hunter long enough to split the proceeds.

A chunk of the table on the top side sheared apart under a bolt, and a couple of thin needles of hot metal tore gashes in my scalp and forehead as they passed by. I was lucky they didn't punch through my skull. Instead I felt warm trickles of blood cooling as they dripped down my head; the trail from my forehead was diverted to the side by my eyebrow, for which I had never been so grateful.

I needed some kind of counterattack. Keeping my body behind the table, I stretched out my right arm and pointed my blaster around the edge, firing off three quick unaimed shots to draw their attention. While they directed return fire there, thinking my head must be nearby, I popped up over the top to locate them and took a careful shot at the easy target, Ruuf Waluuk. I was already ducking back behind my cover as I heard him grunt in surprise, a sound that was followed closely by the clatter of his blaster on the hangar floor and the thump of his body afterward.

I'd seen only a sliver of the Devaronian; more used to fighting than Ruuf, he'd minimized his silhouette by flattening himself on the floor. It was his blaster methodically taking apart the table now. Though the furniture was sturdy enough for the purposes of supporting a light lunch, it had not been built to withstand sustained fire from someone determined to punch through it with a blaster.

I spread myself out flat in imitation of the Devaronian, planning to roll to my left and take shots at him as I moved. Neither of us would have much chance of hitting the other in that scenario, but a second later I had to go with it, because the table developed a hole and the bounty hunter was pouring shots through it with frightening accuracy. He probably had his elbows braced on the ground and one hand supporting the wrist of his firing hand.

Tumbling to my left and squeezing the trigger of my blaster, I hoped some of my shots would be close enough to make him rethink his position or at least slow down his own barrage. If I moved fast enough, I'd put the *Jewel*'s landing ramp between us, and then he would have to move if he wanted a clear shot—and I'd be ready for him.

He saw what I intended and stopped shooting to move first and skew the field of fire in his favor. He was a thin shadow topped with a red globe of a head, and he moved fast. I quit rolling and tried to pick him off before he found cover, but I wasn't accurate enough. He ducked out of sight, and now I had to wonder if he would try to flank me or wait for me to try to flank him.

A loud crack sounded in the hangar and echoed off the walls, almost simultaneously with the taut tapped-cable noise of his blaster firing. Another crack, then silence, and I realized I recognized that pattern.

"It's okay, Luke, he's down," Nakari called. "I just made sure he'll stay down, too." She stepped out from behind the landing ramp, slugthrower cradled in her arms. "You all right? You're bleeding."

"I'll be fine. Azzur Nessin won't, though. Ruuf got him." The cargo magnate clearly should have cultivated the habit of spying on his employees.

Nakari noticed Nessin's bloody remains on the tile floor and said, "Damn. I didn't want our knocking on his door to bring him that kind of end."

"Me, neither. We'd better get out of here if we don't want to end up like him," I said. "Those two might have been acting alone, but they might have also called in some Imperials so they could hand us over."

"Or to serve as backup, yeah," she said. "I think we're just about ready. Status panels are looking green."

"Thanks for the assist, by the way."

She shrugged a shoulder. "Thanks for distracting him. He didn't see me until it was too late."

There was no time and really no need to investigate the body; nothing about the bounty hunter would help us escape the system, and we had to be gone long before local authorities discovered what happened and tried to detain us. We boarded and closed the ramp and I caught Nakari up on what Azzur Nessin had said and the sequence of events before she had gotten involved. I made a quick trip to the bathroom to throw some disinfectant and adhesive on my scalp and forehead, hoping it wouldn't scar.

Artoo reported finding and eliminating not one but five different tracking programs hidden in the nav computer's code sometime during the last few days. Drusil found another he missed, an Imperial Sleeper she called it, tied to the ship's clock. It would become active at a set time, triggered by the turning of the clock, note our current course and position, and send a coded burst reporting it to the nearest Imperial world. There was no way to tell if they had been installed by a single person or several individuals, but at this point we had little choice but to run and hope we had found them all.

Lifting out of the atmosphere was even rougher than descending to the surface; we weren't as streamlined now with the modifications, and at one point a particularly bad stretch of turbulence surprised Nakari, causing her to bite her tongue.

We emerged into vacuum on a heading to the galactic south, where an Interdictor and half a dozen Star Destroyers had bottled up exiting traffic bound in that direction. The Star Destroyers were sending shuttles of troops from ship to ship, inspecting and clearing them, and the Interdictor turned off its projectors periodically to allow cleared vessels to go about their interstellar business.

We traveled with the sublight engines running at about half their capability. The uneven thrust from the replacement had introduced some resistance into turns or rolls to starboard, but otherwise it gave us respectable if not blistering speed.

A curt Imperial query asking for our destination, business, and number of passengers and crew elicited a slightly impatient reply from Nakari, precisely the tone one should take. Once the Imperial traffic controller instructed us to hold course and prepare for boarding and Nakari acknowledged, I asked Artoo and Drusil if they were ready to run east and make the first jump.

"Ready," Drusil said. A clacking noise could be heard through the comm as she ran her fingers over her datapad. "Monitoring Imperial frequencies in system." Artoo confirmed he was ready, as well, so I banked the *Desert Jewel* to port and opened up the engines to full.

It didn't take long for the Empire to notice aloud that we did not appear to be maintaining our course. Nakari ignored two requests to resume previous course and acknowledge transmission. Drusil's voice blared over the intercom, reporting intercepted transmissions she had decrypted.

"Bridge of the Interdictor is talking about us to the bridge of the flagship destroyer in the southern battle group."

"Talking is fine. They can talk all they want."

"The destroyer has assigned a TIE squadron to pursue us," Drusil continued. "I calculate intercept in approximately ten minutes. Too late to capture us before we jump, though they don't know that. A shuttle is following to board us immediately."

"How long until we can jump, Artoo?" I asked.

FOUR MINUTES EIGHT SECONDS, he replied.

"The destroyer captain believes we are the ones they are looking for. He wants the Interdictor to redirect its gravity projectors."

That wouldn't be good. They might be able to do it in time.

"But now a third captain has interrupted from another destroyer," Drusil said. "He argues that we couldn't possibly be going anywhere without an established hyperspace lane in this direction, and it is more likely that we are a distraction. In other words, the real fugitives are already waiting in queue, and once they move the gravity projectors the lane to the south will be open and allow their escape. Amusing."

Nakari laughed in agreement.

"The flagship captain points out that if I am on board, I might be capable of charting a new hyperspace lane on my own. That is sobering. I fear he may be distressingly competent."

"Uh-oh," I said.

"The Interdictor has just sent a request to Polser Couriers on Kupoh to confirm our transponder code and that we are conducting legitimate business on their behalf."

"That's not going to end well," Nakari said.

"But it will take them some time to respond," I reminded her. "Even if it's a minute, that could help."

Drusil continued her reporting. "An argument rages. The flagship captain wants the gravity projectors to be redirected this instant; the other destroyer captain maintains we are a ruse; and the Interdictor captain insists that they wait on an answer from Polser before acting rashly."

Nakari looked at me. "Why doesn't the flagship captain simply order it done?"

"He probably will in a moment. The other captains are making sure their objections are heard and recorded so that if the operation goes badly they can't be faulted for the decision."

"Ah, got it," Nakari said, nodding with comprehension. "Standard operating procedure in a culture of blame where risk taking and initiative are punished. Always tell Lord Vader it was someone else's fault."

"Polser Couriers just simplified matters," Drusil said. "They report they currently have no outbound shipments headed that way and we are not one of their ships."

"That was fast."

"The flagship captain has ordered us stopped now, and the Interdictor captain is complying. Turning off gravitational projector to realign in front of our present course."

"Can they stop us?" Nakari asked.

"Maybe," I said. "Depends partly on the crew and partly on their power situation. They've been conducting operations for a while here, turning the projectors on and off, and their generators might be drained. Or they might not. I haven't done this all that often in raids, much less alone. We'll find out in a couple of minutes. Or less. Artoo, will you throw up a countdown giving us the time until the jump?"

He chirped, and the display indicated we had eighty-nine seconds left.

I've noticed the curious ability of time to linger and stretch instead of pass by under moments of stress or boredom, and yet it can slip past unnoticed during periods of rest and contentment. Right then it was a monstrous, lumbering creature that barely moved as we waited for the seconds to tick by.

With thirty-two seconds to go, Drusil made another

report. "Interdictor captain announced the projector is down and realigning to our sector. Spinning up."

Our intelligence was spotty here. Thirty seconds had to be a minimum time to get a gravity field projected—intelligence suggested it took more like a couple of minutes—but we weren't safely outside of operational parameters yet.

"You know what, Luke? You're kind of cute when you're nervous."

The twin shocks of being called both cute and nervous tore my eyes from the countdown. Nakari was smirking at me. "I also like how you're completely calm when people are shooting at you but are easily rattled by compliments."

"It's not everyone who can rattle me," I said. "Just you." She tilted her head and I added, "But in a good way."

Nakari flashed her teeth at me and said, "Of course. I'm the good kind of rattling."

And she was, because she successfully distracted me from the countdown, and the hyperdrive shot us out of that sector into a region of space more accurately charted by Drusil's equations than any existing star charts.

"Hey. Did we just get away?" I asked.

"Yep. For the moment, anyway. Good job, pilot."

I sighed in relief and knew that Nakari was teasing me again. I'd had very little to do with it—this part of the trip was all made possible by math and physics and brains that could process it far faster and more accurately than I ever could. It wasn't without its own tension, however. Without traveling established lanes, there was a chance we'd never come back into real-space again. But if we did, we'd have a view of the galaxy no one else had ever enjoyed before.

Over the next eight hours, we wound up spending

more time in realspace than hyperspace. Drusil's short jumps dumped us into new systems, and she spent time with Artoo taking readings, scanning the stars, and then tweaking her calculations for the next jump. I encouraged her to take all the time she needed.

Most of the systems we encountered were full of barren rocks and gas giants, but one had a habitable planet with life on it. We lingered there awhile longer, noted the coordinates and the path to get there, and took some preliminary scans of the planet to be analyzed later.

"This might yield something useful for my father," Nakari said. "A consolation prize for losing his advantage on Fex."

"It might also work as a base for the Alliance," I said, making sure Artoo noted weather patterns and took some atmospheric readings. "If the water's okay and it doesn't have predators like Fex, it could be the kind of place Admiral Ackbar is looking for."

The worry of being lost in space got replaced by the worry of running into Imperials again once Drusil and Artoo announced that we were back on established routes, skirting the far side of Hutt Space and traveling to the galactic north, dropping into a deserted system, and then plotting our course from there into Omereth.

Our eventual arrival into the Omereth system was an anticlimax. I didn't realize how tense my shoulders were until I saw no threats on the scanners and hardly any ships at all in orbit around the planet. They were small personal yachts with few weapons.

"Oh," I said, consciously relaxing. "No one's gunning for us. That's a nice change. Kind of the galaxy I want to live in, honestly."

"I'll take it," Nakari said, and then brought up a current view of the planet on the holo. "Whoa. Are we sure there's land on that thing? It looks like a solid blue marble with some clouds swirling above it."

"I assure you that dry land exists," Drusil said over the comm. "I have provided the rendezvous coordinates to your outstanding droid."

"Thanks," I replied, grinning over the fact that Artoo had now been upgraded to *outstanding* in Drusil's eyes. He'd climbed so high so fast. "Artoo, go ahead and put them in and set our course. I'll take back manual control if necessary." His acknowledging chirp provoked a happy sigh from me. I looked over at Nakari and smiled. "Almost through with this mission."

"I know. Part of me can't believe we made it."

My smile faltered and I tensed up again. Destiny sometimes finds it amusing to strike at people who believe they're safe. I rechecked the scanners for threats and made sure the shields were still up and working.

"What?" Nakari said. "Luke?"

"It's nothing," I said. "I have a part of me that can't believe it, either. The war's made me believe that nothing is ever easy. But maybe we really did fake out the Empire with those uncharted hyperspace jumps."

Turned out we did fool the Empire and Drusil was right—they'd never look for her on Omereth. But that's not who was waiting for us to enter the atmosphere.

WHEN THE *DESERT JEWEL* bit into the atmosphere of Omereth, a starboard drag on the stick evolved that was much more severe than when we'd left Kupoh. It got noticeably worse as we descended, until we were flying with blue above and blue below. I didn't see any smoke trail behind us but I almost felt there should be one—I definitely felt tremors in the ship.

"Not good," I murmured. Perhaps I'd pushed the engine too hard in our race to outrun the Empire, or perhaps there was a problem with the aerodynamics— the modifications we'd made to the chassis back there might have degraded in the turbulence of leaving Kupoh and worsened upon entering atmosphere here, introducing a worrisome tug on that side. It significantly reduced the ship's maneuverability, and I doubted that we would find convenient repair facilities on this planet. Banking left was a chore, and banking right was now the ship's default on a dead stick. If I pulled the stick to starboard we'd probably spin out of control.

Nakari grimaced when I explained that to her. "Well,

I suppose the engine served its purpose, right? It was always going to be temporary anyway. Can we make it back to the fleet with just one engine?"

"Sure. It'll be a bit slower, but we'll make it. There's nothing wrong with the hyperdrive. I'm thinking of just killing the engine now. I might get some maneuverability back if it's the engine shaking loose on that side causing the trouble."

I powered down the starboard engine and some of the shaking and drag eased, which was a relief. The stick became more responsive, too, though it still wished to drag us to starboard a little. We lost quite a bit of speed, of course, but I was just thinking we didn't need much anymore when an alarm blatted.

"Luke," Nakari said, "there's something on the scanner. Two somethings. Ships inbound from our rendezvous coordinates."

Drusil heard this over the comm and ventured with a hopeful note in her voice, "Perhaps my family is coming to meet me."

I didn't reply at first, instead studying the data scrolling across the scanner readout. I'd have to tell Drusil that her guess was highly improbable. "I don't think so. Those aren't personal shuttles. They're custom ships like this one, moving very fast. And whoa—they just threw up their deflector shields. Definitely not friendly."

I raised our own shields, and my heart sank as I considered our options. Those ships were much faster than us right now, and might still be faster even if I turned on the starboard engine again. And turning it on would mean I'd lose what little agility I currently had for a speed gain that wouldn't be enough. There were no canyons or other land features for me to exploit, either: We were over open water for kilometers.

"Who are these guys?" Nakari asked.

"Bounty hunters," I grated. Patient ones. And the only way they could have been here waiting for us was if they had followed Drusil's family here. Major Derlin's half of the operation, as I'd feared, had to have been compromised. It was no wonder we'd never gotten any news about it. I hoped the Givin's family was still safe; there was no bounty on them as far as I knew, so maybe the bounty hunters had merely been staking them out, waiting for our arrival. And I hoped the major was all right if he was still on the planet.

Drusil had no comment to make over the comm. She was brilliant, and now that she had new information she could see the probabilities much more clearly than I could.

"Nakari," I said, my voice pitched low. "No matter what I do, we're at a severe disadvantage here. We'd better prepare for an emergency water landing."

"Oh. Right." She nodded and began to unbuckle. "What about your droid?"

"His electrical systems are watertight so he can survive a dunking, but he's not a good swimmer. We'll have to help him get out."

"Got it." She bent to kiss the top of my head as she exited. "Fly well, my pilot."

The bounty hunter ships were designed with narrow silhouettes like the *Desert Jewel* to make them difficult to target. One was dark, flat, and chunky, like a malevolent piece of armed and flying toast, and the other sailed like a vertical needle, similar to a B-wing, cockpit at the top and a rectangular battery of lasers below that fired in sequence and repeated, a barrage of blasts almost impossible to dodge.

Only the needle ship fired, and while I managed to avoid many of the bolts and landed a couple of hits myself, we still got pounded so many times on the first pass that our shields were reduced to dangerous lows. We probably wouldn't survive the next pass.

But a strange situation developed. An angry voice berated the needle ship over an open channel, demanding that it stop firing or be destroyed. Since there were no other ships around, the voice could only belong to the pilot of the flying toast. He took issue with the pilot of the needle attempting to destroy us, since we represented a sizable bounty and they could hardly collect if we disappeared into the ocean. I took advantage by searching for a way out. There was an island ahead and slightly to port, maybe only two or three dozen square kilometers in size, sporting forested hills above a sheltered lagoon with a sandy beach. If we could land on the beach and run for cover that would be best, but I remembered Admiral Ackbar's warnings about the planet's seas, and in case we were forced down before we reached that island, I wanted us to have as little water to cross as possible.

We were functionally on the deck, skimming only thirty meters above the surface of the water and moving slowly. The scanner showed additional ships coming from the rendezvous coordinates to the east—slower and bulkier than the first two but no doubt also piloted by bounty hunters. Regardless of whether they wanted to destroy us or capture us, I began to feel like we were being followed by a flock of carrion birds.

The needle ship fired at me again from its dense battery of cannons, and as it did the flying toast unloaded on the needle, and I thought perhaps I understood why. The needle pilot didn't want to capture us so much as deny our capture to all the others—but especially to the pilot of the toast. There was an internecine rivalry there, and the needle pilot was not playing to win but rather playing to make everyone lose.

We would lose the most. Though I avoided the majority of the bolts, a few landed and overwhelmed our shields, and after that another one struck and damaged our port engine. The ship rocked, and the smoke trail I thought should have been there earlier finally appeared.

I thought that would be the end of us, but the needle's shields dissolved under withering bombardment from the other bounty hunter, and then it was shot down, trailing fiery wreckage into the water. It was a welcome if temporary reprieve, for we looked to share a similar fate. Most of our speed had leached away, and all I could do was fight to keep the nose up and minimize the angle of our dive. I thought of restarting the starboard engine but didn't want the fire to spread there, as well.

"We're going down!" I said.

"Coming!" Nakari said.

I didn't know why she'd be coming forward if the landing ramp was behind the cockpit, but there was no time to argue. I fought the stick and the failing engine as much as possible so that we skipped across the surface once before plowing into the still green waters of the lagoon. Cries of alarm erupted from Nakari, Artoo, and Drusil as they all pitched forward from the impact and joined me in the cockpit. Nakari was carrying in front of her the Kelen Biolabs Emergency Aquatic Something Something—I couldn't catch it all—and it saved her from cracking her head against the dome of the cockpit. She grunted at the collision but then told me to unbuckle as we began to sink into the dark waters of the lagoon that now appeared to be quite deep, even though it was a sheltered cove.

"Don't touch the landing ramp!" she said, tossing me a water filter for my nostrils. She had her slugthrower strapped to her back and her jacket zipped up tight. "We're getting out this way, but we have to do it before we sink too deep."

"How?"

"Manual release and mechanical ejection of the viewport. It'll slide up and away, water will pour in, we grab Artoo and clear the ship, deploy the raft underneath him, ride it to the surface." She twisted black dials and pulled levers in sequence at three points along the outside edge of the cockpit on the copilot's side. "You gotta turn these right and then pull down on your side, too," she said.

I hadn't noticed them before, but the dials and levers were there, blending into the trim of the window. Presumably they released the airtight—and watertight—seal. The atmosphere in the ship had given it a modicum of buoyancy, but we'd be ruining that in a moment and we'd sink faster. I flipped and pulled until a trickle of water began to seep through the edges.

"Ready? Got your breather in? Crouch down by Artoo and we'll do this. Drusil?"

"Ready," the Givin said. She didn't have a breathing apparatus attached to her nose, but any being that could survive in vacuum for a day could survive the water for a few minutes. She was braced against the bulkhead, anticipating the incoming rush of water. Her slicing hardware was slipped into her carry-sack, presumably waterproof, which she slung over her shoulders. I squatted next to Artoo, feet planted wide to brace myself, and Nakari yanked down on a larger lever located above the viewport in the center. The ship shuddered, a metallic clang reverberated around us, and then a loud hiss and *foosh* announced the ejection of the transparisteel from its casing and the concomitant deluge of seawater into the ship. Artoo bleeped in alarm, and I gasped at the shock of cold and threw my arms around the droid to steady both of us.

The cockpit glass slid away as Nakari had said it would, and the ship began to sink more rapidly into darkness as the *Desert Jewel* filled with water. Nakari joined me on the other side of Artoo, her damaged left hand overlapping mine, and together we pushed off from the deck and escaped the ship in a fountain of bubbles.

Unlike said bubbles, we didn't rise. Artoo's weight was dragging us down despite my frantic kicking. Nakari placed her right hand, which held the emergency raft, directly under Artoo and activated its automatic inflation. The compressed canister inside released its gases and a large raft billowed underneath us, folding my legs underneath me and supporting Artoo and Nakari, as well. Our descent halted, turned into a slow ascent, and quickened to an alarming pace as the raft inflated fully. Halfway to the surface, I realized that Drusil wasn't on the raft with us. And a moment later I realized that breaking the surface wouldn't be a gentle exercise. We shot out of the sea and I was thrown several meters in the air. Artoo stayed put, being so much heavier and centered on the raft, but Nakari flew even higher than I did. We both landed back in the sea, leaving Artoo temporarily alone on the raft. A hand grabbed my tunic and lifted as I kicked for the surface; it was Drusil. We emerged next to the raft and held on, and I smiled in relief when I saw Nakari surface a moment later. She returned my grin and pulled herself up into the raft.

"Good flying, pilot."

"Hey, now."

"I mean it. We're still alive and close to shore." She scrambled over to our side and helped us aboard.

"Yeah, but we have no way to get to the rendezvous point."

"One thing at a time. Getting to shore is all I need right now, and I have a chance of making it, so I am content. We made it, Luke."

A low, throbbing whine from above directed our eyes to the sky, where we saw the black flying-toast ship descend on its repulsors and hover perhaps four meters above the center of the lagoon, water rippling underneath it. It was a safe distance away from us—we couldn't get to it without a pair of oars and tremendous effort, while all its pilot had to do to us was pull the trigger. The cockpit of the ship was barely discernible, tinted as black as the rest of it. Even if Nakari was to get her slugthrower into position for a shot, she wouldn't know where to aim—and the bounty hunter was sure to have shields up anyway.

"Every time you say 'We made it,' something bad happens," I said.

"Correlation isn't causation," she replied. "But yeah. Damn."

A flat mechanical voice broadcast from the black ship. "Do not touch your weapons," it said. "You will proceed to the shore, where the Givin—"

Without warning, something truly massive erupted from the lagoon underneath the ship, jaws yawning wide and treating the bounty hunter's ship precisely like the toast it resembled by engulfing it. We heard a squawk from the bounty hunter over his speakers and saw a belated attempt to escape, but the ambush was perfect and he disappeared into the maw of a beast that appeared to be an eel of epic proportions. We could tell that he had begun to fire his blasters before the creature plunged back into the depths, but he would never be able to escape that carcass even if he killed the monster from the inside.

Admiral Ackbar's warnings about the planet were well founded. Our crash landing and subsequent ejection had no doubt attracted the attention of the predator.

A side effect of the beast's appearance was two impressive waves—one for its emergence, and another following afterward caused by its reentry. Both of them lifted us and propelled us toward the shore. Nakari's eyes danced and her eyebrows waggled at me as we cruised onto the beach, but she kept her lips pressed together tightly in a barely stifled smile as we helped Artoo onto the sand.

Once we all had our feet firmly planted on the shore, she said, "What did I say, Luke?"

I stretched out my arm in panic. "No, no, don't say it again—"

Nakari pumped her fist and shouted, "We made it! Wooo!"

And that's when the slower ships I had seen on the scanner before our crash arrived in the sky above the lagoon, searching for us and banking around, their wings bristling with weapons. There were six of them.

CHAPTER 22 $= \dfrac{n!}{(n-r)!r!}$

NAKARI AND I RAN for the tree line right away, making the strategic decision to let Drusil trail behind. We were expendable to the bounty hunters but she was not; from this angle the ships couldn't fire at us without a risk of hitting her first. She effectively served as a shield and allowed us to reach cover. The bounty hunters would have to land and come after us on foot, which would not be as easy.

When we reached the cover of the canopy, Nakari removed her slugthrower from her back and checked to make sure it was still functional after the dunk in the lagoon. Satisfied, she drew her blaster and tossed it to Drusil.

"I think you should stay with Drusil and head for the high ground there," she said, pointing to a promontory to the south. "I'll flank out to your side and take shots at whoever follows you."

"But what if they follow *you*?" I asked.

"I'm taking the droid and our tracks will make that clear. They'd never believe we'd split up and put their big-money target under the protection of an astromech, right? So they'll chase you, and I'll pick them off. You just move as fast as you can."

I nodded. "Right," I said, and we both took a couple of steps in different directions, thinking only of the mission. But then we stopped, thinking of each other, turned back, and froze. Both of us waited for the other to speak first, and we each made one or two halting starts, simultaneously, which caused us to stop and wait for the other to continue, and the awkwardness escalated with every fraction of a second—not to mention the terror. I was mortified that whatever I said next would be precisely the wrong thing—either too much or too little, just wholly inappropriate and not what she wanted to hear. Nakari must have been feeling something similar, and I wanted to say she didn't need to worry, she could say anything to me, but even that would probably be wrong.

"What is happening?" Drusil asked. "I am unfamiliar with this kind of human behavior. Have you lost the power of speech?"

"No," Nakari said, and she closed the distance between us in three long strides. Her head darted forward, lips kissing mine briefly, and then our gazes met. "Be safe, Luke."

It was a very safe thing to say compared to all the other phrases I had been considering, so I nodded with some relief and replied, "You, too."

"That was astoundingly straightforward," Drusil commented, her confusion clear. "What was the difficulty that prevented you from expressing such commonplace wishes?"

The Givin's words evoked embarrassed smiles from both of us, but I was grateful to Drusil for saying them anyway. Nakari's eyes spoke volumes to me, and I hope mine communicated as much to her. What I said, however, was "No time to explain," and I broke eye contact with Nakari to witness the landing of the first of the bounty hunters on the beach. "We have to go." Thinking of the extensive catalog offered by Utheel Outfitters on Rodia, as well as many other such businesses throughout the galaxy, I gave some final instructions to my droid.

"Artoo, make sure you're scanning in the infrared and other channels besides the visual and let Nakari know if you see something she doesn't. These bounty hunters are sure to have some tricks in their arsenal."

He acknowledged with a short electronic burp, and his dome rotated to face the lagoon.

We truly did part after that, and Drusil followed behind me as I picked a path through the trees toward the southern hill. I hoped we weren't rushing to the edge of a cliff; having so many other things demanding my attention on our flight, I hadn't committed the topography of the island to memory—I hadn't even gotten a very good look at it, beyond tagging it as an emergency landing spot.

While we headed due south, Nakari and Artoo swung southeast. In space, that can magnify quickly into vast distances, but on foot on a small island it was only the difference of a hundred meters. Nakari was silent in the forest, but Artoo made enough noise for both of them. Astromechs are the opposite of stealthy and are ill suited to moving cross-country across a largely rocky island covered with a thin layer of fern-dusted soil. The trees were unable to send roots deeply into the stone, so those roots trailed like wooden snakes above the ground, ready to trip us up and slow the progress of rolling droids. Their white trunks were understandably thin, but their canopies of broad leaves cast ample shade.

When I took a brief moment to check my trail, I

saw that Drusil's head was in constant motion, small jerks like those of a bird.

"What are you doing?" I asked.

"Gathering data."

A mechanical whine announced the approach of a swoop bike. One of the bounty hunters must have unloaded one from his ship, thinking to get to us first. The question of when precisely the newer arrivals would turn on one another was a good one; I hoped it would be sooner rather than later. If they focused on getting us first and then fighting through their competition, that would be to our detriment. Far better for them to cannibalize early and reduce their numbers.

"Incoming," I told Drusil, halting for the moment and turning around. "Use a tree for shelter and minimize your profile. I'll present myself as a target." I took a step to the right and spied the skimmer cutting through the trees toward us. It was piloted by a human with goggles strapped to his head, a dark cloak streaming behind him.

"My friend, there is no need," Drusil said.

"What do you mean?"

A crack sounded and the bounty hunter tumbled from the skimmer, sending the vehicle into an uncontrolled dive that resulted in a loud collision with the ground that was half crunching metal and half cracking bones and pulped tissue. A secondary explosion of startled birds from the nearby trees shuddered the air.

"Your mate is an exceedingly good sniper," Drusil said. "The odds were high she would eliminate the threat before we had cause to worry."

"My *mate*?" I said, spinning on my heel to resume running for high ground.

"Are you not mated?"

"I don't know—whatever we are, just don't call it

that, okay? I think that might be the worst possible word to describe a human relationship." I picked up my pace as if I could put physical distance between myself and her word choice.

"The definition has been quite clear in Basic for many years," Drusil persisted, close on my heels. "Is there another word that humans use among themselves?"

"Yeah—pretty much anything else."

"My sincerest apologies," Drusil said, her tone solicitous. "I was unaware of that word's potential to cause psychological trauma in your species."

"It's fine, let's just move on. There are still five bounty hunters, and we have a hill to climb."

"There is little cover beyond the thin trunks of the trees and the occasional flowering shrub," Drusil observed. "These ferns do not even rise to our knees, attractive as they may be."

"We'll have to take what advantage we can of the trees," I said. "And I want you flat on the ground when the shooting starts. Disappear into the ferns."

She didn't answer, probably because the exertion of jogging uphill had us both winded. When we did achieve the summit, I noted with satisfaction that it wasn't the edge of the island; the hill sloped back down to the water on the other side.

There was also an outcropping of boulders nearby that might serve as cover should we need to retreat that way. I didn't want to head there now, however; we had a good field of vision from this spot and little chance of the bounty hunters flanking us from behind. This island was unfamiliar terrain to them, as well.

"Let's set ourselves up behind some trees here," I said, moving to one nearby that afforded a good view down the slope.

"It would be preferable to choose one a little lower," Drusil said.

"Why?"

"Your . . . Nakari Kelen's field of fire would be clearer there."

"How would you know? You don't even know where she is." Nakari had taken cover along with Artoo somewhere off to our right and presumably downhill from our location.

"I do not need that information to decide where to place ourselves. Plot the trees or obstructions on a grid, calculate vectors—taking into account variations in elevation, of course—and it becomes clear that a small descent on our part will maximize her efficacy."

"All right, then. Tell me where we should take cover."

Instead of answering verbally, Drusil picked her way downhill perhaps ten meters and knelt behind a white-barked tree with black spots of old fallen branches, against which her pale head was perfectly camouflaged. She pointed to one immediately adjacent, indicating that I should plant myself there.

Crouching down as I moved, I confirmed visually that we could see the lower ground to our right a bit better from here—and presumably Nakari could see us a little better, too, and anyone approaching our position.

The air grew still. The birds had already taken flight, presumably to a quieter patch of the island or to another island entirely, and even the drone of insects tapered off. I didn't think there were any mammals either to disturb us or be disturbed; I doubted there was a source of fresh water on the island except whatever rain fell.

The hush and tension of a hunt is the wrong kind of

excitement when you're the one being hunted. There had to be at least one bounty hunter approaching us now on foot, if not more, but I saw no movement in the trees and heard nothing but the faint hum of ships powering down in the lagoon or else idling their engines, ready for a quick takeoff.

Checking on Drusil, I noted that she was not unfamiliar with how to handle a blaster; she was even practicing proper trigger discipline, keeping her finger outside the guard for the time being.

Seconds ticked by in near silence and I thought I picked up a low mechanical whir, but that was off to my right and might have been Artoo.

It was Artoo, in fact; he shot a bolt from his ion blaster, the attachment we'd installed on Denon to disable Drusil's security droid, directly across our vision from right to left. The white electric bolt splashed and crackled against an egg-shaped obstruction, which fizzed and popped and then melted away, revealing a Rodian bounty hunter who had been advancing upon us using a stealth-field generator attached to his belt. He was fast: He leveled his blaster and squeezed off three quick shots at the source, hitting at least once, judging by Artoo's high-pitched scream.

He never got off a fourth shot. With his stealth field neutralized, Nakari could see him, and she sent a slug through his eye that exploded the back of his head like a jogan fruit. Two down, four to go.

I hoped Artoo wasn't seriously damaged. I saw a thin trail of smoke rising through the trees, revealing his position, but he was also chattering angrily, so clearly he wasn't completely out of commission.

The problem was that he was making himself an easy target—and Nakari, too, if she was hiding nearby. It would be smart to put some distance between herself and the droid.

Drusil commented on the problem. "The damage to your droid reduces our tactical advantage. Seeing what happened to their colleagues and having a plain target to follow now, the remaining bounty hunters may attack our partners instead of ascending the hill. They could then attempt to flank us. At any rate, Nakari's ability to surprise is negated at this point."

"Maybe we can surprise *them,*" I said in a low voice, and pointed at two tan-skinned bipeds dressed for the desert. "See there? Two more of them advancing through the trees, working together as a team. Weequay."

"I have never encountered the species before."

"Tough hides. Naturally resistant to blasterfire. The Hutts like to use them as bodyguards and bounty hunters."

Drusil looked down, considering her weapon. "If they are resistant to our blasters, what can we do?"

"Resistant doesn't mean invulnerable. Nakari will have a better chance of knocking them down with a slug, of course, but we can probably wound them. Just firing at them will draw Nakari's attention—and theirs—and she can pick them off while we keep them busy."

"If she has the best chance of prevailing then we should let her take it. If you will permit me an observation, there are six functioning ships back at the lagoon to steal. Our odds of surviving without stealing one are quite low."

"Bounty hunters are paranoid," I said, shaking my head. "They'll have identity locks on their ignition sequence and maybe even traps installed so that no one else can fly their ships."

"So? You're with the galaxy's best slicer," Drusil said, and then she shrugged at my reaction. "Or *one* of the best, if I am being modest. Let my injudicious expression of confidence reassure rather than shock you. Get us back to the beach alive, Luke Skywalker, and I will get us a ship."

"How much time would you need?"

"If they are extraordinarily equipped, I may need as much as half an hour, no more. If a certain ship looks too difficult and we are pressed for time, however, we can simply choose another. The odds that all of them will have time-consuming security to overcome are small."

"All right, we'll head back to the lagoon. But we need to take out those Weequay first. Maybe that Rodian will have some extra weapons I can use."

SOMETIMES SIMPLE PLANS are the best ones. Or no plan at all, which is how Han often likes to fight: "If your plan never survives meeting the enemy, kid, why plan at all?" he asked me once. "Wasting time on something that's going to die in the first few seconds—I mean the plan—is a waste of time." When I told him that was circular logic he said to stop wasting his time. "Just blast everything and fly a fast ship. And bring a Wookiee. Works for me."

I didn't have a Wookiee or a fast ship anymore, but I could blast everything. I began shooting at the Weequay to make them take cover and halt their advance to the flank; once they hunkered down and fired back, Nakari would place bullet holes on their temples like periods at the end of a sentence. Drusil joined me and proved to be quite accurate. She took fewer shots but they were well aimed, her very first one striking one of the Weequay on the shoulder and knocking him down. His partner dived into the ferns also, but both of them popped up behind trees and returned fire, wild shots at first that didn't threaten us. I discovered that the trees weren't very good cover when I blasted one and it splintered apart, soft spongy wood spraying out behind yet toppling it forward, the canopy obstructing our view for a few seconds. The bounty hunter took advantage of that to move elsewhere, and the crack of Nakari's rifle sounded twice. I didn't see him fall, but he didn't get up to shoot at us again, either.

The tree trunk behind which Drusil knelt exploded in a blast from the other bounty hunter and fell backward. Drusil rolled away toward me, out of the shadow of its path, and poured four quick shots back at the Weequay. Those might have been shots fired in anger; I still couldn't tell from her expression. Combined with my own firing, one of us hit him and he tumbled back into the ferns—down, but not out.

"He will move and fire from a different position," Drusil mumbled, as much to herself as me, and then added a bit more clearly, "Probably to our left, ten to fifteen meters."

She turned out to be half-right. The Weequay did emerge from the ground cover to our left, but he didn't fire. He rose and sprinted uphill, a move that would eventually place him on our flank and put us between him and Nakari.

Except Nakari wasn't having any of that. He hadn't moved twenty meters before the staccato clap of her slugthrower echoed in the air and punched the bounty hunter off his feet.

"Four down," I said, allowing a note of hope to creep into my voice. We had chosen our positions well, and now there were only two left.

"The Aqualish will be problematic," Drusil said.

"What Aqualish? Where?"

"The one far downhill with a grenade launcher."

Problematic indeed. I didn't see him at first, but eventually I spotted movement through the trees. He was thick-limbed, with two frontal tusks and large dark eyes. These weak trees had already proven to be poor protection, and Nakari and Artoo had nothing else—nor did we. The bounty hunter wouldn't lob a grenade our way for fear of taking out Drusil, but he wasn't approaching us. Nakari was at the top of his list. She had been so effective that she had marked herself as the primary threat.

"We have to bring him down." I raised my blaster and steadied it by cupping my left hand under it and locking my elbows. My first shot was perceptibly in his direction but didn't get too close, since it clipped a tree trunk on its way and its energy was absorbed.

"At this distance and with this number of obstructions, accuracy from a handheld blaster is difficult to achieve," Drusil noted. "We should move closer, yet keep an eye out for the last bounty hunter."

I didn't hesitate. Rising to my feet and scanning ahead, looking for a clear shot, I kept my blaster in a two-handed grip, ready to fire as soon as the opportunity arrived. But the Aqualish saw his opportunity first. He pointed his weapon up, and a huffing noise heralded the launch of his first grenade.

"No," I said, and took the best shot I could. It scored the side of a trunk near the bounty hunter, but he didn't even turn his head. He just fired another grenade as the first one landed and rocked the island with a palpable concussion. It wasn't particularly close to Nakari, nor was the second one, but I think he was merely finding his range.

Giving up on trying to blast him since all I hit were trees, I aimed at the trees instead—ones that might fall on him and cause him to quit firing grenades long enough for me to do more lasting damage. Drusil helped, and several of them began to topple around the bounty hunter, but he managed to fire two more grenades before scrambling out of the way, finally affected by our fusillade.

Desperate, I stretched out with the Force, trying to locate those grenades and divert their path at least a little bit, but I couldn't find them or feel them. I felt Nakari's presence, though, and the Aqualish running for cover, and also the last bounty hunter, a reptilian Trandoshan, crouching in the ferns close to the lagoon and taking in the scene. And I was able to sense all this just as the grenades boomed and shook the ground below us and a cry of pain, cut short, was accompanied by Artoo's wail, and then there was a sharp, empty space in the Force where Nakari had been a moment earlier.

It was a blow to the gut, realizing what that sudden absence meant. I hadn't seen it happen with my eyes, but I had felt Nakari's life snuffed out through the Force, and into that void where she had shone anger rushed in—anger, and a cold sense of raw power and invincibility. With clarity I had never felt before, I knew precisely where the Aqualish had moved and the Trandoshan, too. The latter had decided to go after the Aqualish before coming after us, thinking it best to eliminate the guy with the grenade launcher before tackling the people with the blasters.

I found myself agreeing with him: Eliminate the Aqualish. I took a step to join in the hunt but stopped, breathing heavily, unaccountably sweating even though I felt so cold inside and the power of the Force roiled within me.

"I don't feel so good," I muttered, and when Drusil asked me to clarify, I didn't answer. It was the feeling of invincibility that worried me—I had just learned through the Force that we were definitely not invincible creatures, and yet now the Force suggested that I somehow was. I shook with emotion and power, and none of it felt the way the Force had before—warm and supportive and nurturing. I was frightened both by the unfamiliarity of the feeling and because I didn't know what to do with all that energy.

So I kept still, letting the bounty hunters go after each other and consciously slowing down my breathing, trying to calm myself and control the impulse to lash out unthinkingly. Had the Aqualish been directly in front of me, I doubt I would have been able to restrain that impulse, but he was still a good distance away and had changed tactics now, trying to stalk us and use a blaster set to stun. I sensed that he was unaware of being stalked in turn.

"Luke, you seem unwell. Can I assist you somehow?"

"I need a minute, Drusil," I managed, realizing that she didn't know yet that Nakari was gone. Merely thinking that refilled the empty space in the Force with even more rage, and I saw what kind of a space it was, a black hole that would always be hungry no matter how much I fed it. I might never feel warm again if I didn't get myself under control.

Blasterfire erupted downhill, an exchange of murderous heat between the two bounty hunters, and when the Aqualish's presence disappeared from the Force, I felt a small sense of justice, if not balance. Another deep breath, and I opened my eyes, feeling a semblance of calm return.

"Only one of them left now," I said.

"Are you certain?"

"Positive. The Trandoshan. Did you see him?"

"Earlier, yes, but I was worried about you and took my eyes off him for approximately nineteen seconds."

"Well, we don't have to sit here and wait. Probably better that we don't. We've pushed our luck far enough as it is. Let's get back to the beach like you suggested and steal a ship."

"You are thinking Nakari will shoot the—"

"No," I said, cutting her off and shaking my head. "The grenades."

"Oh," Drusil said, a hand rising to her throat. For the first time I thought I saw emotion on her face. "That is heartbreaking. You saw?"

"No." I looked down, trying to keep it together. "I felt it."

"I am so very sorry."

"Me, too."

The Givin's head turned to gaze downhill. "But then we must worry about the Trandoshan ourselves."

We did, but at some point, the clarity of sense that I'd possessed had faded away along with my anger. I no longer felt the bounty hunter's presence in the Force. All I felt was loss.

"I'm sure he'll be along eventually if we just stay here," I said.

"Wait," the Givin said, staring into the forest. She pointed with a pale finger. "Do you see that thicket of shrubbery between the two trees six degrees left of the y axis from our position? Shoot it."

I squinted through the tree trunks until I found the thicket she spoke of. "Why? Did you see something move?"

"No. But based on available cover, spatial geometrics, and his prior movements, the statistical probability he is there is quite high."

I wasn't going to argue. Even if we missed it would most likely flush him out. "Shoot the center of it?"

"Just to the right of center. I will shoot slightly right of that, nearer the tree. Let us steady our hands, aim carefully, and fire together on my count."

Drusil counted down from three and we fired in tandem into the foliage. We were rewarded with a pained cry of surprise and followed up with a few more shots to make sure. I looked at the Givin, incredulous that she could figure his position so precisely, and she shrugged.

"What can I say? Math."

CHAPTER ± 24

$$\sqrt{\sigma^2 + \varepsilon}$$

A GRISLY YET RELIABLE fact about custom bounty hunter ships is that you can always count on them to have body bags stashed somewhere for the easy transport of their kills. They often had built-in refrigerated storage, too, and a small chamber that served as a brig for those bounties they needed to bring back alive.

Much as it hurt, I searched for and found a body bag for Nakari in one of the ships that had its bay open, then I trekked back into the forest and finally set eyes on her, visually confirming what I had already felt. I couldn't just leave her on Omereth. Fayet Kelen had already had his wife ripped from him with no way to say good-bye and let go. It was the very least I could do to take his daughter home; I owed her far more.

Nakari had ragged holes in her from shrapnel, but I was relieved that she was at least still in one piece and her eyes were already closed. Artoo waited nearby, still smoking from where a bolt had destroyed his ion blaster and part of the socket where it had been attached. The rest of him was coated in a thin layer of black grit and carbon scoring. He greeted me with a morose moan instead of his usual burble.

"We'll get you fixed, Artoo," I reassured him, and then I dropped to my knees next to Nakari, eyes welling up already, and in a strange way I welcomed the blur to my vision and let the tears come; I'd never done so before because it had never seemed the proper time to mourn. Ben had been there when I discovered the burnt bodies of my aunt and uncle and I'd bottled everything up in shock, telling myself that the Empire was hunting us and we had to get to Alderaan. When Vader cut down Ben, there was no time to mourn him, either, only time to escape the Death Star and then join the Battle of Yavin. I lost my old friend Biggs to a TIE fighter during that battle, but I could hardly allow myself to think of that when I had to make my firing run down the trench. Then, incredibly, we won the day and everyone was happy, and there was always more work to do after that. It was never the right time to stop and feel all that I'd lost. But I had the time now: The Empire didn't know where I was, Drusil would wait until I returned, and Artoo wouldn't judge me. So I finally opened up that bottle inside and let the grief pour out. Nakari's smile, Ben's teaching, my aunt and uncle, joking around with Biggs, and so much more—all of it had been ripped from me by the war and I'd repressed it all because I thought I had to. But no more. My throat constricted with emotion and I lowered my head to Nakari's shoulder and allowed myself to feel it all, the complete tragedy that none of them would ever speak to me again—even Ben's voice was gone now.

Though it took a while, eventually I was spent and sat up, brushing a lock of hair away from Nakari's face and hooking it behind her ear. "I'm so sorry. You were more than just good for me. I should have said so." It was wholly inadequate, but I couldn't think of what else to say.

Recalling our conversation last night on Kupoh, I wished I could go back to the Luke of a few hours ago and say, *Tell her how you feel* now, *Luke, while you still have the chance. Because you'll always regret never saying the words.*

I'm not sure why I have such trouble with that. I don't know if it's a natural thing or something I learned from Uncle Owen. I know he had strong feelings, but he wasn't in the habit of giving them words. He would do small things for Aunt Beru, surprising kindnesses, and whenever she came across them her eyes would light up and she would smile and say softly, "Owen." That's how she knew, and that's the example I grew up with: You don't tell people you love them, you show them. Or maybe I'm just terrified of sounding like an idiot when I try to tell someone they make me glad to be alive. I hope my friends know that I would fight and die for them. And I also hope that is enough, though I'm afraid maybe it isn't.

I might have stayed there on my knees staring at Nakari until sunset if I hadn't had Drusil waiting on me in the lagoon. Pointless, really; it wasn't like I would forget the sight anytime soon. But somehow, putting her in the bag meant I had to let her go, and I didn't want to. I needed to, though. I needed to let them all go.

It took some effort and a fresh spring of tears rolled down my face in the process, but I got her inside and asked Artoo if he could make it back to the beach on his own as I gently pulled the zipper closed. He beeped and edged forward as an answer, so I said, "Let's go."

The thin plas material crackled as I picked up Nakari and with some effort hitched her over my shoulder. Her physical weight didn't seem nearly as heavy

as the pressure of my grief, and I knew I'd have to
carry the grief much longer.

We had the pick of six ships on the beach, but Drusil chose the one I had entered to find a body bag.
It was the sleekest design among a heavily armored
bunch, a dark-blue, beetle-shaped crate that may
have belonged to the Dressellian whom Nakari had
shot off the swoop bike. Drusil avoided the cockpit
entirely, searching instead for the guts of the nav computer and the systems service bay. Artoo accompanied her, and I heard him chattering and the Givin
mumbling to him as I gently lowered Nakari's body
to the deck.

Seeing the lifeless black lump of plas that represented her now, a surge of anger and the cold that
came with it rose up inside me again. But I closed
my eyes, focused on my breathing, and remembered
laughing with her. The cold gradually turned to
warmth and I felt much better. Instead of feeling an
impotent rage over all the time we wouldn't have, I
determined to feel grateful for the time we did, because it had all been good and not everyone gets to
enjoy times like those. I carefully sat next to her on
the deck, folding my legs in front of me, determined
to master my emotions. I still had a mission to complete, and it wouldn't do to be ruled by them. The
bounty hunters we'd eliminated here might not be
the only ones on the planet; more could be waiting
at the island for us.

I didn't know how much time slipped past, but when
Drusil entered the bay and told me the ship's security
had been sliced and was now safe to fly, I was ready
and the sun was riding low on the horizon.

"You checked the cockpit, too?" I asked. "There
might be additional traps there."

"Oh, yes. Everything has been seen to."

"All right. Let's get to the rendezvous."

Drusil had fed the coordinates into the computer, and after taking some time to orient myself to the controls, I had the ship rise vertically to a safe height above the ocean before banking west. I didn't want to become a snack for anything underneath the waves.

The scanning equipment on the ship was serviceable but not near the level of the *Desert Jewel*. We got a look at the island, much larger than the one we had left behind, and saw that there were plenty of heat signatures and life readings there, along with a Corellian corvette on the ground that could have anywhere from a dozen to hundreds of people on board. It was one of the combat-outfitted CR90s with six dual turbolasers, and I wondered if Major Derlin could still be there.

If he was, he'd probably seen this ship before, which meant he would shoot at us on sight if he could. I spun the ship into evasive maneuvers just in time as a volley of laserfire zipped past us into the sky. I flipped on the deflector shields, cursing myself for not doing so as a routine precaution, and changed my approach to the island. We'd have to land some distance away and walk in, calling to make sure we weren't ambushed. I didn't know how to hail Major Derlin from this ship—but then I thought maybe Artoo could figure it out, since he was wired into this unfamiliar system. He wasn't in the cockpit, though, and I didn't know which of the auxiliary switches would activiate an intercom link to him. Deciding to go low-tech, I shouted over my shoulder and hoped he would hear me.

"Artoo, can you reach that ship on the island and patch it through if they respond? Tag your query with Alliance codes."

We had to scramble out of the firing range of the other craft for another minute, but eventually a voice came through to the cockpit demanding to know how we had come to possess Alliance codes.

"This is Lieutenant Luke Skywalker. We destroyed all the bounty hunters that came to kill us and I have commandeered this ship. I have Drusil Bephorin on board ready to reunite with her family. Please stop shooting at us and let us land."

After a pause, a different voice replied. There was the unmistakable sound of cheering going on behind him. "Lieutenant Skywalker, this is Major Bren Derlin. So good to hear your voice, sir. Drusil's family is alive and well. You're cleared to land."

"Copy that. Coming around, see you soon."

A noise in the ship startled me—something like a bantha horking up a glob of phlegm the size of a small moon. It turned out to be Drusil reacting to the news; she'd been listening in. Givin don't have mucous membranes similar to humans or even tear ducts, so her loud expression of raw emotion was nothing I would have encountered before.

Bren Derlin's team—a couple of squadrons of experienced troops—was waiting for us outside the ship, weapons ready but lowered, just in case a bounty hunter walked out after all, but they smiled and put away their weapons when I emerged. They looked tired and Derlin's legendary mustache drooped a bit, but they were otherwise in good shape. He signaled to one of his troops and she waved someone forward who was out of sight on the ship, and that turned out to be Drusil's family. Her husband and two children clattered down the landing ramp with excited steps and Drusil ran to meet them. They collided together with outstretched arms and many awkward noises.

"What happened?" I asked Major Derlin. "The bounty hunters followed you here?"

Chagrined, he nodded. "Unavoidable. Just bad timing. We were in the middle of extracting the family when word went out about the bounty on Drusil. Suddenly the family got checked on and we were discovered. We had a firefight getting out of there—I lost three men—and four hunters followed us out of the system. We lost the Empire once we jumped but picked up more hunters as we went—I think some of them called in their friends."

"But they didn't call the Empire?"

"The bounty on the family was too small to fight over, but the money for Drusil was worth a stakeout and splitting the proceeds. We hoped you'd be here waiting and we could take off right away, but instead we had to fortify and try to hold them off."

"Clearly you succeeded."

The major shrugged his shoulders and managed to do the same with his mustache. "They never attacked. They just jammed us to prevent us from broadcasting any messages and waited for you to show up. We couldn't leave the family here on their own or it would have become a hostage situation, and if we tried to pick a fight, we'd have been outgunned."

"Why didn't they just attack you, then? We were coming regardless."

"We made it clear that if they did attack we'd take a couple of them with us. And they made it clear we weren't allowed to leave and change the venue. The smartest choice for everyone was to wait for you to arrive. And since they weren't letting the Empire know we were here, I thought you had a good chance of winning through, and you did."

"Not without cost, though," I said. I bobbed my

head back at the ship. "We lost the *Desert Jewel* back there, and lost Nakari Kelen, too."

Derlin's face fell. "Nakari was with you? They didn't tell me. I'm very sorry, Luke. We met her not long ago. She was a top-shelf sniper, taught me and the boys a few things."

I nodded, keeping my emotions firmly reined in. "She taught me a lot, too." I waved a hand at his corvette. "Are you in good shape? Okay to head back to the fleet?"

"Yeah, we have some scorch marks, but that's about it."

"Can I ride along?"

"Of course."

Drusil came over with her family, elated, and introduced me to her husband and children. They were clothed in something like long, colorful tapestries with a hole for the head and belted at the waist, and underneath were simple black shirts and pants. Her son started to ask me a math question, but Drusil interrupted him. "That's very polite of you, Pentir, but you can dispense with pleasantries in this case."

"Oh. Apologies," he said.

"Not to worry. It's my pleasure to meet you all," I said.

"I'm so very grateful to you and the Alliance for engineering a successful escape," Drusil said. "I'm well aware of the sacrifices you have made to free us. And I have promised you a significant amount of intelligence regarding Imperial codes and search patterns in return. The slicing programs for low-level Imperial encryption that I mentioned, as well as others. Where would you like me to download this information?"

"You can share it with Artoo," I said, "and he'll distribute it as necessary to the rest of the Alliance."

"Excellent. I will begin shortly. May I ask one more favor?"

"Go ahead."

"Considering that this location has been compromised, we will need transport offplanet. May we take the bounty hunter's ship, or might you take us back to the lagoon to secure another? We will settle somewhere else, and I will make contact with the Alliance to set up a continuing employment arrangement."

"You can take this ship," I assured her.

"And I can arrange a dead drop site for you to use once you're safe," Derlin added.

While Drusil huddled with Artoo and transferred files from her hardware to his memory and Derlin busied himself with getting his corvette ready to depart, I transferred Nakari's body from the bounty hunter's craft to the Alliance vessel myself. We would stop at Pasher on the way back to the rebel fleet, and I already knew there was no way to adequately communicate to her father my sorrow at her fate. Even if I could, it wouldn't matter; he would be as inconsolable as I was, for no matter how personally rich and powerful he became, no matter how he tried, he would never have the power to keep everyone safe— nor would I.

After farewells and promises of future contact, we lifted away from Omereth, leaving it to churn and spin in isolation. Major Derlin and his crew kept me occupied and accompanied for much of our very roundabout return to the fleet, but I found myself eating a lonesome bowl of noodles for lunch at some point in the ship's cavernous mess, Artoo by my side but unable to share food or much in the way of conversation. Thinking of my previous small victories with noodles made me miss Nakari again and threatened to set my emotions aboil, but I also recollected the amusement of those times and Nakari's delight in my progress in the Force—or at least her delight in flying noodles. It occurred to me that I would honor her memory much more by continuing to improve rather than by wallowing in a swamp of regret. And that empty space inside me could be filled with pleasant memories instead of anger.

The door to the mess was open and I flicked my eyes that way, listening for a moment to make sure no one was nearby. Once satisfied that I'd be alone for at least a few more minutes, I closed my eyes and stretched out to the Force, recalling that feeling of confidence and encouragement Nakari had given me before. I focused on the fork, currently submerged beneath a carpet of noodles in a vegetable broth. It felt the way it used to, warm and kind rather than that one time it had been cold and implacable. Gently lifting, feeling the Force supporting the fork, I floated up a glob of noodles and then guided it into my mouth, where I bit down and slurped a little bit, holding the fork between my teeth and opening my eyes to make sure this was really happening. I smiled around the fork and some juice leaked out the corners of my mouth, staining my tunic. Of course. That started me laughing, and Artoo seesawed on his arms and tweeted his own amusement. I reached up with my hand to grab the fork before it got any worse.

"That has to be the weirdest way to eat," I said to Artoo. "But Nakari would have loved it."

Artoo chirped his agreement and I took a deep breath and exhaled slowly, arriving at a clear, quiet place in my mind. Using the Force in this way was a gift Nakari had given me, and it would be senseless to let it go to waste.

I would practice, and think of her, and get better at this. Much, much better.

I would still prefer a teacher, of course, but Nakari showed me that progress is possible without one, and so I owe it to her—and to Ben, and everyone else I've lost and might lose in the future—to make what strides I can.

It might take me many years, but I am determined to become a Jedi like my father.

Read on for an excerpt from

STAR WARS: AFTERMATH

Chuck Wendig

Published by Del Rey Books

PRELUDE

Today is a day of celebration. We have triumphed over villainy and oppression and have given our Alliance—and the galaxy beyond it—a chance to breathe and cheer for the progress in reclaiming our freedom from an Empire that robbed us of it. We have reports from Commander Skywalker that Emperor Palpatine is dead, and his enforcer, Darth Vader, with him.

But though we may celebrate, we should not consider this our time to rest. We struck a major blow against the Empire, and now will be the time to seize on the opening we have created. The Empire's weapon may be destroyed, but the Empire itself lives on. Its oppressive hand closes around the throats of good, freethinking people across the galaxy, from the Coruscant Core to the farthest systems in the Outer Rim. We must remember that our fight continues. Our rebellion is over. But the war . . . the war is just beginning.

—Admiral Ackbar

Coruscant

THEN:

Monument Plaza.

Chains rattle as they lash the neck of Emperor Palpatine. Ropes follow suit—lassos looping around the statue's middle. The mad cheers of the crowd as they pull, and pull, and pull. Disappointed groans as the stone fixture refuses to budge. But then someone whips the chains around the back ends of a couple of heavy-gauge speeders, and then engines warble and hum to life—the speeders gun it and again the crowd pulls—

The sound like a giant bone breaking.

A fracture appears at the base of the statue.

More cheering. Yelling. And—

Applause as it comes crashing down.

The head of the statue snaps off, goes rolling and crashing into a fountain. Dark water splashes. The crowd laughs.

And then: The whooping of klaxons. Red lights strobe. Three airspeeders swoop down from the traffic lanes above—Imperial police. Red-and-black helmets. The glow of their lights reflected back in their helmets.

There comes no warning. No demand to stand down.

The laser cannons at the fore of each airspeeder open fire. Red bolts sear the air. The crowd is cut apart. Bodies dropped and stitched with fire.

But still, those gathered are not cowed. They are no

longer a crowd. Now they are a mob. They start picking up hunks of the Palpatine statue and lobbing them up at the airspeeders. One of the speeders swings to the side to avoid an incoming chunk of stone—and it bumps another speeder, interrupting its fire. Coruscanti citizens climb up the stone spire behind both speeders—a spire on which are written the Imperial values of order, control, and the rule of law—and begin jumping onto the police cruisers. One helmeted cop is flung from his vehicle. The other crawls out onto the hood of his speeder, opening fire with a pair of blasters—just as a hunk of stone cracks him in the helmet, knocking him to the ground.

The other two airspeeders lift higher and keep firing.

Screams and fire and smoke.

Two of those gathered—a father and son, Rorak and Jak—quick-duck behind the collapsed statue. The sounds of the battle unfolding right here in Monument Plaza don't end. In the distance, the sound of more fighting, a plume of flames, flashes of blaster fire. A billboard high up in the sky among the traffic lanes suddenly goes to static.

The boy is young, only twelve standard years, not old enough to fight. Not yet. He looks to his father with pleading eyes. Over the din he yells: "But the battle station was destroyed, Dad! The battle is over!" They just watched it only an hour before. The supposed end of the Empire. The start of something better.

The confusion in the boy's shining eyes is clear: He doesn't understand what's happening.

But Rorak does. He's heard tales of the Clone Wars—tales spoken by his own father. He knows how war goes. It's not many wars, but just one, drawn out again and again, cut up into slices so it seems more manageable.

For a long time he's told his son not the truth but the idealized hope: *One day the Empire will fall and things will be different for when you have children.* And that may still come to pass. But now a stronger, sharper truth is required: "Jak—the battle isn't over. The battle is just starting."

He holds his son close.

Then he puts a hunk of statue in the boy's hand.

And he picks one up himself.

Part One

CHAPTER ONE

NOW:

Starlines streak across the bright black.

A ship drops out of hyperspace: a little Starhopper. A one-person ship. Favored by many of the *less desirable* factions out here in the Outer Rim—the pirates, the bookies, the bounty hunters and those with bounties on their heads to hunt. This particular ship has seen action: plasma scarring across the wings and up its tail fins; a crumpled dent in the front end as if it was kicked by an Imperial walker. All the better for the ship to blend in.

Ahead: the planet Akiva. A small planet—from here, striations of brown and green. Thick white clouds swirling over its surface.

The pilot, Wedge Antilles, once Red Leader and now—well, now something else, a role without a formal title, as yet, because things are so new, so different, so wildly up in the air—sits there and takes a moment.

It's nice up here. Quiet.

No TIE fighters. No blasts across the bow of his X-wing. No X-wing, in fact, and though he loves flying one, it's nice to be out. No Death Star—and here, Wedge shudders, because he helped take down two of those things. Some days that fills him with pride. Other days it's something else, something worse. Like he's drawn back to it. The fight still going on all around him. But that isn't today.

Today, it's quiet.

Wedge likes the quiet.

He pulls up his datapad. Scrolls through the list with a tap of the button on the side. (He has to hit it a few extra times just to get it to go—if there's one thing he looks forward to when all this is over, it's that maybe they'll start to get new tech. Somehow, this datapad had actual *sand* in it, and that's why the buttons stick.) The list of planets clicks past.

He's been to, let's see, five so far. Florrum. Ryloth. Hinari. Abafar. Raydonia. This planet, Akiva, is the sixth on the list of many, too many.

It was his idea, this run. Somehow, the remaining factions of the Empire are still fueling their war effort even months after the destruction of their second battle station. Wedge had the notion that they must've moved out to the Outer Rim—study your history and it's easy to see that the seeds of the Empire grew first out here, away from the Core systems, away from the prying eyes of the Republic.

Wedge told Ackbar, Mon Mothma: "Could be that's where they are again. Hiding out there." Ackbar said that it made some sense. After all, didn't Mustafar hold some importance to the Imperial leadership? Rumors said that's where Vader took some of the Jedi long ago. Torturing them for information before their execution.

And now Vader's gone. Palpatine, too.

Almost there, Wedge thinks—once they find the supply lines that are bolstering the Imperials, he'll feel a whole lot better.

He pulls up the comm. Tries to open a channel to command and—

Nothing.

Maybe it's broken. It's an old ship.

Wedge fidgets at his side, pulls up the personal comm relay that hangs there at his belt—he taps the side of it, tries to get a signal.

Once more: nothing.

His heart drops into his belly. Feels a moment like he's falling. Because what all of this adds up to is:

The signal's blocked. Some of the criminal syndicates still operating out here have technology to do that *locally*—but in the space above the planet, no, no way. Only one group has that tech.

His jaw tightens. The bad feeling in the well of his gut is swiftly justified, as ahead a Star Destroyer punctures space like a knife-tip as it drops out of hyperspace. Wedge fires up the engines. *I have to get out of here.*

A second Star Destroyer slides in next to the first.

The panels across the Starhopper's dash begin blinking red.

They see him. What to do?

What did Han always say? *Just fly casual.* The ship is disguised as it is for a reason: It looks like it could belong to any two-bit smuggler out here on the fringe. Akiva's a hotbed of criminal activity. Corrupt satrap governors. Various syndicates competing for resources and opportunities. A well-known black market—once, decades ago, the Trade Federation had a droid manufacturing facility here. Which means, if you want some off-the-books droid, you can come here to buy one. The Rebel Alliance procured many of its droids right here, as a matter of fact.

New dilemma, though: What now?

Fly down to the planet to do aerial recon, as was the original plan—or plot a course back to Chandrila? Something's up. Two Star Destroyers appearing out of nowhere? Blocked comms? That's not nothing. *It means I've found what I'm looking for.*

Maybe even something much better.

That means: Time to plot a course out of here.

That'll take a few minutes, though—heading inward from the Outer Rim isn't as easy as taking a long stride from here to there. It's a dangerous jump. Endless variables await: nebula clouds, asteroid fields, floating bands of star-junk from various skirmishes and battles. Last thing Wedge wants to do is pilot around the edge of a black hole or through the center of a star going supernova.

The comm crackles.

They're hailing him.

A crisp Imperial voice comes across the channel.

"This is the Star Destroyer *Vigilance*. You have entered Imperial space." To which Wedge thinks: *This isn't Imperial space. What's going on here?* "Identify yourself."

Fear lances through him, sharp and bright as an electric shock. This isn't his realm. Talking. Lying. A scoundrel like Solo could convince a Jawa to buy a bag of sand. Wedge is a pilot. But it's not like they didn't plan for this. Calrissian worked on the story. He clears his throat, hits the button—

"This is Gev Hessan. Piloting an HH87 Starhopper: the *Rover*." He transmits his datacard. "Sending over credentials."

A pause. "Identify the nature of your visit."

"Light cargo."

"What cargo?"

The stock answer is: droid components. But that may not fly here. He thinks quickly—Akiva. Hot. Wet. Mostly jungle. "Dehumidifier parts."

Pause. An excruciating one.

The nav computer runs through its calculations.

Almost there . . .

A different voice comes through the tinny speaker. A woman's voice. Got some steel in it. Less crisp. Nothing lilting. This is someone with some authority—or, at least, someone who thinks she possesses it.

She says, "Gev Hessan. Pilot number 45236. Devaronian. Yes?"

That checks out. Calrissian knows Hessan. The smuggler—sorry, "legitimate pilot and businessman"—did work smuggling goods to help Lando build Cloud City. And he is indeed Devaronian.

"You got it," Wedge says.

Another pause.

The computer is almost done with its calculations. Another ten seconds at most. Numbers crunching, flickering on the screen . . .

"Funny," the woman says. "Our records indicate that Gev Hassan died in Imperial custody. Please let us correct our records."

The hyperspace computer finishes its calculations.

He pushes the thruster forward with the heel of his hand—

But the ship only shudders. Then the Starhopper trembles again, and begins to drift forward. Toward the pair of Star Destroyers. It means they've engaged the tractor beams.

He turns to the weapon controls.

If he's going to get out of this, it's now or never.

Admiral Rae Sloane stares down at the console and out the window. The black void. The white stars. Like pinpricks in a blanket. And out there, like a child's toy on the blanket: a little long-range fighter.

"Scan them," she says. Lieutenant Nils Tothwin looks up, offers her an obsequious smile.

"Of course," he says, his jaundiced face tight with that grin. Tothwin is an emblem of what's wrong with the Imperial forces now: Many of their best are gone. What's left is, in part, the dregs. The leaves and twigs at the bottom of a cup of spice tea. Still, he does what he's told, which is something—Sloane wonders when the Empire will truly begin to fracture. Forces doing what they want, when they want it. Chaos and anarchy. The moment that happens, the moment someone of some prominence breaks from the fold to go his own way, they are all truly doomed.

Tothwin scans the Starhopper as the tractor beam brings it slowly, but inevitably, closer. The screen beneath him glimmers, and a holographic image of the ship rises before him, constructed as if by invisible hands. The image flashes red along the bottom. Nils, panic in his voice, says: "Hessan is charging his weapons systems."

She scowls. "Calm down, Lieutenant. The weapons on a Starhopper aren't enough to—" Wait. She squints. "Is that what I think it is?"

"What?" Tothwin asks. "I don't—"

Her finger drifts to the front end of the holograph—circling the fighter's broad, curved nose. "Here. Ordnance launcher. Proton torpedo."

"But the Starhopper wouldn't be equipped—oh. *Oh.*"

"Someone has come prepared for a fight." She reaches down, flips on the comm again. "This is Admiral Rae Sloane. I see you there, little pilot. Readying a pair of torpedoes. Let me guess: You think a proton torpedo will disrupt our tractor beam long enough to afford you your escape. That may be accurate. But let me also remind you that we have enough ordnance on the *Vigilance* to turn you not only to scrap but rather, to a *fine particulate matter.* Like dust, cast across the dark. The timing doesn't work. You'll fire your torpedo. We'll fire ours. Even *if* by the time your weapons strike us our beam is disengaged . . ." She clucks her tongue. "Well. If you feel you must try, then try."

She tells Nils to target the Starhopper.

Just in case.

But she hopes the pilot is wise. Not some fool. Probably some rebel scout, some spy, which is foolish on its own—though less foolish now, with the newly built second Death Star destroyed like its predecessor.

All the more reason for her to remain vigilant, as the name of this ship suggests. The meeting on Akiva cannot misfire. It must take place. It must have a *result*. Everything feels on the edge, the entire Empire standing on the lip of the pit, the ledge crumbling away to scree and stone.

The pressure is on. An almost literal pressure—like a fist pressing against her back, pushing the air out of her lungs.

Her chance to excel.

Her chance to change Imperial fortune.

Forget the old way.

Indeed.

Wedge winces, heart racing in his chest like an ion pulse. He knows she's right. The timing doesn't favor him. He's a good pilot, maybe one of the best, but he doesn't have the Force on his side. If Wedge launches those two torpedoes, they'll give him everything they have. And then it won't matter if he breaks free from the tractor beam. He won't have but a second to get away from whatever fusillade they send his way.

Something is happening. Here, in the space above Akiva. Or maybe down there on the planet's surface.

If he dies here—nobody will know what it is.

Which means he has to play this right.

He powers down the torpedoes.

He has another idea.

Docking Bay 42.

Rae Sloane stands in the glass-encased balcony, overlooking the gathered battalion of stormtroopers. This lot, like Nils, are imperfect. Those who received top marks at the Academy went on to serve on the Death Star, or on Vader's command ship, the *Executor*. Half of them didn't even complete the Academy— they were pulled out of training early.

These will do, though. For now. Ahead is the Starhopper—drifting in through the void of space, cradled by the invisible grip of the tractor beam. Down past the lineup of TIE fighters (half of what they need, a third of what she'd prefer), drifting slowly toward the gathered stormtroopers.

They have the numbers. The Starhopper will have one pilot, most likely. Perhaps a second or third crew-member.

It drifts closer and closer.

She wonders: *Who are you?* Who is inside that little tin can?

Then: A bright flash and a shudder—the Starhopper suddenly glows blue from the nose end forward.

It explodes in a rain of fire and scrap.

"Whoever it was," Lieutenant Tothwin says, "they did not wish to be discovered. I suppose they favored a quick way out."

Sloane stands amid the smoldering wreckage of the long-range fighter. It stinks of ozone and fire. A pair of gleaming black astromechs whir, firing extinguishing foam to put out the last of the flames. They have to navigate around the half dozen or so stormtrooper bodies that lie about, still. Helmets cracked. Chest plates charred. Blaster rifles scattered and broken.

"Don't be a naïve calf," she says, scowling. "*No*, the pilot didn't want to be discovered. But he's still here. If he didn't want us to blast him out of the sky out *there*, you really think he'd be eager to die in *here*?"

"Could be a suicide attack. Maximize the damage—"

"No. He's here. And he can't be far. Find him."

Nils gives a sharp, nervous nod. "Yes, Admiral. Right away."

Read on for an excerpt from

STAR WARS: BATTLEFRONT: TWILIGHT COMPANY

by Alexander Freed

Published by Del Rey Books

THE RAIN on Haidoral Prime dropped in warm sheets from a shining sky. It smelled like vinegar, clung to the molded curves of modular industrial buildings and to litter-strewn streets, and coated skin like a sheen of acrid sweat.

After thirty straight hours, it was losing its novelty for the soldiers of Twilight Company.

Three figures crept along a deserted avenue under a torn and dripping canopy. The lean, compact man in the lead was dressed in faded gray fatigues and a hodgepodge of armor pads crudely stenciled with the starbird symbol of the Rebel Alliance. Matted dark hair dripped beneath his visored helmet, sending crawling trails of rainwater down his dusky face.

His name was Hazram Namir, though he'd gone by others. He silently cursed urban warfare and Haidoral Prime and whichever laws of atmospheric science made it rain. The thought of sleep flashed into his mind and broke against a wall of stubbornness. He gestured with a rifle thicker than his arm toward the nearest intersection, then quickened his pace.

Somewhere in the distance a swift series of blaster shots resounded, followed by shouts and silence.

The figure closest behind Namir—a tall man with graying hair and a face puckered with scar tissue—bounded across the street to take up a position opposite. The third figure, a massive form huddled in a tarp like a hooded cloak, remained behind.

The scarred man flashed a hand signal. Namir turned the corner onto the intersecting street. A dozen meters away, the sodden lumps of human bodies lay in the road. They wore tattered rain gear—sleek, light-weight wraps and sandals—and carried no weapons. Noncombatants.

It's a shame, Namir thought, *but not a bad sign.* The Empire didn't shoot civilians when everything was under control.

"Charmer—take a look?" Namir indicated the bodies. The scarred man strode over as Namir tapped his comlink. "Sector secure," he said. "What's on tap next?"

The response came in a hiss of static through Namir's earpiece—something about mop-up operations. Namir missed having a communications specialist on staff. Twilight Company's last comms tech had been a drunk and a misanthrope, but she'd been magic with a transmitter and she'd written obscene poetry with Namir on late, dull nights. She and her idiot droid had died in the bombardment on Asyrphus.

"Say again," Namir tried. "Are we ready to load?"

This time the answer came through clearly. "Support teams are crating up food and equipment," the voice said. "If you've got a lead on medical supplies, we'd love more for the *Thunderstrike.* Otherwise, get to the rendezvous—we only have a few hours before reinforcements show."

"Tell support to grab hygiene items this time,"

Namir said. "Anyone who says they're luxuries needs to smell the barracks."

There was another burst of static, and maybe a laugh. "I'll let them know. Stay safe."

Charmer was finishing his study of the bodies, checking each for a heartbeat and identification. He shook his head, silent, as he straightened.

"Atrocity." The hulking figure wrapped in the tarp had finally approached. His voice was deep and resonant. Two meaty, four-fingered hands kept the tarp clasped at his shoulders, while a second pair of hands loosely carried a massive blaster cannon at waist level. "How can anyone born of flesh do this?"

Charmer bit his lip. Namir shrugged. "Could've been combat droids, for all we know."

"Unlikely," the hulking figure said. "But if so, responsibility belongs to the governor." He knelt beside one of the corpses and reached out to lid its eyes. Each of his hands was as large as the dead man's head.

"Come on, Gadren," Namir said. "Someone will find them."

Gadren stayed kneeling. Charmer opened his mouth to speak, then shut it. Namir wondered whether to push the point and, if so, how hard.

Then the wall next to him exploded, and he stopped worrying about Gadren.

Fire and metal shards and grease and insulation pelted his spine. He couldn't hear and couldn't guess how he ended up in the middle of the road among the bodies, one leg bent beneath him. Something tacky was stuck to his chin and his helmet's visor was cracked; he had enough presence of mind to feel lucky he hadn't lost an eye.

Suddenly he was moving again. He was upright, and hands—Charmer's hands—were dragging him backward, clasping him below the shoulders. He snarled the native curses of his homeworld as a red storm of particle bolts flashed among the fire and debris. By the time he'd pushed Charmer away and wobbled onto his feet, he'd traced the bolts to their source.

Four Imperial stormtroopers stood at the mouth of an alley up the street. Their deathly pale armor gleamed in the rain, and the black eyepieces of their helmets gaped like pits. Their weapons shone with oil and machined care, as if the squad had stepped fully formed out of a mold.

Namir tore his gaze from the enemy long enough to see that his back was to a storefront window filled with video screens. He raised his blaster rifle, fired at the display, then climbed in among the shards. Charmer followed. The storefront wouldn't give them cover for long—certainly not if the stormtroopers fired another rocket—but it would have to be enough.

"Check for a way up top," Namir yelled, and his voice sounded faint and tinny. He couldn't hear the storm of blaster bolts at all. "We need covering fire!" Not looking to see if Charmer obeyed, he dropped to the floor as the stormtroopers adjusted their aim to the store.

He couldn't spot Gadren, either. He ordered the alien into position anyway, hoping he was alive and that the comlinks still worked. He lined his rifle under his chin, fired twice in the direction of the stormtroopers, and was rewarded with a moment of peace.

"I need you on target, Brand," he growled into his link. "I need you here *now*."

If anyone answered, he couldn't hear it.

Now he glimpsed the stormtrooper carrying the missile launcher. The trooper was still reloading, which meant Namir had half a minute at most before the storefront came tumbling down on top of him. He took a few quick shots and saw one of the other troopers fall, though he doubted he'd hit his target. He guessed Charmer had found a vantage point after all.

Three stormtroopers remaining. One was moving away from the alley while the other stayed to protect the artillery man. Namir shot wildly at the one moving into the street, watched him skid and fall to a knee, and smiled grimly. There was something satisfying about seeing a trained stormtrooper humiliate himself. Namir's own side did it often enough.

Jerky movements drew Namir's attention back to the artillery man. Behind the stormtrooper stood Gadren, both sets of arms gripping and lifting his foe. Human limbs flailed and the missile launcher fell to the ground. White armor seemed to crumple in the alien's hands. Gadren's makeshift hood blew back, exposing his head: a brown, bulbous, wide-mouthed mass topped with a darker crest of bone, like some amphibian's nightmare idol. The second trooper in the alley turned to face Gadren and was promptly slammed to the ground with his comrade's body before Gadren crushed them both, howling in rage or grief.

Namir trusted Gadren as much as he trusted anyone, but there were times when the alien terrified him.

The last stormtrooper was still down in the street. Namir fired until flames licked a burnt and melted hole in the man's armor. Namir, Charmer, and Gadren gathered back around the bodies and assessed their own injuries.

Namir's hearing was coming back. The damage to his helmet extended far beyond the visor—a crack extended along its length—and he found a shallow cut across his forehead when he tossed the helmet to the street. Charmer was picking shards of shrapnel from his vest but made no complaints. Gadren was shivering in the warm rain.

"No Brand?" Gadren asked.

Namir only grunted.

Charmer laughed his weird, hiccoughing laugh and spoke. He swallowed the words twice, three, four times as he went, half-stuttering as he had ever since the fight on Blacktar Cyst. "Keep piling bodies like this," he said, "we'll have the best vantage point in the city."

He gestured at Namir's last target, who had fallen directly onto one of the civilian corpses.

"You're a sick man, Charmer," Namir said, and swung an arm roughly around his comrade's shoulders. "I'll miss you when they boot you out."

Gadren grunted and sniffed behind them. It might have been dismay, but Namir chose to take it as mirth.

Officially, the city was Haidoral Administrative Center One, but locals called it "Glitter" after the crystalline mountains that limned the horizon. In Namir's experience, what the Galactic Empire didn't name to inspire terror—its stormtrooper legions, its Star Destroyer battleships—it tried to render as drab as possible. This didn't bother Namir, but he wasn't among the residents of the planets and cities being labeled.

A half dozen Rebel squads had already arrived at the central plaza when Namir's team marched in. The rain had condensed into mist, and the plaza's tents and canopies offered little shelter; nonetheless, men and women in ragged armor squeezed into the driest corners they could find, grumbling to one another or tending to minor wounds and damaged equipment.

As victory celebrations went, it was subdued. It had been a long fight for little more than the promise of a few fresh meals.

"Stop admiring yourselves and do something *useful*," Namir barked, barely breaking stride. "Support teams can use a hand if you're too good to play *greeter*."

He barely noticed the squads stir in response. Instead, his attention shifted to a woman emerging from the shadows of a speeder stand. She was tall and thickly built, dressed in rugged pants and a bulky maroon jacket. A scoped rifle was slung over her shoulder, and the armor mesh of a retracted face mask covered her neck and chin. Her skin was gently creased with age and as dark as a human's could be, her hair was cropped close to her scalp, and she didn't so much as glance at Namir as she arrived at his side and matched his pace through the plaza.

"You want to tell me where you were?" Namir asked.

"You missed the second fire team. I took care of it," Brand said.

Namir kept his voice cool. "Drop me a hint next time?"

"You didn't need the distraction."

Namir laughed. "Love you, too."

Brand cocked her head. If she got the joke—and Namir expected she did—she wasn't amused. "So what now?" she asked.

"We've got eight hours before we leave the system," Namir said, and stopped with his back to an overturned kiosk. He leaned against the metal frame and stared into the mist. "Less if Imperial ships come before then, or if the governor's forces regroup. After that, we'll divvy up the supplies with the rest of the battle group. Probably keep an escort ship or two for the *Thunderstrike* before the others split off."

"And we abandon this sector to the Empire," Brand said.

By this time Charmer had wandered off, and Gadren had joined a circle with Namir and Brand. "We will return," he said gravely.

"Right," Namir said, smirking. "Something to look forward to."

He knew they were the wrong words at the wrong time.

Eighteen months earlier, the Rebel Alliance's sixty-first mobile infantry—commonly known as Twilight Company—had joined the push into the galactic Mid Rim. The operation was among the largest the Rebellion had ever fielded against the Empire, involving thousands of starships, hundreds of battle groups, and dozens of worlds. In the wake of the Rebellion's victory against the Empire's planet-burning Death Star battle station, High Command had believed the time was right to move from the fringes of Imperial territory toward its population centers.

Twilight Company had fought in the factory-deserts of Phorsa Gedd and taken the Ducal Palace of Bamayar. It had established beachheads for rebel hover tanks and erected bases from tarps and sheet metal. Namir had seen soldiers lose limbs and go weeks without proper treatment. He'd trained teams to construct makeshift bayonets when blaster power packs ran low. He'd set fire to cities and watched the Empire do the same. He'd left friends behind on broken worlds, knowing he'd never see them again.

On planet after planet, Twilight had fought. Battles were won and battles were lost, and Namir stopped keeping score. Twilight remained at the Rebellion's vanguard, forging ahead of the bulk of the armada, until word came down from High Command nine months in: The fleet was overextended. There was to be no further advance—only defense of the newly claimed territories.

Not long after that, the retreat began.

Twilight Company had become the rear guard of a massive withdrawal. It deployed to worlds it had helped capture mere months earlier and evacuated the bases it had built. It extracted the Rebellion's heroes and generals and pointed the way home. It marched over the graves of its own dead soldiers. Some of the company lost hope. Some became angry.

No one wanted to go back.

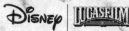